MOMENT OF DESTINY
ONE DAY IN ORAN

An Alternative History

of

The Second World War

and

The Post-war World

ROGER BRANFILL-COOK

Trafford
PUBLISHING™

*We at Trafford believe that it is the responsibility of us all, as both individuals
and corporations, to make choices that are environmentally and socially sound.
You, in turn, are supporting this responsible conduct each time you purchase a
Trafford book, or make use of our publishing services. To find out how you are
helping, please visit www.trafford.com/responsiblepublishing.html*

*Our mission is to efficiently provide the world's finest, most comprehensive
book publishing service, enabling every author to experience success.
To find out how to publish your book, your way, and have it available
worldwide, visit us online at www.trafford.com/10510*

www.trafford.com

North America & international
toll-free: 1 888 232 4444 (USA & Canada)
phone: 250 383 6864 ♦ fax: 250 383 6804
email: info@trafford.com

The United Kingdom & Europe
phone: +44 (0)1865 722 113 ♦ local rate: 0845 230 9601
facsimile: +44 (0)1865 722 868 ♦ email: info.uk@trafford.com

10 9 8 7 6 5 4

In memory of my good friend Jim Rankin

With thanks to my Son Leo for his continued encouragement

PREFACE

Discussing the Second World War with a friend one day, seated in a French café in Haywards Heath in West Sussex, I pondered a multitude of "What if's". Inspired by the milieu, my thoughts turned to the tragedy of Mers el-Kébir and the senseless waste of life and fine ships, which cemented the Vichy Régime's hatred of Britain, and effectively removed France from the struggle against the Axis powers.

That rumination resulted in this alternative history of the Second World War.

So many similar works which ask the old question "What if?" are based on just one basic premise, and all too soon the authors run out of fresh ideas, or introduce something which stretches the bounds of realism and credibility.

To avoid these pitfalls I have carried my narrative through to the inevitable end, using only logical progressions based on what would have been possible, given the one initial change.

Familiar personalities act out their drama on the stage, but not necessarily in the same way and at the actual time. Those of them who died in real life do so in my version of events but again, not necessarily in exactly the same way. It would have been satisfying to have saved Erwin Rommel, and to have had the opportunity to interview him in old age, so I have saved him in my version. He is just one of countless millions whose lives were not to be cut short. On the other hand, what I have read of Admiral Darlan leads me to conclude that he was not the best choice to lead France into the Post-War period of prosperity and peace, so I have had to let him go, and allow Charles De Gaulle to fulfill his destiny.

The result is, I admit, both satisfying and at the same time depressing. For so much has been lost which would otherwise have been saved, so many lives wasted unnecessarily, and the World diverted from the true path of Human progress by immense evils.

But it did not have to be so.

Ivoiry

July 2007

ii

Author's Note

Real life is far stranger than fiction. In a world full of startling coincidences, here is one more to ponder on.

Having set the scene, I wondered how Admiral Somerville might have found an alternative way out of the dilemma he faced that dark day at Mers el-Kébir. To his dying day, Somerville must have gone over and over in his mind what he should have done.

Then one day the obvious answer came to me, and I typed it out, just as if I had always known it.

Much later, I was astounded to discover that he died the day I was born.........

Perhaps now, Admiral James Somerville, your ghost can rest in peace.

HEALTH WARNING

In the following narrative, beginning at the point where Admiral James Somerville contemplates the dilemma he faces, the depiction of the events described and the majority of the illustrations, are of the Author's creation.

The eye witness descriptions, including those of actual historical characters, are based on what they could have related in the circumstances of this narrative. But in every case the words used are those of the Author.

Contents

Chapter One
A BRAVE NEW WORLD   page 1
The Old Rivals
Setting for a Tragedy
The Prize

Chapter Two
FATEFUL DAY   page 16
A Sea Change
Point of No Return
De Gaulle
Victory in the Mediterranean

Chapter Three
THE BATTLE OF BRITAIN   page 39

Chapter Four
OPERATION BARBAROSSA   page 45

Chapter Five
BATTLE OF THE ATLANTIC   page 51

Chapter Six
THE SAMURAI CONNECTION   page 63

Chapter Seven
SUCCESS IN RUSSIA   page 68
Western Stalemate

Chapter Eight
JAPAN MAKES HER MOVE   page 85
A Nasty Surprise
Allied Riposte
Monster Bombs

Chapter Nine
SHOWDOWN IN THE EAST   page 96

Chapter Ten
DE GAULLE REBUILDS THE
ARMOURED DIVISIONS   page 119

Chapter Eleven
SECOND BATTLE OF FRANCE   page 128

Chapter Twelve
ENDGAME   page 145
Japan

Chapter Thirteen
AFTERMATH   page 166

Annexe One
TIMELINES   page 169

Annexe Two
NAVAL COMPARISONS OF 1940   page 184

Annexe Three
REALITY VERSUS FICTION   page 190

Annexe Four
COUNTERPOISE   page 203

LIST OF ILLUSTRATIONS

Page 3

The Battle of Trafalgar by Turner, 1822-24. Admiral Darlan's first meeting with the British Admiralty took place in a room dominated by a painting of Trafalgar. (©National Maritime Museum London)

Page 5

Hitler stamps his foot in delight on hearing the news the French had requested an Armistice. A still from the ciné film shot by Walter Frentz at Führer Headquarters "Wolfsschlucht" in Brûly-de-Pesche on June 17th 1940. In an attempt to ridicule the vicious dictator, this film would be doctored by Documentary Filmmaker John Grierson to make it appear Hitler was dancing a jig. (Imperial War Museum Neg. NYF 37082)

Page 12

Richelieu – the guns that crippled Giulio Cesare and Bismarck. These are 15in/50 calibre weapons firing an 884kg shell to a maximum of 35 km. (©www.mariusbar-photo.com)

Page 12

Heavy Cruiser Algérie, probably the best of the Treaty Cruisers of the 1930s. Her eight 8in/50 calibre guns fired 127kg shells to a maximum of 31 km. (©www.mariusbar-photo.com)

Page 13

Minelayer Cruiser Emile Bertin. Capable of 40 knots plus. (©www.mariusbar-photo.com)

Page 13

Super-Destroyer Le Malin. All of the Class were very fast ships. One of her sisterships, Le Terrible, reached 45.02 knots on trials, a speed record for large full-displacement vessels which has never been exceeded. (©www.mariusbar-photo.com)

Page 16

Map of Oran and Mers el-Kébir, showing the general area before the construction of the port. (François Beltra)

Page 17

A sketch map shows the defences and the positions of the French ships on 3rd July 1940.

Page 28

Obverse and reverse of one of the new coins planned for Pétain's short-lived Vichy régime, showing the fascist style inscription.

Page 43   *René Mouchotte in the cockpit of a Hawk 81A-1 (the export designation of the P-40), one of 140 produced by Curtiss for the Armée de l'Air, but delivered to Great Britain instead. Note the lack of an armoured windscreen, and the ring-and-bead gunsight.*

Page 49   *A knocked-out example similar to the 'lone KV-1', no doubt after target practice by the Germans, showing the multiple hits these tough armoured vehicles could survive. Note the four 5cm AP shot embedded in the hull side. Despite all the superficial damage, only one shot in the turret angle and another in the turret ring, both by the 8.8cm FlaK gun, actually penetrated all the way through the armour.* (AKG Images)

Page 72   *Two views of a wrecked Soviet destroyer, the Lenin, scuttled by her crew when the onrushing panzers capture the last Russian naval base in the Black Sea.* (Siegfried Breyer Collection)

Page 74   *A confident Erwin Rommel framed by the flames from the sabotaged Baku oilwells.* (Bundesarchiv Koblenz)

Page 78   *Red Air Force wrecks litter the airfield now used by the 109s of Hans Joachim Marseille, the "Young Lion", which are lined up in the background. The disparate collection of wrecks appears to be a graveyard of several different models, collected together by the Germans for scrapping.* (Keystone)

Page 86   *Japanese "peacekeepers" arrive in the Dutch East Indies* (The Mainichi Newspapers)

Page 87   *Outnumbered KNIL soldiers surrender to Japanese "peacekeepers".*

Page 91   *HMS Anson as built with 9 x 16-inch guns in triple turrets in place of the 10 x 14-inch guns of her earlier sisters of the KGV Class. The photo was taken just after the Battle of the Indian Ocean, in which Anson was credited with sinking the Nagato.* (Original photo from the collection of Alan Raven)

Page 95   *Shinano joins her sisters. A poor-quality photo, taken by a foreign naval attaché in secret at long range, at dusk, but the only one showing the three super-dreadnoughts together, for the first and last time.* (Original photo from National Archives and Records Administration)

Page 111   *Yamato at high speed, under attack by Tallboy bombs.* (Original photo from National Archives and Records Administration)

Page 113   *Yamato explodes, while the last of her attackers fly away.* (Original photo of *Yamato* from National Archives and Records Administration)

Page 121   *A prototype of the M6 Heavy Tank, armed initially with a 3-inch gun and a co-axial 37mm.* (The Tank Museum, Bovington)

Page 123   *De Gaulle at Aberdeen Proving Ground compares an M6 prototype modified to his specifications with the first model armed with two coaxial cannons. The modified M6 is seen here seen behind the General: the main gun has been upgraded to 90mm, and the co-axial 37mm has been replaced with a .30 cal machine gun. In order to make space for the recoiling breech of the larger cannon, the rear turret machine gun has been removed, and the radio has been moved from inside the turret to an armoured box welded on the turret rear. The General has donned his old tanker uniform to ride inside the M6, and his white gloves prove the inside of these prototypes had been cleaned to a high degree for the occasion.* (Original photos of the M6 from The Tank Museum, Bovington; original photo of Général De Gaulle from the Fondation et Institut Charles de Gaulle)

Page 130   *Operation Aphrodite – the Invasion of Southern France – a production M6 christened "Verdun" with 90mm gun comes ashore from an LST. Note this early model still carries the cumbersome twin MG mount in the hull front. In later models this will be replaced with the simplified hull MG ball mount copied from the Sherman.* (Original photo from National Archives and Records Administration)

Page 133   *Map of the re-activated CORF defence lines at the Mediterranean end of the Alps, showing how the interlocking fields of fire from the Ouvrages cover each other and also the advance posts and blockhouses.* (Inspired by Lt-Col Philippe Truttmann)

Page 136   *General de Lattre de Tassigny with Swiss soldiers.* (Keystone Switzerland)

Page 137   *Typical Swiss "Toblerone" anti-tank defences* (Jean-Charles Moret)

Page 139   *Long-range Swiss 10.5cm fortress gun similar to those which stopped Blaskowitz's XIXth Armee. The rubber tubes hanging from the ceiling attach to face masks worn by the gun crew, allowing them to breath fresh air when firing instead of inhaling the propellant gases* (Jean-Charles Moret)

Page 140   *A Swiss 7.5cm fortress QF gun in a concrete emplacement* (Jean-Charles Moret)

Page 149   *The Consolidated B-32 long-range bomber, a development of the B-24 Liberator, was planned as a fall-back insurance against possible failure of Boeing's B-29 Superfortress. Originally named the Terminator, for political reasons after the War it was rechristened the Dominator. This is a fully-armed production model.* (National Archives and Records Administration)

Page 150   *A pair of the specially converted B-32 "nuclear bombers", with full cabin pressurization and armament reduced to just a pair of .50cal guns in the tail turret. The aircraft will be repainted in RAF "PRU Blue" just prior to the operation which would culminate in the Chernobyl attack.* (Original photo Imperial War Museum Neg. 30745)

Page 155   *The Zoo FlaK Tower in Berlin with destroyed SS panzers.* (Original photo of the Flakturm from the Landesarchiv Berlin; original photo of the Königstiger from The Tank Museum, Bovington)

Page 157   *Wehrmacht soldiers hoisting the old German flag on the Reichstag*
                  building after the swastika has been torn down.

Page 162   *Japanese Kairyu midget submarines in Dry Dock, Kure. Although*
                  not specifically intended for suicide attacks, their fragility and
                  low endurance meant that each and every mission was a one-way
                  journey for the dedicated crews. (National Archives and Records
                  Administration)

Page 163   *Pre-attack reconnaissance photo composite of Nagasaki.*
                  (National Archives and Records Administration)

Page 164   *Nagasaki after the attack. A photo taken by one of a party of*
                  visiting Royal Navy sailors. (Private collection)

Page 191   *The small target presented by Richelieu head-on, compared with*
                  the length of Bismarck broadside-on. (Siegfried Breyer)

Page 191   *Richelieu's side and deck armour compared with that of*
                  Bismarck. (Siegfried Breyer)

Page 192   *Bismarck's limited A-arcs of turrets Anton and Bruno trained*
                  astern. (Siegfried Breyer)

Page 198   *Nose of a production B-32.* (National Archives and Records
                  Administration)

Page 200   *Mers el-Kébir on 3rd July 1940. High drama in the port:*
                  In the centre, behind the oiler, the battleship Bretagne's aft
                  magazines explode, killing almost 1,000 of her crew.
                  To her left the battlecruiser Strasbourg begins to move, avoiding
                  a salvo of shells falling in her berth.
                  On the left of the photo, the battleship Provence has just fired her
                  opening salvo, firing between the masts of her flagship alongside
                  (out of the picture).
                  In the left foreground the destroyer Tigre or Lynx heads for the
                  gate in the anti torpedo nets.
                  To the right the large seaplane carrier Cdt Teste will help rescue
                  survivors from Bretagne; Cdt Teste herself avoids damage.
                  (Marine Nationale, Toulon)

Page 201	*A painting of the same scene: Flagship Dunkerque struggles to free her moorings but is about to be hit and crippled by a salvo of three 15in shells* (Marine Nationale, Toulon)
Page 201	*A 15-inch shell hits the super-destroyer Mogador, setting off her depth charges.* (Marine Nationale, Toulon)
Page 202	*A view of the battle from neighbouring high ground. In the harbour, Bretagne burns furiously before capsizing. In the foreground is the explosion of Mogador's depth charges. She survived the attack, although badly damaged aft.* (Marine Nationale, Toulon)
Page 202	*Mers el-Kébir today.* (Private collection)

I would like to express my particular thanks to the following individuals for their help and patience:

David Fletcher of the Tank Museum, Bovington

Louise Macfarlane of the Imperial War Museum

Andrea Peterhans of Keystone Zurich

Barbara Schäche of the Landesarchiv Berlin

Sarah Beighton of the National Maritime Museum

B. Castel of Editions Marius Bar

Commandant Masson and **Laurent Bouillon** of the Marine Nationale, Toulon

Michel Metallo of the Fondation et Institut Charles de Gaulle

Yao-Hsiang Tsui of Mainichi Newspapers

Gérard Klopp

Jean-Charles Moret

Alasdair Farquharson

Michael Foedrowitz

François Beltra

Klemen L.

Randy Short and **Cindy Ferguson** of Snyder & Short Enterprises

Alan Raven

Seigfried Breyer

Chapter One
A BRAVE NEW WORLD

The long-anticipated announcement that the United
Nations Mars Mission is go for launch from Grissom
Base in the Sea of Tranquility in 18 months time has
galvanised the World's financial markets. In the wake of
the Dow's 700 point rise, Tokyo was up 395, and London
followed with a rise of 360. The sharpest percentage
rise, however, was in the Saigon Exchange, where local
electronics and robotics firms' hopes of supplying the
equipment for the French Commonwealth's contingent led
to a twenty five per cent rise in quoted share values in
just one morning.

Reuter
10/09/1991

In the harbour of Mers el-Kébir, to the west of Oran, during the dark, desperate days of July 1940, two men met under tense circumstances. The first, a French Admiral, gave a promise and his word of honour to the second man, an English Admiral. The latter was ordered by his Government to ignore this gesture.

The immediate result was bloody conflict, more than a thousand dead, a generation of bitterness and recrimination, and a great opportunity lost.....

The ramifications spread far and wide, and for long after the Second World War ended... An old Empire was to fall, and a newer, more perverted Empire was to come close to World domination. Uncounted millions were to die all over the World in the next 50 years, until the fall of that second, evil Empire.......

As Shakespeare so eloquently penned, *"There is a tide in the time of men which, if taken at the flood, leads on to greater things"*.

Stopping the German Blitzkreig in its tracks was beyond the capabilities of two great Armies, turning the tables on the Luftwaffe in

1

the heady Summer of 1940 took the unremitting efforts and sacrifice of thousands of brave men and women.

It is given to few men to change the course of History itself by their own acts, and to fewer still to change it for the better.

But two such men were James Somerville and Marcel Gensoul that Summer's day in the Bay of Oran at the place called Mers el-Kébir.

And could everything have turned out so very differently?

It has long been fashionable in Britain and America to write off the French Navy, based mainly on its lamentable performance during the French Revolutionary War and the Napoleonic era. Both Nations should remember that it was French naval successes just thirty years earlier which allowed the arming of the American Colonists with thousands of Charleville muskets, and permitted their ultimate victory.

And so much depends on individuals. One has only to compare the decisive orders given by Nelson before the Battle of Trafalgar with the clumsy manoeuvring of Villeneuve during the battle itself. What if by some "accident of birth" Nelson had begun his naval career as a privateer sailing out of Saint-Malo?

Admiral Darlan, as the new commander of the French Navy, visited the Admiralty in London for talks on inter-naval cooperation. He was ushered into a meeting room dominated by an enormous painting of the Battle of Trafalgar.

Darlan drily commented that his Grandfather had been killed in that battle. This was hardly a propitious start to a relationship.

The Battle of Trafalgar by Turner, 1822-24. Admiral Darlan's first meeting with the British Admiralty took place in a room dominated by a painting of Trafalgar.

THE OLD RIVALS

Anglo-French rivalry could be traced back to the day when William, Duke of Normandy, defeated Harold Godwinson and was crowned King of England. Having increased their territorial holdings out of all proportion, it was natural for the Norman rulers to pursue their claim that they should also be considered Kings of France. The scene was thus set for the continual confrontations which blighted Anglo-French relations down the centuries, and culminated in the naval race of the 1870s. That Britain won this race conclusively was admitted by the Emperor Napoleon III, when he ruefully referred to *HMS Warrior* and *Black Prince* as 'the black snakes among the rabbits'.

Common sense prevailed when the Royal Navy realised that the biggest threat to its dominance came, not from our closest neighbours, but from their sworn enemies, the new German Empire. Thus it was that the Entente Cordiale was forged, which passed the test of the greatest bloodletting in history, in the years between 1914 and 1918.

Although the inter-war years saw some minor resurgence of the old rivalry in some parts of the world, notably the Middle East, the Anglo-French naval race turned to commercial one-upmanship, whereby the *Normandie* and the *Queen Mary* vied for custom on the prestigious North Atlantic passenger routes.

And in military matters the two allies were as close as ever. Behind the scenes, Royal Navy constructors helped the French Navy with the design of the carrier *Béarn*, lending plans of her RN counterpart HMS *Eagle*, and when La Royale was drawing up plans for the battlecruisers *Dunkerque* and *Strasbourg*, once more the Royal Navy came forward with details of the construction and performance of both the tower bridge, and the main armament layout, of the latest RN battleships *Nelson* and *Rodney*. Faced with the threat of Luftwaffe land-based bombers, the Royal Navy commenced construction of armoured-deck aircraft carriers. The plans of these vessels were passed to the French, who began building two new carriers of their own.

On land, the prototypes of the British Churchill infantry tank and the giant 'TOG' assault tank both carried the same 75mm Bourges hull-mounted cannon as used on the French Char B1 bis. Each month, nine examples of the B1 bis itself were to be allocated to Royal Tank Regiment units, in exchange for hulls for the Hotchkiss H-39 tank to be cast in Britain.

In the air, an early Spitfire Mk I was tested by the Armée de l'Air, details of the Hispano 20mm aircraft cannon were shared with the British, and plans were made to fit Rolls-Royce Merlin engines into French Dewoitine fighters.

The old alliance was beginning to pull together to fight the common enemy.

All this good work, however, was to be dashed in ruins by the dramatic events of May and June 1940.

SETTING FOR A TRAGEDY

On 21st June 1940, Adolf Hitler staged one of his theatrical coups, when he exacted revenge for the humiliation of the Imperial Germany Army in which he had ended the Great War as a corporal.

Hitler stamps his foot in delight on hearing the news the French had requested an Armistice. A still from the ciné film shot by Walter Frentz at Führer Headquarters "Wolfsschlucht" in Brûly-de-Pesche on June 17th 1940. In an attempt to ridicule the vicious dictator, this film would be doctored by Documentary Filmmaker John Grierson to make it appear Hitler was dancing a jig.

In the Forest of Compiègne, in the very same Wagon Lits railway carriage used for the Armistice signing in 1918, Hitler had arranged for the French Government delegates to sign the Armistice agreement ending fighting between Germany and France. In the newsreel of the occasion, Hitler lurks in the background as the 'éminence grise". In fact he took no direct part in the process, waiting only for Keitel to read the preamble to the document before contemptuously leaving for his forest hideout in Brûly.

In six weeks of fighting it was the French Army which had suffered the most. The majority of its tanks and armoured vehicles, and most of its field artillery, were destroyed or in German hands. Tens of thousands of troops lay dead and over a million men were prisoners. The French Air Force, on the other hand, ended the battle with many more, and much more modern, machines than it had started with. Negligent, or deliberate, mismanagement had meant that hundreds of modern aircraft lay around the rear airfields immobilised for the lack of one or more vital parts, a propeller here, a gunsight there, others lacking machine guns.

The French Navy too had escaped relatively unscathed. True, they had suffered grievous losses in destroyers in the desperate fighting in Norway and off the Dunkirk evacuation beaches, but at the time of the Armistice the French Navy was still the fourth most powerful in the World, behind Britain, the United States and Japan.

As had happened with the surrendered German High Seas Fleet at the end of the Great War, all interested eyes turned towards this glittering prize. From a French point of view, the Fleet was their greatest, and virtually only, bargaining counter. The Germans and Italians would dearly like to see some means of getting their hands on these fine naval vessels, if indeed the French could not be persuaded to throw in their lot with the Axis. For Britain, the game was entering a frighteningly dangerous phase, for Italy's late entry into the War had threatened to tip the balance of power in the Mediterranean decisively against the hard-pressed Royal Navy, with its large but ageing fleet.

Desperate hours breed desperate men, and Winston Churchill had played dangerous games before. On August 2nd 1914, as First Lord of the Admiralty he had set in hand drastic steps to stop the Turks taking possession of their new battleship *Sultan Osman I*, completed at Armstrong's Works in Newcastle. The *Sultan Osman* had been paid for with mainly public donations, raised to exact revenge from the hated Greeks - the women of Anatolia cut off and sold their hair to buy the ship. But her new crew, marching along the quay from the steamer which had brought them from Turkey, was confronted by detachments of soldiers blocking the gangplanks, armed with machine guns. Furious, they were forced to return home empty-handed. Retribution for this act was not long in coming, for only eight days later, the German battlecruiser *Goeben* arrived in Istanbul after her breathless flight from the Royal Navy. Admiral Souchon cleverly played on the current anti-British sentiments by offering *Goeben* to the Turks as a replacement for the *Sultan Osman*. Their acceptance of his offer sealed Turkey's entrance into the Great War on the side of the Central Powers.

It was to be hoped that this experience might make Churchill more cautious the next time, especially when the ships at stake formed the fourth strongest navy in the World, but it was not to be. To galvanise the British into action after the defeats in Norway and then France, Churchill decided on a campaign of firmness and determination. He had already refused Reynaud's desperate pleas for more Fighter Command squadrons to help in France. Now, in the face of the threatened German invasion, the "Stay-behind" terrorist groups were recruited, and the question of the French Fleet was to be settled in the most ruthless manner.

As Allied military resistance crumbled, many French ships had escaped to temporary refuges.

The old dreadnoughts *Paris* and *Courbet* had found their way to Britain, where the latter ship under the command of Philippe Jubelin was to play a significant part in the anti-aircraft defence of Portsmouth, firing at German raiders until her 75mm AA gun linings were worn out.

The engines of the giant submarine *Surcouf*, dismantled for repair at the time of the collapse, were hurriedly reassembled and she managed to reach Britain.

The brand-new battleship *Richelieu*, one of the most powerful in the World, sailed from the port of Brest, where she was due to run full-power engine trials, with all the midshipmen from the French Naval Academy on board, and made her way to Dakar in West Africa.

Her sister ship *Jean Bart*, still under construction at Saint-Nazaire, had a near miss with the German panzers which were rushing towards that port. The earth dike sealing off her construction berth was dredged away to let her out. Engine parts still in crates were hurriedly installed and, with no time to test-run the two turbines ready in place, she sailed in the nick of time. Only one of her two quadruple main armament turrets was on board, no guns were ready to fire, so several anti-aircraft guns were craned aboard and lashed in position, and her systems were all in local manual control as she set out. Nevertheless by a brilliant feat of seamanship she succeeded in reaching Casablanca harbour, at an average speed of 21 knots. A merchant ship setting out with some of her missing 15in gun barrels was sunk in the Gironde by a Luftwaffe plane.

Churchill was already smarting from one broken promise. Reynaud had agreed to transfer more than 400 captured Luftwaffe aircrew to England for safe-keeping. However, the new Vichy régime had handed them back to the enemy, and, as Churchill bitterly observed, now the RAF would have the job of shooting them down all over again. At least he had secured the rescue of all the Polish aircrew serving alongside the French Air Force, who had safely arrived in England to continue the fight from a third country.

But two of the terms of the Franco-German Armistice agreement caused dismay and consternation in Britain:

```
Article 8. The French War Fleet, with the exception
of that part permitted to the French Government for
the protection of French interests in its Colonial
Empire, is to be assembled in ports to be specified
and disarmed under German or Italian supervision.
The choice of these ports will be determined by
the peacetime stations of the ships. The German
Government solemnly declares to the French Government
that it does not intend to use for its own purposes
in the war the French Fleet which is in ports under
German control, with the exception of those units
needed for coastal patrol and for minesweeping.
Furthermore, it solemnly and expressly declares
that it has no intention of raising any claim to
the French War Fleet at the time of the conclusion
of peace. With the exception of that part of the
French War Fleet, still to be determined, which
is to represent French interests in the Colonial
Empire, all war vessels which are outside French
territorial waters are to be recalled to France.
```

Article 8 was the result of a cunning plan by Hitler to bend the French to his will. While stating the expected, it also holds out the promise that the French will be able to negotiate for the continuing use of its fleet overseas in respect of the part "still to be determined".

A French protest that they would return no ships to Northern and Western ports now in German hands, with which the Germans concurred, was not conveyed to the British.

It was to be the original French word 'contrôle' in Article 8 which would create the most alarm in Britain. The French interpretation of the word would mean "under inspection", or "verification", whereas in the desperate days of 1940 it was all too easy for the British to interpret the word in its English form of "control" or "direction". A fatal "faux ami".

> Article 9. The French High Command is to provide
> the German High Command with detailed information
> about all mines laid by France, as well as all
> harbour and coastal barriers and installations of
> defence and protection. The clearing of minefields
> is to be carried out by French forces to the extent
> required by the German High Command.

Another reasonable requirement on the face of it, but the scope of the declarations was not limited to those ports in German hands, and handing over details of coastal defences in Mediterranean ports could facilitate the sudden seizure of war vessels at some future date.

The overriding impression given by these Articles is one of consideration for the susceptibilities of a beaten enemy, and a genuine concern to work in concert with the French. At that time the utter ruthlessness and immorality of the Nazi regime was suspected by some, such as Churchill, but the majority of politicians hoped against hope that the Germans were still capable of negotiating and concluding deals in good faith.

Thus the scene was set for bloody, and needless tragedy. It was inconceivable that the French sailors would either allow their fine ships to be seized by their late enemies, or that they would readily sail under German or Italian control and open fire on British ships or installations. Nonetheless, on 3rd July 1940 the Churchill Government conceived and executed Operation Catapult, to seize or immobilise the French Fleet. In Britain the only blood spilt was in a dramatic confrontation in the wardroom of the submarine *Surcouf*, where three Royal Navy submariners and one French officer were killed and several others injured in an exchange of gunfire.

The confrontation off Oran promised to be a far more dangerous affair.

THE PRIZE

In June 1940 the French Navy, known popularly inside France as 'la Royale', was the fourth most powerful fleet in the world, behind the Royal Navy, the US Navy and the Imperial Japanese Navy (See the Comparison Chart in Annexe 2).

The French had the *Richelieu* running trials and the *Jean Bart* nearing completion, two more units of the class on the stocks, plus the two potent modern battlecruisers, backed up by three older dreadnoughts and one old aircraft carrier. Two modern aircraft carriers were on the stocks.

In cruisers the French were very strong: seven impressive heavy cruisers, and 11 modern light cruisers (plus one more on the stocks).

The fleet of 67 French destroyers included the largest and fastest of their type in the world, and eleven more were under construction.

In submarines the French had commissioned 73 units and were building a further 34 - intentionally to match their traditional rivals the Italians.

Richelieu – the guns that crippled Giulio Cesare and Bismarck
These are 15in/50 calibre weapons firing an 884kg shell to a maximum of 35 km

Heavy Cruiser Algérie, probably the best of the Treaty Cruisers of the 1930s
Her eight 8in/50 calibre guns fired 127kg shells to a maximum of 31 km

Minelayer Cruiser Emile Bertin. Capable of 40 knots plus.

Super-destroyer Le Malin. All of the Class were very fast ships. One of her sisterships, Le Terrible, reached 45.02 knots on trials, a speed record for large full- displacement vessels which has never been exceeded.

Although numerically the Italian Navy built up by Mussolini outstripped the French fleet in capital ships, destroyers / torpedo boats and submarines, the French were closing the gap in terms of submarines, and were far ahead of the Italians in terms of the fighting power of the individual heavy units.

Italian ships had traditionally traded protection for speed, and the sleek greyhounds of Il Duce's fleet were no exception.

The French Navy also had one crucial advantage over its Mediterranean rival: greatly superior morale. The Italians could display exceptional courage and skill at times, notably their special underwater and explosive motorboat attack teams, but on the whole the Italian crews were poorly motivated and led, and one is led to the conclusion that the Italian Nation as a whole, and its Navy in particular, had little stomach for Mussolini's grandiose schemes of conquest, if they involved coming up against determined Allied opposition.

Such a powerful fleet in being was an irresistible prize for the conquering Germans. The recent Norwegian invasion had been a disaster for the fledgling Kreigsmarine: it had lost half its cruisers and half its destroyer force in that otherwise successful campaign. In such a weakened state, with the first of its large modern battleships not expected to be ready for almost a year, Raeder's fleet was patently incapable of forcing the issue in the English Channel - as required by Operation Sealion.

Add even a proportion of the modern French ships to the equation and the situation for Germany would be transformed. This was the reality behind Churchill's waking fear in late June of 1940.

Equally well, however, the chance to keep such a powerful up-to-date fleet fighting on the Allied side would tip the balance conclusively - and irretrievably - against the Axis Powers.

In London, General De Gaulle was trying to pull together a force of French warships and crews, and build a new navy from scratch. It was an uphill struggle, as he quickly discovered.

On the other hand, back in France, the head of the French Navy, Admiral of the Fleet Jean Louis Xavier François Darlan, (or 'Popeye' as he would irreverently be called by the Americans), desired above all to preserve his fleet as a viable institution, with all the advantages of its control structure, its training and resupply echelons. A staunch right-winger, as could be expected of a career naval officer of his generation, he nevertheless viewed with disdain the Pétain régime's choice of Vichy as its seat of government, with its undertones of having to take the 'cure', to purge the body of its afflictions....

The French Navy had acquitted itself well in action, and it remained the only institution of the French State which was untarnished by the stain of failure and defeat, as were the Army and Air Force, or of impotence as had been the crack fortress troops bypassed and shut up in the CORF defence lines.

Unusually for a naval officer, Darlan also had political ambitions. If an elderly Marshall of the discredited Army could bring himself out of retirement and claim to represent France, then why not a virile Admiral of the unvanquished Fleet, twenty five years his junior?

Chapter Two
FATEFUL DAY

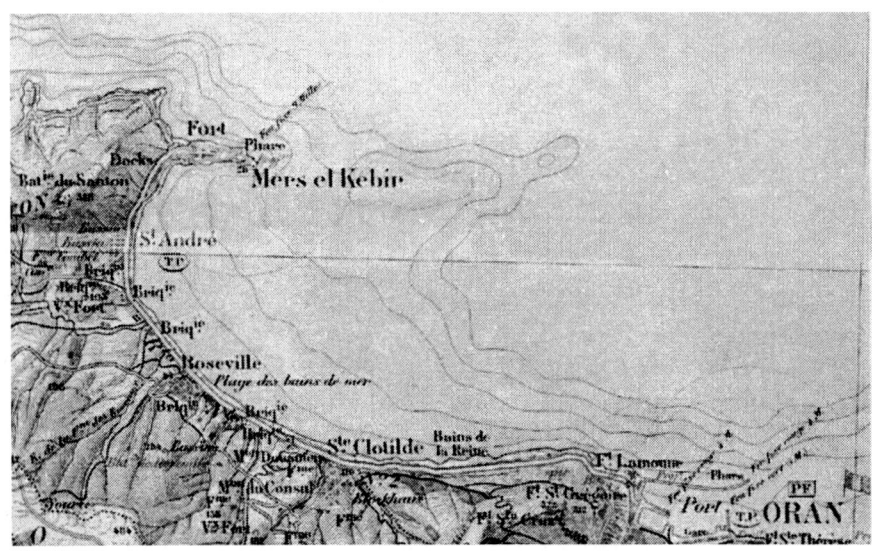

The Bay of Mers el-Kébir, before construction of the naval base

Mers el-Kébir – its Arabic name means "The Great Harbour" - was a new naval base, long planned but barely started in July 1940. It was positioned so as to lie beyond the normal range of Italian bomber aircraft. However, only half the projected breakwater had been completed, and the ships moored inside had to augment their defences with anti-torpedo nets.

Even worse, under the terms of the Franco-German Armistice, work had started on demilitarising the guns of the coast defence batteries, and many breechblocks had already been removed.

At the nearby airbase of La Sénia, there were some 50 Morane 406 fighters, and a similar number of modern twin-engined bombers.

The main targets for Somerville's Squadron would be the two modern battlecruisers *Strasbourg* and *Dunkerque*, the two older battleships *Provence* and *Bretagne*, and the large seaplane carrier *Commandant Teste*. In addition, the base sheltered six large destroyers. Another dozen or more destroyers and sloops were stationed in the Port of Oran itself not far away along the coast. Several submarines completed the French offensive power, but they had been in the process of unloading their torpedoes, and one had disembarked her battery.

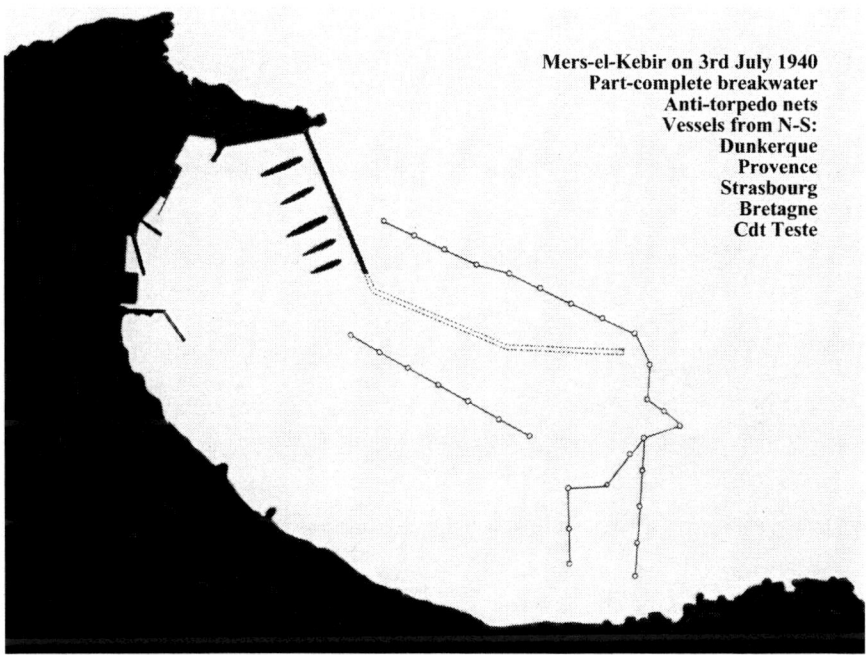

Mers-el-Kebir on 3rd July 1940
Part-complete breakwater
Anti-torpedo nets
Vessels from N-S:
Dunkerque
Provence
Strasbourg
Bretagne
Cdt Teste

The battlecruisers were fast and well armed, but the older *Dunkerque* had a thinner armour belt than normal, since she had been designed to counter the German panzerschiffe of the *Graf Spee* type. In addition, they were normally moored stern on to the breakwater, and all their main armament was concentrated up front. To swing them at anchor to face the British squadron might be taken as a hostile act and the precursor to opening fire.

The pair of battleships, design contemporaries of the old British *Iron Duke* Class of the First World War, had received a few modifications since completion, but their thin deck armour over the magazine spaces meant they were ill-equipped to survive a stand-up fight against dreadnoughts armed with 15-inch guns, especially when caught in the confines of a narrow harbour. Lieutenant de Vaisseau Cherrière, Gunnery Officer of the *Provence*, was confident of his ability to slug it out with the *Hood*, but his gun turrets were masked by the superstructure of the flagship *Dunkerque* alongside.

The big ships under Somerville's command included the battlecruiser *Hood*, at the time the largest warship in the World, the newly-rebuilt *Valiant*, and the older *Resolution*, all armed with eight 15in guns apiece. This was certainly an adequate force on its own to enforce Churchill's dictat, and the French were heavily outgunned.

The British had the air cover given by *Ark Royal's* obsolescent Skua fighter / dive bombers, which in theory could be overwhelmed by the modern French fighter and bomber squadrons, but, as Gensoul knew very well, French land-based bombers could play no part in the stand-off at Oran. Because of recent defections by aircrews fleeing North Africa for Gibraltar, all the French bombers had been immobilised by deflating their tyres, draining their fuel tanks and disabling the propeller pitch mechanisms.

A SEA CHANGE

On the bridge of the *Hood*, Admiral James Somerville read for the fifth time the last signal he had received from the Admiralty *"Settle the affair quickly or you will have reinforcements to deal with."*. He crumpled the message sheet in his hand and threw it on the chart table.

His mind went back to the last written response he had received from the French, passed on by Captain Holland of *Ark Royal* .....

"Admiral Gensoul can only confirm the reply already given. Admiral Gensoul is determined to defend himself with all the means at his disposal. Admiral Gensoul draws the attention of Admiral Somerville to the fact that the first shot fired would have the practical effect of putting the whole French Fleet against Britain, a result which would be diametrically opposed to that sought by the British Government.".
And Gensoul, damn his eyes, was right, of course.

As Lord Somerville recounted many years later in his autobiography *"Engage the Enemy More Closely"*:

'Things were getting tense, very tense indeed .... We knew we had the firepower and the will to force the issue. On the one hand we had what I knew was the Prime Minister's direct order, and on the other the French were trying to bluff it out, but they were caught like rats in a barrel and they knew it............

We were in the business of risk taking, all of us at sea facing unseen enemies every day, but they had to be calculated risks, and I was not prepared to gamble recklessly on the very survival of my country and everything we stood for.'

I paced up and down on the quarterdeck of *Hood*, and suddenly found myself asking what would our most popular and successful Admiral have done? We had spent countless hours at Dartmouth poring over his tactics, and more than anything else, his bold and daring moves to seize the initiative. "Launch a sudden and devastating attack on the French!" he would have cried.... But these were not the rabid forces of the Revolution nor the fascist lackeys of Napoleon's empire. I had to consciously put aside the traditional enemy of hundreds of years of naval conflict and remind myself that these Frenchmen were now our friends and erstwhile allies, the citizens of a free democracy not unlike our own - but with those annoying little differences, not least the damning traditional arrogance which Gensoul seemed determined to display at this very moment, of all the times!

What had Nelson done at Copenhagen? Gone in and neutralised a potentially hostile fleet. The Danes still hate Nelson for what he did that day, no hero to them. I strode towards the superstructure ladder.

Reaching the bridge I paused, then re-read the first Most Secret message which had set in motion this deadly train of events. My eyes dwelt on the final paragraph

(C) If none of the above alternatives is accepted by the French, you are to endeavour to destroy ships in Mers-el-Kebir, but particularly Dunkerque and Strasbourg, using all means at your disposal............

I turned into the dawn's rising light, and shaded my left eye with my hand. Holding the message chitty up to my right eye, I declared to Captain Holland "I see nothing here which obliges us to kill our friends and allies. They will not evacuate their ships, which we have been ordered to destroy. The message says nothing of causing the unnecessary deaths of thousands of crewmen.".

Calling away my barge, I paused to draft out a brief signal to Gensoul "Admiral at sea to Admiral ashore STOP Short of supplies STOP Especially coffee and croissants STOP Request permission to land my plane in harbour STOP Somerville".

Without waiting for a reply from the no-doubt bemused Gensoul, I descended to my barge with Holland and Jeffries, my Flag Lieutenant, inwardly cursing the fact that *Hood* had not yet been rebuilt with a hangar for Walruses - as I had seen on the provisional plans for her reconstruction.... Then, I reflected, on the other hand time WAS passing, we were taking no offensive action, and the longer a standoff lasts, the less is the chance of hurried, reckless violence....

Reaching *Valiant*, I paused at the foot of her ladder and asked Jeffries to bring with him my Admiral's flag which fluttered at the barge's stern. Five minutes later, we were strapped into our seats in the cabin of the clumsy, but reassuringly solid, Walrus amphibian perched on the trolley of the athwartships catapult. Poor Jeffries had had the unnerving task of clambering out along the port wing to firmly fasten my flag to the rear strut where it could be plainly seen by all. The French, I remembered, had an inbuilt love of pomp and ceremony, after all. Only then did I remember my dislike of flying, and the fact that I had never before experienced the dubious excitement of a catapult launch sideways across a deck...

Banking over the mole, I asked our young pilot, Sub-Lieutenant Fletcher, to waggle his wings in greeting. My flag flapped energetically on its strut, and I prayed that the sight of it would prevent any hothead opening fire on us. We picked out the flagship *Dunkerque*, dropped gently down into the smooth waters of the harbour, and taxied slowly up towards her bows. We could see the heads of hundreds of curious onlookers staring down on us from the decks of *Dunkerque* and the other

French warships. Not every day an Admiral of the Fleet drops in by private aeroplane.

I could have chosen to land our amphibian at the airport outside town, but chose the harbour for two very good reasons. Firstly, it was much nearer, and secondly its waters were our common ground. And, my business was with the French Navy, not officials and Army officers ashore.

Gensoul had called away a barge to meet us. The boat and crew were very smartly turned out. We were conveyed to the flagship, and went on board to a very subdued reception - the men who lined the side did not know what was happening, but their officers had been made aware of the general tenor of our threats and the greetings were distinctly frosty. I now regretted my earlier order to *Foxhound* to flash signals all around the bay inviting the French crews to sail out and join us.

Capitaine de Vaisseau Seguin ushered us below to wait in Gensoul's private quarters for the Admiral to arrive. With the ship at action stations all the doors and scuttles were fastened shut, and I remember the heat was stifling. I noticed on one side wall the framed photograph of *HMS Hood* he had been presented with, when he had commanded the squadron searching the North Sea for German raiders only a few short months ago.

He arrived some twenty minutes later - twenty of the longest minutes of my life, as we stared at the floor, the furnishings, and everywhere except at Capitaine Seguin. A dark thought had briefly crossed my mind - What if Winston had insisted our ships open fire immediately, even with us here on board? I remember thinking, they had better not, or there would be the merry hell to play once I got back home .....

Finally Marcel Gensoul entered. I remember thinking he reminded me of my old Grammar School Deputy Headmaster. I later learned that he had, in fact, been involved in setting up and running various training courses for young French officer cadres...... I also later found out the reason for the delay. Gensoul had finally seen fit to transmit to his boss Admiral Darlan the last peaceful option I had sent to him earlier that morning: to demilitarise his ships in this North African port and send the crews ashore.

After the exchange of courtesies, conducted by Captain Holland - my French was passable, but we had determined to try to avoid any possibly fatal misconceptions creeping into our dialogue - we set to work in earnest.

I began, "You cannot have failed to notice our little fleet cruising the pleasant waters of this peaceful part of the Mediterranean.". I paused to let Holland translate, but Gensoul, who spoke perfect English (as I was later to discover, his Wife was of English descent), nodded in silence, awaiting yet another ultimatum. "I have to tell you that I am ordered by my Government to launch an attack on, and neutralise, a potentially hostile force of ships" - he stared defiantly into my eyes, and made as if to reply, but I continued - "but I see no hostile ships here, only friends."

Gensoul stared at me. I smiled. He looked up at the low ceiling, without smiling - I was to remember that no smile would cross his lips until the Nazi jackboot was removed from his country's throat - but his mouth and eyes relaxed.

Just for a fleeting moment, then he turned and snapped his fingers to an aide. "Your supplies, Admiral" was all he said. Orderleys entered carrying our breakfast, trays of warm, freshly baked croissants and pain au chocolat, followed by steaming jugs of hot French coffee.

As we sat down to break bread together, in the Continental way to which I had taken such a fancy in my landlubber expeditions, we talked briefly of news from France, of the rest of the Fleet scattered far and wide, and of how best to move forward in a spirit of co-operation.

Gensoul asked our pardon to signal his C-in-C. When the aide had left the Admiral turned to me and said simply "Voilà. I have set things in motion. Thanks to you we will prevail" - he paused - "together".

Cognac followed breakfast, then we strode together on his quarterdeck, smoking the excellent cigars I had had Jeffries bring from my day cabin. Just astern and above us, young Sub-Lieutenant Fletcher was being shown over *Dunkerque*'s Loire 130 floatplane perched on her stern catapult, and we could hear his enthusiastic questions of his opposite number. We ourselves said little, and I knew Gensoul was waiting for something.

It arrived, in the form of the same, but now breathless, young aide who handed his chief a signal sheet. Gensoul ran his eyes over it, paused to take in its significance, hesitated, then held it out for Holland and I to see. "Alors, ça commence - So, it begins!" was all he said. I did not need Holland to translate the signal sheet for me.

On it we read <<AAMIRAL ORAN STOP IMPERATIVE CONTINUEZ NEGOTIATIONS STOP MARINE FRANÇAISE AGIRA À COTÉ DES ALLIÉS STOP AUCUN VAISSEAU FRANÇAIS NE S'UNIRA AVEC L'ENNEMI STOP DEVEZ GAGNER DU TEMPS STOP>> and then the clinching signature <<DARLAN>> *(1)*.

We looked at each other - the man was signing his own death warrant. So what did he plan? We were soon to find out.

Admiral Somerville has turned a Nelsonian blind eye. He orders his squadron to disperse, and only then informs Whitehall of his decision, quoting the Darlan message.

As might be predicted, Churchill is furious, and Somerville is recalled to London. The Prime Minister talks openly of having him shot for treason, in the manner of poor Admiral Byng *(2)*.

At the end of the day Somerville is summarily dismissed his rank, and leaves the Navy without a pension. Such a talented officer could not long be kept out of the limelight, however, especially in his country's hour of greatest need, and a year later he is quietly reinstated to Flag rank when the advantages of his masterly inaction begin to filter through. For his part in the drama, Captain Holland of the *Ark Royal* is also vilified, resigns his commission and even, for a brief interlude, serves as a common soldier in the Home Guard, until being quietly re-admitted to the Navy.

Behind the scenes, President Roosevelt has carried out the first and perhaps the most decisive of his many interventions *(3)* on behalf of Western Democracy.

---

1   <<To Admiral Oran STOP Imperative you continue negotiations STOP French Fleet will work alongside the Allies STOP No French vessel will go over to the enemy STOP You must gain time STOP>>.

2   Admiral John Byng was shot in 1757 for dereliction of duty in the face of the enemy, having abandoned the Royal Navy's base in Minorca to a powerful French attack the previous year. Made a scapegoat by the Government, he gave rise to Voltaire's famous comment that in England they shoot an admiral from time to time "to encourage the others".

3   Such as secretly supplying the RAF with 100 Octane fuel during the Battle of Britain, the transfer of the 50 four-stacker destroyers, Lend Lease and the Manhatten Project.

Shocked by the military collapse of France and the fall of the Third Republic, and disappointed by the French lurch to the Right and their rapprochement with the Nazis, he had ordered his special envoy Robert D Murphy at the American embassy in Paris to travel to Clermont-Ferrand and make discreet contact with Admiral Darlan.

Darlan was inwardly seething at what he saw as the failure of the French Army to protect La Patrie. He could count on the absolute loyalty of the largely intact French Navy, and saw this arm as a possible means of restoring the 'Honneur' of France, the word which is so proudly displayed in large brass letters above the quarterdeck of each major French warship.

The secret deal brokered with Roosevelt was that if he, Darlan, agreed to continue the fight from North Africa and brought the Navy over to the Allied side, Roosevelt would guarantee him full political, financial and material support. This would mean cutting himself and his fleet off from its logistical and ship-building base, but Roosevelt promises the full ship-repair and naval construction facilities of the United States will be put at Darlan's disposal to refit and re-arm his ships and, if necessary, replace any combat losses.

The Admiral had promised to sleep on this proposition, but the very next morning the news of the deadly stand-off at Oran had arrived, and Darlan began his day in a mood of dark foreboding. Why would the British risk ruining everything by their high-handed demands?

Darlan was about to leave Clermont-Ferrand for his new ministerial post in Vichy, but he had been delayed by Murphy's visit, and now the serious development off Oran put all thought of moving out of his mind for the moment. It was at this juncture that he received Gensoul's signal that the British would accept demobilization of the vessels, and the germ of a plan started in Darlan's head.

He decides to use the situation at Mers el-Kébir as the excuse to order all remaining French naval units in Southern ports to sortie, and then to converge on North Africa, with the aim of reinforcing Gensoul outside Oran. This movement was what had prompted the final urgent Admiralty signal to Somerville.

Then comes the bombshell message from Gensoul that Somerville was prepared to defy his Government - and Darlan's mind is made up.

Calling his trusted Flag Lieutenant he dashes off the signal Gensoul and Somerville were to read on the Dunkerque's quarterdeck, and immediately calls for his car. Driving to the nearest airbase, the two men commandeer the fastest aircraft available and fuelled to go - a LéO 451 bomber - and head for North Africa. Keeping strict radio silence, Darlan at first heads out East, and only turns South once they are safely out to sea.

Back at French Naval Headquarters an anxious Vichy signals officer paces up and down in indecision for valuable minutes, then telephones Admiral Le Luc. Thirty minutes later, Marshall Pétain stares long and hard at the copy of Darlan's message, and then reaches for the telephone.

At low level, and full throttle, the fast LéO is way beyond the reach of the squadron of Bloch fighters Laval orders in pursuit. The bird has flown.

Darlan has also taken the opportunity to radio to the *Richelieu* at Dakar, ordering her commander, Capitaine de Vaisseau Marzin, to make every effort to gain the confidence of the captain of HMS *Dorsetshire* and the other Royal Navy units cruising off that port. Acting on these orders, Capitaine Marzin slips out of port with the connivance of, instead of the opposition of, the blockading RN squadron, and the *Richelieu* makes her way to Mers el-Kébir.

Arriving in Algiers, Darlan marches on the military headquarters with a Colonial Marine escort. There he establishes himself as the de-facto head of the local authorities. He telephones Pétain to explain the tenor of his exchange of messages with Gensoul. He is determined to preserve the French Fleet at all costs, hence his apparent willingness to join with the Royal Navy, a ploy to keep Somerville from opening fire. Despite appearances, he reaffirms his commitment to Pétain's 'Révolution Nationale' and his personal bond of loyalty to the Head of State. Thus reassured, the aged Marshall endorses Darlan's initiative and he is confirmed in his new post.

To keep up appearances Darlan reinforces the guards on aircraft and minor vessels which his predecessors had instituted - as René Mouchotte discovered almost at the cost of his life during his own dash for Gibraltar and freedom. These actions have the hidden advantage of preserving as many planes and crews as possible for Darlan's own plans.

Although the Germans must be placated, Darlan is extremely popular with the French hierarchy when he publically rattles his sabre in the direction of the treacherous Italians of Il Duce. He issues veiled threats against Italian territorial encroachments, and they dutifully recoil. But behind the scenes he is working to fill all top posts with his nominees such as Admiral Duplat, who he is sure will follow him on the dangerous path he plans to take.

In the tense, spy-ridden atmosphere of French North Africa, which has become polarised between two great political extremes, the Vichy authorities become suspicious of the activities of this Admiral who is slowly supplanting subordinates who had previously sworn loyalty to the new régime.

POINT OF NO RETURN

Matters come to a head when Darlan orders the Fleet to sortie to intercept and turn back an Italian re-supply convoy heading for Tripolitania, covered by their two rebuilt dreadnoughts battleships and an Italian flying boat.

Seeing the approach of major warships, the cargo vessels of the convoy and their destroyer escort turn back, covered by the *Conte di Cavour* and *Giulio Cesare*. The dreadnoughts move into position to shield their charges from what they first believe to be an attack by the Royal Navy, the French fleet being dismissed by the Italians as a spent force.

The crew of the flying boat signal to Admiral Iaschino in *Julio Cesare* that in fact the new arrivals are flying the French Tricolore.

Turning straight towards them, the contemptuous Italians fire several warning shots across the bows of the leading French ship, the *Dunkerque*. The French response is immediate, and they quickly find the range. In the fierce exchange of fire, *Dunkerque* is hit in a boiler room and temporarily forced to heave to. But *Richelieu* accurately straddles *Gulio Cesare* with a salvo of 15in shells. The Italian lightweight is squarely hit and in her turn is brought to a stop. She loses all power, and as the French Fleet closes in for the kill, Admiral Iaschino transfers his flag to *Cavour*. *Cesare's* crew are taken off by destroyers, bravely coming alongside under heavy fire, scuttling charges are set, and she is abandoned. Scuttled or not, her sinking is proudly claimed by the Captain of *Richelieu*.

Pétain is furious, and demands Darlan returns to Vichy forthwith to explain himself. Knowing that this would be a fatal mistake, Darlan refuses and instead puts into action his planned coup d'état. The Admiral declares himself de-facto provisional head of the Fourth Republic.

Hitler is apoplectic with rage, tears up the Armistice Agreement and orders the invasion of Unoccupied France. Vichy is virtually stillborn. The ageing Marshall is left to oversee a puppet state, but all French institutions are overthrown. His new currency, substituting 'Patrie, Famille, Travail' for the familiar 'Liberté Égalité, Fraternité' on the obverse and the Francisque, a Gallic double-headed axe, in place of the head of Marianne on the reverse, is never officially issued, and sometimes turns up today as a curio in coin collections.

Obverse and reverse of the new coins planned for Pétain's short-lived Vichy régime, showing the fascist style inscription.

French North Africa declares for the Allies. Admiral Darlan becomes head of the Free French forces and calls on the colonial authorities worldwide to rally to the new Fourth Republic. Predictably, the conservative nature of the old colonial administrators and military commanders makes most of them hesitate before declaring their support. However, the news of the German takeover of Unoccupied France galvanises them into action.

French Equatorial Africa is a key prize, since more than two thousand tonnes of gold from France, Belgium and Poland has been deposited at Kayes, 125 kilometres inland from Dakar, ever since the French surrender. Darlan sends General Weygand to Dakar in the heavy cruiser *Suffren* as his personal emissary to ensure the adherence of the colony and, more importantly, to organise the transportation of the gold bullion to safety in Oran.

From Brazzaville, Leclerc has already set out with his flying column, observing radio silence. They succeed in crossing the Sahara and fall upon the hapless Italian garrison at Kufra Oasis. The French troops are heavily outnumbered by the Italians, and have only one 75mm mountain gun with them. Leclerc has his men drive round and round the isolated outpost, firing the lone 75 from several different positions, and directions, and keeping up a continuous bombardment from the back of the truck. Deceived into thinking they are facing an overwhelming enemy force well-supplied with artillery, the Italian garrrison surrenders.

Madagascar is briefly threatened with turmoil by Japanese-inspired agitators from the local indigenous nationalist movement. Order is restored by a force of 1,000 French Colonial Marines carried there in a light cruiser and four sloops, and the island is secured for the Free French.

Syria threatens to cause serious problems, but the arrival of a powerful French naval squadron and the personal intervention of Darlan himself defuses the situation. The pro-Vichy General Dentz is removed by a deputation of his top officers, and replaced by General Catroux. At the press conference in Acre the otherwise dramatic takeover is marked by one amusing incident. A tipsy Australian photographer trips over a power lead and blacks out the neighbourhood for almost five miles around. In the darkness an unknown souvenir hunter takes advantage of the confusion and makes off with Catroux's ornate gold-leaf kepi, which is never recovered.

French Indo-China rallies enthusiastically to the cause. The Siamese attempt to make territorial gains at the expense of the colony before military aid can arrive from the West. However, in the short but vicious Battle of Cam Ranh Bay, the small local French squadron comprising the light cruiser *Lamotte-Piquet* and the sloops *Dumont d'Urville*, *Amiral Charnier*, *Marne* and *Tahure* makes a surprise attack on the two Thai "pocket heavy cruisers" *Ayuthia* and *Dhonburi*, sinking both vessels plus two torpedo boats and disabling the rest of the Thai fleet, thereby restoring the status quo.

The small islands of St-Pierre and Miquelon, however, situated not far from the North American continent, hold out for Vichy. Darlan orders the giant French cruiser submarine *Surcouf* to overawe the local authorities with the power of her twin 8in guns. She makes a spectacular entrance, surfacing off the capital St Pierre at dawn on 25th December 1940. It does not take long for her landing party to persuade the local officials where their best interests lie.

Meanwhile, from his North African power base Darlan has dominated the Western Mediterranean. He has chosen as his Fleet Commander Admiral Godfroy of Force X in Alexandria, and this dynamic officer continues the work of bottling up the Italian Navy, which will lead to its virtual elimination in the daring aerial torpedo raid on Taranto.

As for Admiral Gensoul, he is named as Darlan's go-between with the Royal Navy. Marcel Gensoul is a confirmed Anglophile, he speaks excellent English, and has carried out several official visits to UK ports in the pre-war years. Gensoul has previously reported on the primitive Anti-Submarine equipment of French destroyers and escort vessels compared with their Royal Navy counterparts.

He is now given the task of sharing Allied technology and bringing the French vessels up to scratch in terms of Asdic (sonar), depth charges and their throwers, and the new-fangled RDF (as the British call their version of Radar). At the same time the French and British experiences at Narvik have highlighted serious deficiencies in Anti-Aircraft firepower. Fearing that the supply of spares and ammunition for their 25mm and 37mm AA guns will soon dry up, Gensoul negotiates for large numbers of American-built 20mm Oerlikon and 40mm Bofors guns to be supplied on a 'Lend-Lease' basis and fitted to French vessels.

The battlecruisers *Dunkerque* and *Strasbourg* have always experienced problems with their 13-inch main armament turrets, and accuracy at long range is especially disappointing, with a wide spread of shot from each salvo.

Royal Navy gunnery experts from HMS Excellent are brought in to study the problems and suggest solutions. They have much experience with barrel interference in the turrets of the *Nelson*, *Rodney* and Town Class cruisers. The measures proposed – including staggered salvo firing to avoid close interference of the shells in flight, and a change in the head radius of the shells' ballistic caps - bring a partial solution to the problems of long-range accuracy. These features are also introduced on *Richelieu*, and later *Jean Bart*, and greatly increase the effectiveness of their 15-inch main turrets.

It is this intimate co-operation between the British and French which will bear such fruit in the coming Battle of the Atlantic.

GENERAL DE GAULLE

The sudden French about face has brought in its train the problem of how to accommodate General Charles De Gaulle.

On the imminent collapse of France, De Gaulle had fled to England with his wife. He established himself in London, and was attempting to gather around his person like-minded Frenchmen who would continue the struggle against the Nazis.

On 18th June he had broadcast his famous rallying call on the BBC World Service, which began with the words <<La France a perdu la bataille. La France n'a pas perdu la guerre>> (4)

At the time, very few Frenchmen had actually heard the message, preoccupied as they were with other things.

Officially, to Vichy he was a traitor, and a price was placed on his head. Although De Gaulle's last position in the Third Republic was as Undersecretary of State for War, his actual seniority in the military hierarchy meant that in terms of rank he was quite low down in the pecking order of General Staff officers.

When Darlan defects from Vichy and is likewise declared a traitor, subject to summary arrest and Court Martial, the General's position is eased somewhat.

Darlan dislikes De Gaulle as much as Roosevelt does, but De Gaulle is a dedicated patriot and the Free French have need of his technical expertise.

---

4   *"France has lost a battle. France has not lost the War ".*

For the next six months De Gaulle is based in London, in charge of rallying Frenchmen inside Metropolitan France to either defect to freedom – usually via Spain and Portugal or across the Mediterranean direct to North Africa, although a significant number did manage to give the Germans the slip and cross to the UK in small fishing craft – or organise inside the country and carry out acts of defiance and sabotage.

The Communist Party is a thorn in the side of De Gaulle and his Resistance fighters, under orders from Moscow to support the Germans. Only later, when Hitler invades his erstwhile ally's country, will the French Communists waver, and then finally throw their hand in with the Resistance when the Wehrmacht gains the upper hand in Russia. De Gaulle's support and popularity will rise as that of his Communist opponents will decline.

VICTORY IN THE MEDITERRANEAN

The French Navy patrols the Mediterranean, joining the overstretched Royal Navy, relieving Malta and bottling up the Italian Fleet.

The latest Italian battleships *Vittorio Veneto* and *Littorio* have only been completed in May 1940 and could in no way be considered battleworthy. The rebuilt *Conte di Cavour* and *Giulio Cesare* alone could not have hoped to stand up to the French fleet, and already *Cesare* lies at the bottom of the Mediterranean. The Italian cruiser force is impressive to look at but untried. Its ships have clocked some very high speeds but these were achieved on trials with no armament fitted, and their staying power in actual combat is suspect.

Darlan has capitalised on the French Navy's desire for revenge against the Italians who are seen as having stabbed France in the back in June 1940, and before the effects of the invasion of Unoccupied France have demoralised his men. He therefore determines to launch knockout blows against the Italian Fleet. Darlan must move fast because he knows the Luftwaffe will swiftly come to the aid of Germany's weaker Axis partner.

This fear seems justified in the Corsica débâcle. A major Allied setback occurs when Darlan attempts a political takeover of the island. His officers seize control of Ajaccio but reinforcements carried by sea are set upon by Luftwaffe aircraft and driven off with heavy loss. To reassert their authority the Germans resort to a mass paratroop drop. Darlan's troops on the island resist bravely but are quickly overwhelmed. The German paratroops who land by parachute and glider take disproportionate losses (one in four of the men parachuted in, is killed) but the Fallschirmjaeger emerge from the Battle of Corsica with their reputation enhanced. Partisan activity, however, fuelled by agent and supply drops from North Africa, will continue to be a thorn in the Germans' side.

With the Wehrmacht in the South of France, the Luftwaffe can strike at North Africa and the fledgling Fourth Republic. Conversely the French can attack Southern France. The local Luftwaffe units, however, are weakened by having planes withdrawn to throw their weight into the Battle of Britain, and for Hitler and Goering, settling the score with the renegade French of North Africa will have to wait for the moment.

If and when the Luftwaffe return in strength the major French warships would need to be withdrawn eastwards under effective Allied fighter protection. However, the North African French now receive large numbers of modern fighter and bomber aircraft from the USA, and the Americans send 'volunteers' to man a new *Lafayette Escadrille*, successor to the famous American fighter unit of the Great War.

There are several major, but inconclusive naval actions in July and August 1940. The Italian Fleet sorties from port, but on hearing of the presence of major French or British units, the Italians invariably turn and run for home. Then, on the last of these fruitless sorties, the heavy cruiser *Pola* takes a torpedo hit from a Swordfish at dusk, and is brought to a standstill off Cape Matapan. Her sister ships *Zara* and

Fiume are ordered by Admiral Iachino to stand by the cripple and bring her back to port. What they do not know is that the radar-equipped British Mediterranean Fleet is closing with the Italian force during the night. All three heavy cruisers are caught completely by surprise, their main turrets trained fore-and-aft in the searchlights' glare, and they are literally blown to pieces by the 15-inch guns of *Warspite* and *Valiant*.

Finally, the Fleet Air Arm attack Taranto, covered by RN and French units, and put several major Italian ships out of action.

On land, on 9th December 1941 the British Army of Egypt, under Major-General R. N. O'Connor, launches a counter-attack against the Italian forces of Marshall Badoglioni.

At the same time the French Army of North Africa under General Legentilhomme sorties in strength from behind the Mareth Line and attacks the Italian rear in Libya.

Caught between a rock and a hard place, the dispirited Italians have no stomach for an extended struggle. Just fourteen days later, Marshall Graziani agrees to the surrender of all Italian forces in Libya, totaling over 200,000 men, with significant amounts of weapons and equipment. Two days later, the forces of the Duke of Aosta in Somaliland also surrender, and several hundred thousand more Italians go into the bag.

A participant on the French side was Caporal "Paul Lebel", who despite his given name was an Italian, serving during the Libyan campaign in the 13th DBLE:

> You might ask how I, a native Italian from Calabria, felt about facing my fellow countrymen in combat. This would not be my first time, however. As a committed member of my local Communist Party, I had volunteered to fight the *fascisti* in Spain's Civil War, and on many occasions I crossed swords with the Black Shirt fanatics who blindly followed Il Duce. When I saw the Republic's days were numbered, I took ship from Barcelona with Captain "Potato" Jones *(5)* on one of his last life-saving runs through the enemy blockade.

---

5   *Captain Jones (a distant cousin of the Author) ran the Nationalist blockade on several occasions, carrying potatoes into besieged Barcelona – hence his nickname - and returning with refugees.*

But the disgrace of defeat, the stain of running away, the impossibility of returning to my home town while the *fascisti* were still in power led me to sign up for the five years in the Légion, which I joined in 1938.

So it was that just two years later, I found myself invading "my" province of Libya in the ranks of the 13th Demi Brigade of the Légion Etrangère. Strangely enough one of our officers was also Italian. Of my previous history no questions were asked, which is the usual way in the Family of the Légion. But my previous combat experience showed through in training, and here I was holding down the rank of Caporal, in charge of a small section of legionnaires, most as hard bitten as myself, but none so scarred as old "Karl", baptized in the hell hole of Verdun...

I had mixed feelings about our coming attack on the Italian Army. My fellow countrymen I had fought in Spain were mostly dedicated *fascisti* fanatics; now I would be facing young Italian conscripts and second-line older soldiers, many of whom felt little affection for the political ambitions of Il Duce.

On the other hand, the Frenchmen in our expedition felt a bitter hatred towards the Italians facing them and were spoiling for revenge: they could never forget Mussolini's treacherous stab in the back when he attacked France on the Alpine Front, when her armies were already reeling under the Nazi Blitzkreig.

Their animosity was only strengthened when we learned from an Italian prisoner captured in the Matmâta Hills, that he had been an Alpini thrown in vain against the Maginot defences in the Alps. After the French surrender, their unit had been ordered to board Luftwaffe transport planes, to be flown to the rear areas of the Maginot defences, to claim they had broken through! They were waiting on the airfield when they heard the German reaction to this outrageous request. It was colourful, to say the least!

Our plan was for the main body of the Army to move out of the Mareth Line defences and make a demonstration in front of the Italian defences centred around the town of Medenine. Meanwhile we would form part of a desert force which would swing south of the Matmâta Hills, drive through the Tebaga Gap, turn to the south-east and pass Ksar Rhilane, cross the parched Dahar region and turn north to Foum Tatahouine. From here we would press on towards the coast, completely outflanking the Italian defences.

Of course, the execution of the plan was somewhat more difficult than this simple description. My fellow Légionnaires were well seasoned desert veterans, and we were preceded by scouting groups of the Chasseurs d'Afrique, also well-versed in this kind of terrain. Facing us, however, were the equally experienced Italian cavalry units equipped with the Autoblinda 40 armoured car. Many of these, as well as a large number of their trucks, were armed with the Breda 20mm cannon, which deserved respect. Unfortunately for these desert patrols, we were also well-equipped with *soixante-quinze* field guns carried *en portée* on the backs of trucks, an idea we copied from the Laffley anti-tank guns of June 1940, and Leclerc's more recent exploit with his single mountain gun at Khufra. The thin skinned Italian vehicles could not stand up to our 75s, and we made rapid progress.

After my bitter experiences in Spain, my major fear was attack from the air. In the narrow hill passes there was no room to manoeuvre, and on the open desert there was no cover. The German Condor Legion was adept at dive bombing and strafing, and they had contributed greatly to the collapse of the Republican armies. But the cream of the Regia Aeronautica was far away to the east, struggling against the English, or cowering on their bases in Sicilia. We were attacked a couple of times by old CR.32 biplanes – I recognized them from Spain - and once by a light Ghibli, but our air cover soon saw them off. They had been no match for the Dewoitines over the Alps in the Summer, and these guys were rear echelon pilots, the Poverini! Most Italian planes we saw were burnt-out wrecks destroyed on their airfields, which pleased me a great deal.

Once we reached the coast road, the encircled Italians in Medenine surrendered en masse. I had expected a hard fight, but to my relief most of my fellow countrymen proved only too eager to throw down their arms. Not for them the death or glory of the Black Shirts. Talking to prisoners it was all too clear to me that "Signor Turgido" was not as popular as he imagined, whether the trains now ran on time or not.

To be fair to my fellow Italians, apart from the proven mediocrity of their leaders, the quality of weapons they had been given to fight with left a lot to be desired... the three different calibres of smallarms ammunition for rifles and machine guns, a quartermaster's nightmare, the impressive Austrian anti-tank guns with mediocre armour piercing performance, the small fragile tanks known even to their own crews as the "Mobile Coffins".

Mussolini spent a fortune on constructing the grandiose "Via Balbia" coast road, and now we appreciated its firm surface as our trucks and armoured vehicles sped eastwards – Grazie, Amigi! – quickly capturing Tripoli, Homs, Misurata and Sirte. Meanwhile the English had made a grand cross-country sweep to Beda Fomm, cutting off Graziani's retreat. His replacement, old "electric whiskers" Bergenzoli, sent out from Italy just days before to help retrieve the situation, fell into the hands of our advance guard outside the little town of El Agheila, and the game was up.

We had lost few men in our rapid advance, and happily my poor misguided fellow countrymen lost not many more. Our greatest problem was how to cope with the tens of thousands of prisoners we now had to feed and house and guard. Being Italian, I was drafted in to help with translating, and I was also able to help prevent too much revenge-taking on the part of the French.

Mussolini faces disaster on land, at sea and in the air. The Libyan and Eritrean fiasco follows closely on the Italian failure in their invasion of Greece. Il Duce's modern fleet has been trounced by the British and French, and his large air force reduced to impotence.

To try to redress the balance the OKW draw up a plan to send Erwin Rommel to the Western Desert with an "Afrika Korps" expeditionary force, but the prospects for successful transportation and supply are minimal, in the face of overwhelming Allied naval supremacy, and Hitler vetoes the adventure.

German Generals are also keen to seize the Balkans, to secure the southern flank of the planned invasion of Russia, but Hitler also vetoes this as a dangerous diversion of forces, and a potential cause of delays in his overall plan. He also has a deep respect for Turkish military prowess, and wishes to avoid coming into direct contact with Turkey. Greece will remain neutral, although strongly inclining towards the Allied side.

Marshall Badoglio, with the agreement of King Victor Emmanuel, signs an Armistice with Britain and the Fourth Republic, and Italy drops out of the War, much to the relief of her hard-pressed population. To avoid the risk of a German counterstroke and invasion, the Italians ensure that one term of the Armistice is given full publicity, which categorically states that Italy will remain neutral and allow no armed forces of any nation to pass through or occupy any part of Italian territory.

As for Mussolini, having led Italian Arms in their greatest defeat since Caporetto, he is forced from office in disgrace and is imprisoned in the mountain ski resort of Monte Grosso.

Hitler has plans to rescue his old ally, but he now has to consider the prospect of invading Italy as well. It does not suit his purpose in late 1940 / early 1941 as he wishes to concentrate all available forces for Barbarossa. However, he orders the OKW planners to set in hand detailed proposals for an invasion of Italy at a future date.

And, to hedge his bets, he orders that the CORF defences of the "Maginot Line in the Alps" must be maintained in fully working order, just in case he needs to face off an Allied invasion using Italy as the stepping stone to Southern Europe. This plan will eventually backfire on the Germans, but in the late Summer of 1940 it seems like a prudent move.

Italian Fascists who are unable to come to terms with their fall from grace and the humiliation of the Armistice declare an independent state in Northern Italy, the RSI or Republica Socialista Italiana. The central government, never traditionally strong, is for the time being unable to crush this upstart state, and the RSI receives covert military aid from Germany. The RSI question will have to await the final outcome of the wider War.

Chapter Three
THE BATTLE OF BRITAIN

Meanwhile, a thousand miles and more to the North, the Battle of Britain takes place against the sober realisation by Grand Admiral Raeder, that with many French warships available to Britain the Kreigsmarine cannot hope to gain anything more than temporary local superiority in a small area of the Channel, to cover *Operation Sealion*. The plans are changed to encompass massive airborne forces, with airlifted tanks included in the attack for the first time - carried in huge gliders nicknamed the 'Gigants'. The lumbering transports will need absolute air superiority, however, and the Luftwaffe makes an all-out attempt to break Fighter Command.

Reports coming back to Luftwaffe Headquarters tell of massive victories over RAF fighters in the air, and devastation caused on the ground to fighter airfields. These German over-estimates of success will be fatal, however, for they allow Goering to change his tactics, and head for the knockout blow. He will divert his bombers to attack London, thereby achieving multiple desirable ends – the final destruction of Fighter Command, stung into marshalling its surviving fighters to defend the Capital, and the destruction of London itself, which should bring about the psychological collapse of the British and their will to continue the fight. Either way, whether by opening the way for Operation Sealion, or by forcing a surrender all by itself, the Luftwaffe is on target to win.

Fighter Command has a breathing space, and regroups its forces. Lord Beaverbrook has done a marvellous job of relocating strategic aircraft production facilities away from the immediate target areas, and the "shadow" factories are turning out a steady stream of replacement Hurricanes and Spitfires. The RAF's overriding concern is its shortage of trained pilots, and especially fighter pilots. In desperation Fighter Command trawls other areas of the Service, retraining twin-engined Blenheim pilots on single-engined fighters, and even taking pilots from the Fleet Air Arm. The margin between survival and defeat is, however, frighteningly slim.

At this critical juncture, overtures by Churchill result in Admiral Darlan agreeing to second fifty experienced French fighter pilots to Fighter Command for the defence of Britain, and they begin to arrive by air from North Africa, staging through Gibraltar and making a wide detour around their home country up the Bay of Biscay.

There they are hurriedly retrained on the Curtis Hawk 81A-1, similar to the radial-engined Hawk 75A many of them flew in France and North Africa. These aircraft had been ordered by the French Air Force but had not been delivered before the Armistice. Britain has taken over the contract, but they have been delivered complete with French metric instrumentation. Most significantly, the Hawks have throttle levers which work the French way, i.e. they open backwards. The French fighter pilots, however, feel completely at home with these features.

As each Escadrille of Hawks reaches combat proficiency, they are fed into the Battle with orders to avoid Messerschmitt fighters and concentrate on the German bombers. Despite this, French pilots keen on revenge for the rape of their homeland build up healthy tallies of German fighters shot down. The French also lose heavily, but many pilots parachute to safety to fly again, whereas each German who bales out is captured by the vigilant Local Defence Volunteers. Slowly the tide turns against the Luftwaffe.

A typical French fighter pilot who made such a significant contribution to winning the Battle of Britain, is René Mouchotte, who had escaped to Gibraltar from North Africa even before Darlan changed sides:

> After our dramatic arrival at Gibraltar in the Goeland – with both propellers locked in "fine" pitch in a vain attempt to prevent our escape - and our transfer to England, I expected to get stuck into the Nazi swine who had brought my beloved France so low. They certainly were appearing in the blue sunny skies over England in increasing swarms that unforgettable Summer.
>
> At first the RAF did not seem to know what to do with us. They were an extremely traditional – some said conservative - Service, and

many good fighter pilots were being lost unnecessarily through Fighter Command's adherance to the flight or "Vic" of three planes, flying in close formation, which was totally unsuited for modern, high speed combat. There were language problems, and the most intractable of all was a basic difference in our flight training.

In all modern French warplanes, to accelerate one *pulls back* on the throttle lever. For some unknown reason, the Anglo-Saxons had reversed this, and to accelerate a Hurricane or Spitfire it was necessary to *push forward* on the throttle. This seemingly minor difference could instantly take on life-threatening significance in a tight situation. For when one is landing and an obstacle looms, instantaneous action is required to open the throttle. When inbred instinct takes over and pulls the throttle shut instead of opening it, disaster is not far away. Similarly, when a fighter pilot was living on his nerves in the middle of a flashing dogfight, to stop for even a fraction of a second to double-check which way the throttle should be moved could bring a hail of 20mm MGFF shells in your direction.

Imagine our relief, then, when our French-manned squadron was ordered to ferry back to base a number of Hawk 81A-1 fighters. Those of us who had flown the sturdy Hawk 75A, with its bulky but reliable radial engine, felt completely at home in the Model 81. For it was basically a water-cooled, inline-engined version of our older Hawk, and now nicknamed the "Tomahawk". Best of all, these Tomahawks had originally been ordered from Curtiss by our very own Armée de l'Air, and we were delighted to see that all the instruments were calibrated in metric and labelled in good old French! And the throttle levers, well of course they were of the French variety, being pulled backwards to open the throttle. With them, our accident rates in training dropped to near zero, and I was told our RAF caretaker bosses felt that we could at last take our place in the English sky, to help our hard-pressed Fighter Command colleagues face up to the Nazi aerial armadas.

The Tomahawk showed a fair turn of speed, almost 360 miles per hour – that is around 575 kilometres per hour on our French airspeed indicators – but their solid construction, which was to bring many of us home from a desperate fight, mitigated against any form of rapid climb or tight manoeuvring. The Hawk 81 had already begun to put on an alarming amount of weight compared to its older sibling, with all the armour plate, self-sealing tanks and extra wing guns fitted on arrival in Britain. We could dive at high speed, however, unlike our RAF counterparts whose Merlin engines would cut out if you nosed straight down in pursuit of a fleeing 109.

So we evolved a different type of attack tactic – somewhat akin to what those of our pilots who came to us from the old French Bloch 152 had been forced to learn: Gain height, come in very fast, firing when in range, then cut and run to climb back up again. Never slow down, never turn, never climb when pursued by enemy fighters.

This type of tactic stood us in good stead when attacking the lumbering bomber streams, with hundreds of clumsy Heinkels, Dorniers and Junkers loaded down with bombs meant for English fighter bases and other strategic targets. And my twin synchnonized Browning 50 calibre heavy machineguns, mounted in the nose of our Tomahawks, seemed better able to punch through the armour plate the Luftwaffe had been forced to fit behind engines and crew compartments in their fat bombers. The synchronizing gear cut down on the speed of each big Browning, but I knew they gave me the great advantage of outranging the poor defensive gunners in the bombers, with their puny 7.92mm machine guns.

More times than I care to remember, I was jumped by escort fighters, usually Bf 109s. Twice my poor old Tomahawk received such a battering from cannon shells that I was forced to take to the silk. But I got my own back. Three of Monsieur Messerschmitt's twin-engined "Destroyers" fell to my guns, and at least one Bf 109 – more by luck than judgement, for they were small, agile and VERY fast in acceleration. Their turning circle seemed nothing to write home about, but then I met up with one of their "experte", and he really put me through my paces. I had seen him pull a very tight turn and get on the tail of a circling Hurricane, which to my surprise he shot down. I had tried to intervene, but my tracers flashing past his starboard wing served only to announce to this "experte" that I was in the locality. Finding him on my tail, the hunter had become the hunted, and I pulled out all the stops to try to shake him. A 450 mile-an-hour dive down to sea level, and he was STILL in my mirror. With my face mask running in sweat, I jinked port and starboard to try to avoid the showers of spray his guns were raising, when abruptly he stopped firing, pulled up alongside me, gave the thumbs up and peeled off back in the direction of France. Out of ammunition, or low on fuel, or both.......

I gave Bf 109s a wide berth thereafter.

René Mouchotte in the cockpit of a Hawk 81A-1 (the export designation of the P-40), one of 140 produced by Curtiss for the Armée de l'Air, but delivered to Great Britain instead. Note the lack of an armoured windscreen, and the ring-and-bead gunsight.

Twelve of the original fifty French fighter pilots are killed in the Battle, and eighteen more wounded, some seriously, but their contribution is out of all proportion to their numbers and the heavy losses they have taken. Remarkable personal scores have been built up by pilots such as Pierre Le Gloan and Edmond Marin le Meslée, who were already "aces" by the end of the Battle of France.

The nightly Blitz on London and other UK cities begins, and Churchill decides to retaliate in kind. Bomber Command is rapidly expanded and begins the bombardment of the Ruhr.

Fighter Command follows up the Battle of Britain with fighter sweeps over occupied France and the Low Countries, but the British fail to realise that the Luftwaffe is controlling its fighter defence using a sophisticated early warning radar system. This allows just one Jagdgeschwader, JG26, to fend off all the British incursions, with disproportionate losses to the intruders.

In the meantime, the Luftwaffe's virtually-total commitment to the Battle of Britain, and the disproportionately heavy losses they have suffered, have allowed Darlan to proceed largely unhindered with his knockout blows against Mussolini in the 'Mare Nostrum'.

Chapter Four
OPERATION BARBAROSSA

Operation Barbarossa - the invasion of Soviet Russia - is put into effect in the early Spring of 1941.

The OKW planners had worked on multiple variants of the invasion plans for months. *'Barbarossa'* was the codename given by Hitler to the final version, put together by Brauchitsch and Halder. As the Fuehrer announced on 31st July 1940, the invasion would commence in March 1941 and last for five months, culminating in the capture of Moscow and seizure of the Baku oilfields.

Despite being warned by the 'Lucy Ring' of spies inside the German High Command, the Soviets are taken completely by surprise when the storm breaks on their front lines at dawn on March 1st, 1941.

Snorkel tanks originally designed for *Operation Sealion* heave themselves up the eastern banks of the River Bug, and fall on the sleeping Russian defenders. Overhead the Luftwaffe fly thousands of sorties and pulverise the Soviet air force, mainly on the ground. In the first two days of fighting the Soviets lose over two thousand aircraft, and their bomber leader, Lt-General Kopets, commits suicide.

While JG26 holds the Allied fighters at bay in the West, the vast bulk of the Luftwaffe can be deployed in support of *Barbarossa*. Only three NachtGeschwaderen are retained in Germany proper, to fend off the almost nightly Bomber Command incursions.

Hans-Joachim Marseille continues his rise to become Germany's leading fighter ace with a tally of victories which will eventually top 400.

Hundreds of thousands of demoralised Soviet troops are surrounded and forced to surrender.

Only in isolated locations such as the Citadel of Brest-Litovsk, and at Rostov, do the Germans encounter firm resistance.

The steppes are the perfect terrain for deployment of the panzers in 'blitzkreig' tactics. However, two serious problems soon come to light: the troops are overwhelmed by the seemingly endless, and mainly featureless, spread of the Russian steppe, and the dust of summer churned up from the dirt roads soon clogs tank motor filters and begins to degrade all the Germans' machinery.

Despite this, Rommel will enhance his reputation by leading his 7th Panzer Division clear across Southern Russia in a brilliant campaign, eventually seizing Baku and the oilfields of the Caucasus. Each time his advance is held up, General Rommel is to be found at the front line, personally directing his panzers or setting up defence lines of anti-tank guns.

The newest Soviet tanks, the excellent T-34 cruiser and the heavy KV-1, have been in production for less than eight months, and with the T-34, production has run into serious teething troubles, especially with the transmission and the supply of V-12 diesel engines.

Kurt Mayer rode with the 12th SS Panzer Division 'Hitler Jugend' and has left these memories of the early advances:

The resistance shown by the average Russian soldier was incredible. Units reported back on groups of men, cut off from their regiments, who fought on like tigers until they were dead, or wounded, or they ran out of ammunition. We were warned to look out for desperate tricks, some Russians would come towards us with their hands behind their heads in surrender, and when near enough they would suddenly fling the grenade they had been concealing behind them. Others would lie down as if dead, and would spring up behind our troops to take a pot shot. One of our drivers reported an old peasant who simply walked out of a roadside hut as the column passed and stood there for a moment. Suddenly he flung a grenade which took out a truck and killed three men.

The action was infrequent, but incredibly violent. Then we just rolled on and on at a steady speed of some 30 kilometres an hour, over the seemingly endless plains. I was brought up in a land of forests, valleys and rivers. The steppes of Russia simply have to be seen to be believed. Some of us thought this vast land extended off for ever, to the edge of the world! How would we ever succeed in making ourselves masters of this emptiness? Only now could I begin to understand our Fuehrer's talk of 'lebensraum', the free space which would give full rein to our national ambitions!

The key to this place is going to be the towns and cities, where most of the people congregate. The Soviets try to carry out a scorched earth policy, but the speed of our advance often beats them to it. Everyone has to bear in mind the problem Napoleon faced before us. He captured Moscow, but it was put to the torch. We need to have good solid winter quarters to shelter us when the snows hit. We won't make the same mistakes as the French did, forewarned is forearmed, and our Fuehrer will have taken this into account in his overall strategy.

We began to hear scare stories about new Soviet 'supertanks', but the types we encountered were only the old BT-type cruisers, fast and manoeuvrable, but armed only with a 4.5cm gun.

Their inexperienced crews were no match for our hardened veterans, and they usually caused us little trouble. On the rare occasions when the Soviets managed to mass a large number of tanks to oppose us, they usually rushed forward en masse like cavalry. Our tactics in these circumstances were to disperse, go hull-down, or turn aside from the rush and let the Russkies dash themselves to pieces on our PaK screen, which was never very far behind the armoured spearhead. On one occasion we heard about a whole Red tank regiment which slavishly followed their political commissar into a marsh and got bogged down. They lost every single tank.

Then one day in April my unit was hit by a small Red Army tank force of only half a dozen vehicles. They rushed straight at us from the cover of a small village. As we began to turn aside from the charge according to the normal plan, I was amazed to hear our Company Commander on the radio, yelling that he was firing his 5cm gun into the glacis plate of the leading tank, but the shells were simply bouncing off the armour! I tried to raise him but his radio had gone dead.

In the swirling dustcloud up ahead, which accompanied our every movement in this dry land, I saw the plumes of smoke rising from what I took to be burning tanks. I had just ordered my driver to spread out further to the right, when my gunner shouted 'Here they come!' and a rush of Soviets bore down past our left flank.

As the leader went past we flung a couple of hastily aimed 7.5cm rounds into him, but with no apparent effect! The first glimpses I caught of this enemy showed the tanks to be of a new type we had never seen before – I later came to know them as the T-34 model – and they were certainly an impressive sight .... their steeply sloping armour like nothing we had encountered before. As a tanker I would have had to admit they were beautiful machines, but at that moment we were involved up to our necks in a desperate firefight ..... The Soviets tore through our dividing column and raced on down the road, firing wildly to left and right.

Our anti-tank screen threw themselves desperately behind their long-barrelled 5cm PaK guns, and let fly. Lucky hits at point-blank range stopped two of the Russkies, but the other four continued on unscathed. I was astounded.

Desperate calls for help rang out over the radio, and more palls of smoke erupted behind us. Things were going badly for our unit, when at last the T-34s ran into our hastily-deployed line of FlaK guns, firing on their wheels. As in France the previous year, the huge 8.8s soon put paid to this short-lived Soviet rush.

As we stopped to regroup and lick our wounds, I took the opportunity to examine one of the T-34s which remained more or less intact. The 5cm AT round had penetrated a set of road wheels and then gone through the side of the engine compartment. The crew had baled out, and their crumpled bodies lay by the side of the road where our machine gunners had cut them down. The tank had not burned, and I was surprised to see that the engine apparently ran on Diesel, which would have given it a major advantage over our petrol engines in both range and fire resistance.

The long main gun, of around 7.5cm calibre, was a big improvement over our long 5s and short 7.5s, and had certainly created havoc among our leading platoon, which lost four tanks destroyed and three crews.

I noted again the steeply sloped front glacis, and also the sloping sides and rear, an excellent design which increased the effective resistance of any given thickness of armour plate. Looking back at my old faithful Mark IV, she looked high and square-set beside this new greyhound.

The column lost many men and machines, and just this one attack left 43 dead and another 22 wounded. Thank God the Soviets had not so far managed to build more of these new T-34s.

There were also rumours of a new super-heavy tank, the *Klimenti Vorishilov*, or KV-1, named after some Soviet hero or other, but we never met any of these in our sector, as they were comparatively rare.

Other Germans do cross swords with the KV-1, and a very tough opponent it proves to be, in the hands of a capable crew. 6th Panzer

Division faces a lone KV-1, blocking a narrow gap between a marsh and the impenetrable forest. Its crew calmly destroy a dozen trucks, then shoot up two 5cm PaK guns at 600 metres range, their return shots hardly denting its armour plate. The Germans bring up their ace in the hole, an 88 FlaK 36, but at an incredible 800 metres range the Russian crew knocks it out before it can begin to fire. Sappers are sent out to attack it by night, but fail. Only after two days of stalemate can a second 88 disable the Russian tank, while its crew are distracted by Pz IIIs, two AP shot out of seven finally penetrating the KV's armour at 800 metres range.

To be certain of knocking out one of these tough AFVs, the Germans learn they have to risk their powerful 10cm field guns in a forward anti-tank role for which their bulk and clumsiness make them far from ideal.

A knocked-out example similar to the 'lone KV-1' probably used as a target, showing the multiple hits these tanks could survive. Note the four 5cm AP shot embedded in the hull side. Despite all the impressive superficial damage, only one shot in the turret angle and another in the turret ring, both by the 8.8cm FlaK gun, actually penetrated all the way through the armour.

Rommel is the supreme tactician, and in being given the task of securing the Baku oilfields, he realises that he is faced with not only geographic, strategic, logistical and purely combat considerations, but he must also take into account the possibility that the commisars will order the sabotage of the oil wells.

In another example of thorough German attention to detail, one of his Engineer officers is given the role of preparing for this eventuality. He seeks advice from the only specialist source available to the Axis powers – the managers and technicians working in the Roumanian oilfields of Ploesti. At the same time, Wehrmacht sappers are asked to provide examples of how they themselves would set about destroying or disabling the oil wells. The Roumanians and sappers between them devise plans to cope with most foreseeable contingencies.

Rommel feels he is as prepared as he can be, for such a far-reaching and bold endeavour. He is, as usual, just the right man for the job, in the right place at the right time.

Chapter Five
BATTLE OF THE ATLANTIC

Meanwhile, in the first three months of 1941, dozens of French destroyers and escort vessels help the Royal Navy crush Raeder's first great U-boat offensive in the North Atlantic, and Allied convoys continue to reach Britain and the Mediterranean bringing enormous quantities of American food and military supplies: ammunition, planes, tanks and armoured vehicles, field guns, anti-aircraft and anti-tank artillery, trucks, machine guns, radar and radios, medical supplies and uniforms.

Capitaine de Corvette (Lieutenant-Commander) Vassaux and his crew were participants in one of the climactic battles which followed:

While our aerial comrades were fighting so hard alongside the RAF in what would be known as the Battle of Britain, we were training very hard for what we all knew would be our own testing arena, the battle for the Atlantic seaways.

With our family name referring to our feudal military service in allegiance to the King, my father had been surprised when I opted for La Marine! In mid-1940 I found myself in command of the *Bombarde*, one of the small ("600 Tonnes") *escorte*-type vessels. Our Admiralty had sent my ship with half the flotilla, to join our Royal Navy comrades for joint anti-submarine training. It had been planned to fit us up with the latest ASDIC submarine detection gear and also one of the new British radar sets, which they called "RDF".

However, the severe winter weather which set in following the Battle of Britain soon showed up the deficiencies of these small ships, designed for the calmer seas of the Mediterranean. Eleven days before Christmas of 1940, one of our flotilla, the *Branlebas*, had foundered in a storm near the Eddystone lighthouse, with heavy loss of life. We were shocked and saddened by this tragedy, for we lost many good friends. But worst of all was the realisation that we would not be able to take the fight to the U-Boats in mid-Atlantic in such small and unstable craft. It seems from the inquiry into the tragedy that the boilers of our class were much too big and tall for such a small hull, which gave rise to a lack of GM. In the heavy seas for which she had never been designed, the light hull construction worked alarmingly. This may have been the cause of the *Branlebas'* final demise. It was reported by one of the few survivors that she suffered a major engine breakdown when trying to keep the ship head to the enormous seas. With power lost she swung broadside on and broached to.

A final blow was the realisation that our operational radius in bad weather was derisory. We would be unable to accompany a convoy even to mid-Atlantic without ship-to-ship refuelling, which we had never practised, and which was practically impossible in any case in the depths of winter. *(6)*

The British had experienced stability problems with one of their classes of escort destroyer as well, from a desire to cram as much offensive armament into the ship as possible. The first 23 ships of the *Hunt* Class had to give up one of their three twin 4-inch gun mountings, and later versions were widened to increase stability.

Well, here we were with a well-trained crew, eager to get at the enemy, so it was with some relief, but much trepidation, that we heard we were to be transferred to a brand-new British escort vessel. My first sight of the *Coquelicot*, of the *Flower* Class, in Portsmouth Dockyard, caused my heart to sink.... Instead of a lithe, if fragile, young greyhound, I found myself staring at what seemed to be a converted fishing trawler design, bluff in the bows and tubby in the midriff. I soon learned that her ancestors had been walecatchers in civilian life – quite appropriate for her mission to hunt underwater prey. Our first seagoing trials in fine weather confirmed my worst suspicions, as she made only 16 knots absolutely flat out, as compared to our *escorte*'s 34 and a half.

What she lacked in grace and speed, however, our little *Coquelicot* made up in sheer guts. In the heavy winter seas of our training grounds, she pitched and she heaved and she rolled, but she always managed to come up again from under tons of water, shaking herself like a shaggy dog....... We all came to love and respect our little ship, especially when she demonstrated her smart turning circle, spinning almost like a top to drop our practice patterns of depth charges on an imagined foe far below. In place of our long 10cm main guns we had but one stubby 4-inch, still well able to deal with any surfaced U-Boat.

---

6 *This would be a problem with several classes of older Torpilleurs and Contre-Torpilleurs, optimized for high speed in calm weather Mediterranean conditions. In many cases the ships would sacrifice one boiler room with its attendant funnel, for additional fuel bunkerager, trading off a drop in speed against vastly improved range.*

Aft of her single funnel – in place of our puppy greyhound's two – was a single 2-Pounder gun, our meagre anti-aircraft armament but with a good rate of fire against surface targets. To boost our firepower I had scrounged a pair of French twin 13.2mm Hotchkiss heavy machine gun mountings, and somehow the Dockyard had squeezed these onto the extended bridge wings. One feature gave away our little vessel's mercantile origins – her foremast was positioned between our forward gun and the bridge, just like in her whalecatcher ancestors. But, how would she fight?

It was several months before we would find out, and be put to the supreme test. First we had to train, and train, and train again, endless practice sessions involving ranging on submerged wrecks, which took a good pounding from our depth charge patterns, then chasing the obliging little "clockwork mice", as our tame submarine targets were affectionately called. Whatever their crews thought of acting as practice targets for us rookies, when they must have been itching to set off for enemy-held waters to try out their own torpedoes on live targets, we can only guess at. They were very obliging, and in honing their own techniques of underwater evasion, they forced us to pull out all the stops to corner them.

Finally we sailed for gunnery practice, and fired so many rounds through our little 4-inch that it almost needed a new barrel. My Number Two had taken over this little baby as his own pride and joy, and the results his gun team achieved were very reassuring. And just as well, as things turned out.

In March of 1941 we sailed as part of the escort for a West-bound convoy of empty merchantmen, heading to replenish with thousands of tonnes of desperately- needed war materials from that industrial powerhouse, the United States. We picked up several shadowing U-Boats on our RDF screen, but every time we were ordered to run them down on the surface, these low-lying craft had spotted our approach and dived to the obscurity of the depths. It was then that I craved for more speed, not in the final cornering and running to ground of a submerged prey, but in order to close the scene of action before the U Boat could make its getaway underwater, passing beyond the limited range of our detection gear.

And then, one late afternoon in April 1941, everything changed.

Grand Admiral Raeder and his U-Boat commander Donitz had been concerned at the numbers of ships in convoy reaching harbour safely, despite the desperate efforts of his highly-trained, and equally highly-motivated, U-Boat crews. The Germans were losing the Battle of the

Atlantic. There were simply too many escort vessels, destroyers, frigates and corvettes. Every Wolfpack massed attack was detected on RDF, and, with so many escorts available, several could be detached to run down the surfaced U-Boats, leaving enough to still screen the merchantmen. Alert German lookouts and their sophisticated passive listening devices meant that in most cases the U-Boat had plenty of warning to submerge and slip away. But as long as they were kept submerged, the convoys could pass by out of range and largely unscathed.

So the U-Boats were ordered to close with the escorts, take the fight to them in stand-up contests, then win through to the vulnerable merchant ships inside the screen.

Ironically, the blows did not fall against the belligerent Allies' ships, but against the nominally "neutral" US Navy. President Roosevelt had ordered the US Navy to ensure the safe convoying of Allied merchant ships to the mid-Atlantic crossing point, where we and the British would take over and bring our charges safely through the Western Approaches to the British Isles and more distant destinations.

It was the escort of one large convoy, comprising thirty six heavily-laden merchantmen and tankers, on which Donitz's first major effort was concentrated. The U-Boats had planned their attack to take place only some sixty nautical miles from the meeting point, when the American sailors would be looking forward to handing over their burdensome charges to us, and perhaps would be beginning to relax their guard. No attacks would have been carried out prior to this point in order to lull the targets into a sense of false security, that perhaps this convoy would prove, after all, to be just another "milk run". And sixty nautical miles would mean that our screen of corvettes like our own *Coquelicot* would still be a good four hours' steaming away at full speed, too late to intervene, but in plenty of time to find the debris from sinking ships filling the sea for many miles around.

Fortunately our Intelligence services had caught wind of something in the offing, and the Admiralty had ordered us to increase speed to meet the Americans around forty nautical miles further West than normal. Thus it was that we were only just over an hour from the convoy when the German attacks materialised......

During that hour, we were assailed by frantic messages for help, of S.O.S. messages from torpedoed ships, escorts as well as merchantmen, and we guessed that this must be a big push by the Nazis to try to cripple a major convoy. Our inexperienced American counterparts were fighting for their lives, as well as those of their charges. They were holding up well, but more and more U-Boats were concentrating, and the escort was on the verge of going under. My chief engineer created miracles, and kept our single-screw reciprocating engine going at maximum speed. I even remembered the old trick I had read from the Falklands Battle, when the captain of HMS *Kent* had sent large numbers of his crew to the stern of the cruiser, dipping her screws deeper in the water and giving them more bite, such that she exceeded her maximum design speed by at least a couple of knots. Alas, my own modest efforts in this direction failed to noticeably register on the patent log, but we all felt we had to try to do something – anything – to help our hard-pressed friends tantalisingly close, just over the curve of the horizon.

At one point in our mad dash there was a heart-stopping explosion which we could clearly see, although the ammunition ship itself which had been blown to atoms was beyond our range of vision. Further away, a greasy smudge of smoke told where a tanker had been hit. Had she been carrying the 100 octane aviation fuel which Roosevelt was sending to our fighter pilots, she also would have gone up like a bomb. As it was, she was badly on fire. Our arrival might persuade her crew to stay on board and fight the flames. She still might just survive to reach port, these tankers were extremely tough, and the oil in her undamaged tanks would help keep her afloat. Unless a second torpedo found her...........

Finally, after an agonizing wait, we arrived on the scene, one of indescribable chaos. The convoy had not scattered, but had held its formation of three columns, although the entire collection of ships was zigzagging as a unit, kept together by the force of personality of their commodore. All around the convoy individual ship against submarine combats were being bitterly contested, with huge columns of white foam indicating the exploding depth charges. One of the American captains later told me that his own ship was down to his last four charges when we hove into sight............ An old American four-stacker destroyer had already been sunk with heavy loss of life. Hit amidships by a torpedo, she had broken in two and quickly sunk, her ancient bulkheads giving in rapidly to the pressure of water.......

To starboard a large destroyer of the *Mahan* Class, which I recognised from her pennant number as the USS *Keeling*, was dead in the water from a torpedo hit to her stern, which had blown off her propellors. Her assailant had actually surfaced to finish her off, but was being driven off by a hail of well-aimed 5-inch shells from *Keeling*'s aft guns. Before we could intervene, the U-Boat dived, and put a second torpedo into the *Keeling* just under her bridge. We had been told that these modern destroyers could survive with two compartments flooded, as long as the hull girder remained intact. Three compartments filling with water, and it was unlikely she would remain afloat. A third torpedo would settle the matter beyond any doubt. So, we had to do something, and do it quickly.

We were close enough to actually see the attacking U-Boat's periscope eyeing her stricken victim. In order to get her attention, I ordered my Number Two to plaster the periscope's position with 4-inch shells, less in the hope of hitting such a tiny target than to force her commander to turn to face us instead. My strategem worked, only too well. The lookout on the port bridge wing yelled "Torpedo approaching", a second before my hydrophone operator chimed in with an identical warning, adding course and estimated speed of closing. The target, why our own little *Coquelicot*, of course. The 200 kg warhead of one of those torpedoes impacting our small hull would be enough to blow us all to kingdom come – in spite of my affection for our little craft I bore no illusions about her ability to survive even one torpedo...... But in return our small size and handiness made us a difficult target to hit. Our helmsman swung the wheel this way and that on my orders, and we were all mightily relieved to see the torpedo wake cross our stern only some twenty metres away.

But now it was our turn to strike back. Already our ASDIC operator was calling out the ranges to our unseen adversary, and we were running him down extremely quickly. Even our slow ship seemed like an express train compared with his maximum underwater speed of just nine knots, which he could only keep up for a very short time. I could imagine the orchestrated panic on board the U-Boat. Having missed with his torpedo the commander would now be shouting out orders to take the boat deep, and do it quickly. Our old RN "mice" had told us in post-training de-briefings that one of their favourite tricks was to send as many hands as possible racing through the submarine to the bow compartments, to hasten her crash-dive on our approach, and I was certain that was what our prey would be doing at this very moment.

I ordered a full pattern at medium-depth settings, and we stormed in to the attack. Depth charges raining off our throwers to port and starboard and tumbling off our two stern racks. One problem with a maximum of only sixteen knots is that you can get badly shaken by your own exploding depth charges as you exit the scene at our modest turn of speed. But I was prepared to take that risk, spun her around in a tight turn and then, hoping against hope that our previous pattern might have exploded below the plunging U-Boat, blowing him upwards towards the surface, I ordered a second full pattern, this time on shallow setting. And to hell with the risk of blowing off our own stern!

Suddenly a cry went up from several observers, and I turned in the direction they indicated to see the U-Boat, streaming water, burst to the surface just two hundred metres to starboard. Immediately every gun we had which would bear opened up on her, with no need to await my bidding. A 4-inch SAP shell seemed to hit her at the turn of the hull smack below the conning tower. Our twin Hotchkisses on the starboard bridge wing cut down her gun crew as they raced along the casing towards the long 10,5cm gun mounted there, and our Pom-Pom shells could clearly be seen exploding in a very satisfying manner against the top of the conning tower itself. Several more hits by the 4-inch, and it was clear our U-Boat was going down, but no longer under her captain's orders. Her bows swung up and over as she slipped rapidly downwards at the stern, canting over to port and exposing the shattered planking of her upper deck to our astonished eyes. Then she turned right over on her side, and seemed to hang there for several agonizing seconds, before pointing her bows skyward once more and slipping rapidly below the waves, stern-first, plunging to her eventual resting place on the bed of the Atlantic.

All our men topside raised an enormous cheer at the sight of our enemy's death, especially heartening for those of us whose homes and loved ones lay under the heel of the invader, but I had no time for such reflections, intent as I was on rejoining the main battle.

Over to port, a huge column of water amidships signified the torpedoing of one of the largest merchantmen at the head of the convoy. My signalman told me, to my dismay, that she was flying the pennant of the convoy commodore. I could only hope that doughty old warrior, brought out of naval retirement to put his Great War command experience to use running and marshalling this convoy, might get to one of the boats or rafts before she went to the bottom.

But nemesis was approaching, in the shape of our plucky *Coquelicot*. Tearing over at our maximum sixteen knots to the spot where my ASDIC operator had warned me the attacking U-Boat was lurking, we ran over his position literally showering him with high explosive. Once more the giant columns of tortured water, and once more the heart-stopping sight of a U-Boat blown to the surface by our charges! Spinning round in almost our own length, we were on him like a tigress. In my eagerness to finish him off, I ordered our helmsman to ram, until I realised that this prey was one of the larger Type IX U-Boats, which was probably bigger than we were, and certainly with a very tough outer skin! So at the very last moment we veered off to starboard, virtually running alongside the stranded U-Boat which was pitching and rolling, dead in the water while he struggled to start his diesel engines for an escape bid on the surface. But he was not to get away, as a couple of depth charges at minimum settings rolled off our racks, virtually under his stern as we fled at our modest top speed. As I spun us away to starboard again to clear the arc of fire of his after torpedo tubes, we all saw the stern of the U-Boat blown clear up and out of the water by our exploding charges. Once more, the stricken lurch, then she also slipped sternwards to oblivion. Two down, in under ten minutes!

The story is much the same all around the embattled convoy that afternoon and well into the evening. *Coquelicot* was to share in the destruction of at least two more U-Boats before dawn, and the pride of Donitz's wolfpacks suffer the loss of no less than eight of their number, although at least two other boats which were claimed by the Allies eventually manage to limp home to their refuges in Occupied France. The butcher's bill? Just four merchantmen sunk and three damaged, plus two American destroyers sunk and one, the *Keeling*, abandoned under tow when the weather deteriorated the next morning and sunk by a "friendly" torpedo from one of her compatriots. Hardly a score in the U-Boats' favour, and the first of many similar nails in their "iron" coffin.

To try to stop the rot, Raeder pulls together a task force comprising *Bismarck*, *Scharnhorst*, *Gneisenau* and *Prinz Eugen*, and they sortie in May 1941 to seize control of the Atlantic sea routes.

Richelieu – by far the strongest of the Allies' battleships – the battlecruisers *Strasbourg* and *Dunkerque*, together with the heavy cruiser *Algérie*, join forces with *Prince of Wales*, *King George V*, *Suffolk* and *Norfolk*, escorted by several flotillas of destroyers. The Allied force falls on the Germans as they debouch from the Denmark Strait. In the ensuing battle *Prince of Wales* is severely damaged by *Bismarck* and *Gneisenau*, but in return the combined firepower of *Richelieu*, *Prince of Wales* and *King George V* smash the *Bismarck* into a blazing hulk. Her crew set scuttling charges, and the pride of Hitler's High Seas Fleet vanishes beneath the waves. The shattered wreck of *Scharnhorst*, torn apart by a large number of the 55 torpedoes launched at her, follows *Bismarck* to the bottom an hour later. More than four thousand German sailors perish. Despite taking heavy damage, *Gneisenau* and *Prinz Eugen* make a high speed dash for safety, give their pursuers the slip and return to Germany.

Karl Reinar was an official photographer for 'Signal' Magazine. He observed the battle from the Admiral's bridge on *Gneisenau*, and has left this patriotic, but highly vivid description:

Today in the Arctic half-light we witnessed the heroic sacrifice of more than four thousand brave German sailors in their fight to break the enemy's stranglehold in the Atlantic Ocean.

We sailed together from Norway to break the economic blockade which threatens the peoples of Europe. Never again must the British be allowed to starve women and children through their food blockade of the European mainland. Our glorious Kreigsmarine will ensure freedom of the sea lanes for German ships and German goods, whatever the cost. Heil Hitler.

The Fuehrer had ordered Grand Admiral Raeder to sortie in strength to sweep the Atlantic of enemy shipping. Through spies our departure was observed and our course plotted. This enabled overwhelming enemy surface forces and aircraft to ambush our valiant squadron as we debouched from the Denmark Straits.

I asked an officer how many ships the enemy had concentrated against us. He replied the lookouts had identified five battleships and battlecruisers so far, plus an equal number of heavy cruisers. The whole enemy fleet was shielded by more than twenty destroyers, whereas our own destroyers had been detached on a diversion to the south of Iceland while the heavy ships forged ahead into the rising swell.

The *Bismarck* opened the battle by taking the lead enemy ship under fire of her 38 cm guns. Their blast lit up a whole section of the horizon, and for a heart-stopping moment it seemed she must have blown up. The next second we saw her rush through the smoke of her own guns, her huge battle flags proudly streaming as she made full speed for the thick of the action.

Almost immediately our own ship opened fire, quickly followed by *Scharnhorst* and *Prinz Eugen*. Soon came the enemy reply, lifting huge geysers of coloured water on our starboard side. The enemy shells fell some distance away, between ourselves and the *Scharnhorst*. Suddenly a yell went up from the gunnery officers - two heavy shells had exploded together on the second enemy ship. I asked who had hit her and one of our officers said it was shells from *Gneisenau*. We could see flames leaping up from the after deck of the enemy ship which we had hit, and suddenly she turned through 90 degrees and veered out of the battle line. The Kapitan announced to the crew that an English battleship of the latest King George V Class, perhaps even the Royal Navy Flagship herself, had been badly hit and was withdrawing. A huge cheer went up from our men in exposed positions around the superstructure, a cheer which was abruptly cut short by the crushing concussion of our next salvo.

By now, however, every gun on the remaining enemy ships seemed to have targeted the *Bismarck*, our leading vessel. At times she completely disappeared behind a curtain of water thrown up by the exploding shells. Now and again we could see orange flashes burst through this curtain, and I asked one of our officers if this was her guns firing. He sadly replied that most of *Bismarck*'s guns appeared to be out of action, and the flashes were the explosions of enemy shells on her thick armoured hide.

We could only watch as, like a hunted beast at bay, the *Bismarck* turned first one way and then the next to try to throw the hunters off the scent. All to no avail, since the enemy were present in overwhelming strength. I have since learned that at least three renegade French vessels took part in this engagement, and it is to be hoped that they suffered heavily for their treachery.

Suddenly we saw *Bismarck* hove to and dead in the water. Her funnel casing had been shot away, and her engines were stopped. Huge shell bursts were still rising around her, but the enemy was now shifting target to bracket our ship. *Gneisenau* weaved to port and starboard at high speed, and we were literally thrown from one side of the Admiral's Bridge to the other. Suddenly there was a huge rushing sound like an express train, and the whole ship shuddered as if she had been struck by a giant hammer. The very deck plates leapt like live things, and we were thrown off our feet for a second time.

When I regained the bridge rail, I saw that we were heading at high speed in the opposite direction to our original course. Leaning out over the rail I could just make out a smudge of black smoke astern which I assumed hid the *Bismarck* from our gaze, then the scene was gone beyond my field of vision.

Ahead of us, just off our port bow, steamed the reassuring sight of the *Prinz Eugen*, her stern throwing up a huge cataract of water as her propellers thrashed the water into foam. Her aircraft catapult was hanging down over the side of the ship, and when she turned to avoid the next enemy salvoes I could see the guns of Anton turret pointed skywards at a strange angle. Like us, however, she was still steaming at full speed, a magnificent sight with her battle ensigns streaming straight back in the wind.

I asked a communications officer if he had news of our other ships. He answered that *Bismarck* was sinking when she was last seen. *Scharnhorst* had disappeared off to the south, shrouded in shell bursts, but we had high hopes that she would be able to use her superior speed and, like us, break free of the enemy's entrapment and make it back home. Sadly, this was not to be, and to date we have no news of the fate of this fine vessel and her brave crew.

The Führer has ordered all available U-Boats to converge on her last known position. Sieg Heil!

Hitler is once more enraged. In a tirade he sacks Raeder, and orders the *Gneisenau*, the newly completed *Tirpitz*, the Panzerschiffe and the cruisers laid up and disarmed. Their guns are brought ashore and most are employed on railway mountings for use on the Eastern Front which is about to open. In all, 8 x 15in, 21 x 11in, 16 x 8in, 75 x 5.9in and 78 x 4.1in guns are made available. Those ex-naval guns which are turned against Leningrad will make a significant contribution to crushing the spirit of the Soviet defenders.

The U-boat fleet is not immediately rebuilt, so very few Allied planes are diverted into maritime patrol. With the German Fleet immobilised and disarmed in German waters, the ships cease to be a bomber priority for the time being. Regular photo reconnaissance missions are flown, however, to keep an eye on the hulks - and the uncompleted carrier *Graf Zeppelin* - in case the Germans ever decide to reactivate them.

Hitler is persuaded by Dönitz to allow the development of the high-submerged-speed Type XXI U-boat, along with more experimental Walther type U-boats driven by closed-circuit hydrogen peroxide fuel. With the successes of Barbarossa, however, U-boat construction is given a low priority. One underlying reason is that the SS are at the forefront of the land advances which are creating the dreamed-of *liebensraum*, and the SS are not at all interested in U-boat warfare.

The temporary German withdrawal from the Battle of the Atlantic brings an unexpected bonus. Several *geschwader* of long-range four-engined Focke-Wulf Condors are withdrawn from maritime reconnaissance. Their crews are experienced in long-distance navigation, but they are also well-trained bombing exponents.

In searching for a role for these expensive aircraft, the Luftwaffe offers them to Barbarossa, to carry out long-range bombing missions against Soviet arsenals - in particular those producing armoured vehicles – and also railway marshalling yards. In this way the supply of new tanks from the factories is severely disrupted. Long range fighter escort is provided by Bf110Ds carrying drop tanks. The Soviet Air Force is geared to battlefield support missions, so the early Condor raids are virtually unopposed. When the Russians belatedly allocate several squadrons to factory defence, the fast but poorly armed MiG-1s and MiG-3s of the PVO *(7)* are no match for the highly experienced German *experte* in their deadly *Zerstörer.*

The missions are so successful that Focke-Wulf is authorised by the RLM to develop a more powerful strategic bomber version of the Condor, restressed and strengthened throughout to take four BMW 801 radial engines, and with the outer wing panels covered in metal in place of fabric.

---

7 *Both models of MiG were armed only with a single 12.7mm Beresin BS and two 7.62mm ShKAS machine guns, barely able to hurt a heavily-armoured Condor.*
PVO : Protivovozdushnoi Oborony or Protective Air Force, a point-defence force.

Chapter Six
THE SAMURAI CONNECTION

Without time-consuming diversions into the Balkans, Adolf Hitler is free to concentrate on his declared main purpose, the destruction of the Bolshevik Soviet Union and the seizure of Leibensraum.

Hitler has, for a long time, been trying to persuade his eastern Axis partner to strike at the Soviets across their common border in Manchuria. He knows this will cause a fatal diversion of Russian effort, and the Soviet Union will be unable to sustain a fight on two fronts. This scenario would ironically bring the ex-Corporal a great deal of satisfaction, since it was the need to fight for so long on two major fronts during the Great War which he felt had robbed Imperial Germany of the victory she and her Army so richly deserved.

However, the Japanese Army is still smarting from the overwhelming defeat they suffered at the hands of Marshall Zhukov at the battle of Khalkhin Goll near Nomonhan in Manchuria in 1939, and they persistently refuse to consider affronting such a powerful opponent.

Sensing that his allies feel they are technically far outmatched in the East, Hitler proposes a way of breaking the stalemate. Just as a previous generation of Soviet military hardware was tested - and found wanting - in the bloody Spanish Civil War (which in many ways was used by the fascists and communists as a practice ground for their coming great conflict), he wants to try the mettle of the latest Soviet armoured forces and the tactical and strategic abilities of their generals.

Hitler therefore despatches a technical military mission to Tokyo, headed up by the redoubtable Panzer specialist General Von Manstein. His role is to help bring the Japanese Army up to strength in terms of modern armour and panzer tactics.

To everyone's surprise, the Japanese react favourably. As they have so amply demonstrated ever since the arrival of Perry and his 'Black Ships', they are keen to learn from the 'gaijin' and especially to absorb the latest foreign military technology, which they have become so adept at first copying, and then adapting to their own needs.

And this new rapprochement turns a drawback into an advantage. Ever since the Allies'overwhelming naval strength has driven the German merchant marine from the high seas, capturing or sinking their freighters or forcing them to seek refuge in neutral ports, Germany has been smarting from a shortage of raw materials. One critical element is tungsten, an essential material not only in modern anti-tank projectiles but also vital to make the machine tools which make the machines which run modern warfare.

Doenitz's U-boats have tried, and failed, to bring back meaningful supplies of tungsten from the Far East. U-tanker boats, no longer needed since the Kreigsmarine's temporary withdrawal from the Battle of the Atlantic, have been bravely attempting the long return journey to Japan. But these huge, clumsy boats are far too easy to detect from the air, and all too easy to destroy once they submerge. Losses have been crippling, and Doenitz reluctantly admits defeat.

At this juncture, the large Japanese merchant marine steps in. At the close of 1941, with the spectre of large scale conflict postponed for some time, the Japanese announce that they will take on the maritime task of supplying Germany with the raw materials she so sorely needs. Large fast Japanese Marus, often disguised merchant cruisers with concealed 5.5-inch guns and torpedo tubes, make regular supply runs to Germany *(8)*.

---

8 *It is possible that an encounter with one of these disguised Japanese Armed Merchant Cruisers may have been responsible for the mysterious loss of the Australian light cruiser Sydney. She disappeared without trace after a desperate engagement with the German auxiliary cruiser Kormoran, which sank in the battle. It has been suggested that Kormoran may have been heading for a re-supply rendezvous with a Japanese AMC when she met Sydney and was forced to fight. The Maru which closed the scene would then have been in a position to torpedo the crippled Australian vessel without warning, perhaps when pretending to offer assistance. Ominously, no confirmed trace of Sydney's crew, no bodies, wreckage, boat or liferaft, have ever come to light, apart from one body thought to be from her crew, found much later in a bullet-riddled liferaft.*

In the event of them being stopped by the Allies for inspection of their cargo manifests, the materials in their holds are officially destined for Scandinavia. Once safe inside the private German lake which the Baltic has become, the ships make straight for northern German ports.

In this way Hitler's war machine receives massive injections of tungsten, and mercury, and many other vital war supplies.

The empty ships load with the latest German military and aviation technology, to help bolster the Japanese military and make Hitler's dream of a war against the Soviets on two fronts come one step closer to realisation. They carry back the latest Nazi designs, ground and air-interception radar sets, anti-aircraft and aircraft cannons, prototype jet engines, squeeze-bore and other advanced anti-tank guns, and armoured vehicles.

Mitsubishi Industries and Daihatsu set up new production lines to produce Japanese variants of, respectively, the Panzer Mk IV and the Sturmgeschutz III. These Japanese versions at first faithfully follow the plans and pilot models provided by the Manstein Mission, but they are powered by Japanese diesel engines.

At the same time Von Manstein and his subordinates work hard to retrain the Japanese in the use of these new tanks. Traditionally the Imperial Army has regarded the tank as merely an adjunct to the infantry. To take on the Soviets and beat them on the steppes, theJapanese will need to absorb the lessons of the type of fast-movingBlitzkreig campaign which Hitler, and Zhukov, have so successfully used, the latter against the Japanese themselves.

These tactical lessons are much harder to put over than the technical material advances, however, and when Von Manstein and his men are recalled to Germany to add their experience to the push against Stalin in the West, they are not certain that their Japanese understudies have fully absorbed all the lessons.

In fact Hitler's ploy has failed to hit the target, and the Japanese will after all continue to refrain from going head-to-head with the Soviets. Instead they prefer to use their new panzers in China, where they will be instrumental in crushing at least one Communist foe, namely the peasant Red Army of Mao-Zedung. After a long and bloody conflict in China's North-Western Shaanxi Province, the Red leader is captured by the Imperial Kwantung (Guandong) Army in Yan'an and sent to a jail outside Tokyo. At the end of the War he will be handed over to the Kuomintan Nanking Government and be transferred to prison on Formosa, where Mao lives out his remaining years in the company of convicted Japanese war criminals. The last inmate of the prison, he eventually dies on 9th September 1976, forgotten by most of the outside world.

The very same Panzer IVs and StuGs will be a thorn in the sides of the American garrison and relief forces during the bitter fighting for the Phillipines.

One other side-effect of this military co-operation is the aid the Germans provide to the Japanese Air arms.

Before the War, Ernst Heinkel - thwarted in his ambition to build fighters for the Luftwaffe by political insistence that his factories concentrate on building only bomber aircraft - has tried to export his shapely He 112 fighter, the unfortunate rival to the Messerschmidt Bf 109. One customer was Japan, who eventually purchased two demonstrators, the 5th and 11th prototypes - the latter fitted with a DB600 engine - plus a small production run including 27 of the redesigned He 112B model.

In the event, the Japanese reverted to type and eschewed the high level and diving speed characteristics of these modern Heinkels in favour of their traditional dogfighter aircraft, with the emphasis on manoeuvrability above all else. Sadly, the Heinkels ended their days as instructional airframes for budding Japanese air mechanics.

Undaunted by this setback, Ernst Heinkel's sales team continue to court the Japanese. When the RLM's veto on Heinkel fighter aircraft struck down their excellent He 280 twin jet fighter, the first of its kind anywhere in the world, Heinkel turn to the Japanese. The deal is struck, manufacturing rights are assigned, and Mitsubishi and Rikugun set to constructing the revolutionary new fighter as the J7M1 Type He for the Navy and the Ki-66 for the Army respectively.

These new fighters enter service in very small numbers only, but their existence is known to Allied intelligence, and they spur the counter development of single- and twin-engined jet fighters by the British and Americans... The threat of Japanese jet fighters will also be instrumental in forcing the B-29 strategic bomber force to switch from day to night-time bombing raids on the Japanese Home Islands during the closing stages of the War in the Pacific. Lacking AI radar compact and sophisticated enough to be operated by the single crewman of the jets, the Japanese fighter force is practically impotent against these raids, despite having pioneered the "schräge musik" angled cannon installation in its night fighters.

Chapter Seven
SUCCESS IN RUSSIA

The Wehrmacht now sees itself as the successors to the Teutonic Knights.

Its speedy advance has brought the Germans to the very gates of Moscow. This huge city, with its population of more than three million people, is likely to be even more of a problem to Hitler's legions than it was to the Grand Army of his predecessor Napoleon in 1812.

The Soviets organise the population of Moscow for its defence – 160,000 volunteers are formed into 16 divisions, and a further 4 engineering regiments are founded - while hundreds of thousands more dig anti-tank ditches around the city. The defenders are perilously short of tanks and heavy artillery, however, and the Soviet officials harbour doubts about how long they can resist a seige.

The German armies surge past Moscow on both sides, and complete the encirclement of the Russian capital. Initially their attacks are limited to reconnaissance probings into the outlying suburbs. The task facing any force which tries to penetrate into the interior of Moscow proper is a daunting one. In the meantime, the Luftwaffe carries out daily pinprick raids to keep the defences on the alert and deny the men and women in the trenches any sleep or respite. All approaches are systematically mapped by aerial reconnaissance planes, ready for the big push.

Before the Germans can fully commit themselves to the attack on Moscow, Marshall Zhukov suddenly arrives from the East with the Siberian Army and hundreds of new T-34 tanks - virtually the entire production built to date - to break the German blockade of the capital. Aided by a co-ordinated infantry sortie from the eastern defence lines of the city, he manages to create panic in the German centre, but the Wehrmacht stand firm on each flank.

The Germans have great trouble overcoming the T-34's – and only captured French 75s can guarantee defeating their armour. Luckily after their experiences at the start of Barbarossa they have modified hundreds of 75s, mounted on 5cm PaK carriages, with hoops to reinforce their barrel to take a more powerful propellant charge, and a huge perforated muzzle brake screwed on the end to try to reduce the fearsome recoil. Using captured Polish AP shot, it can defeat even the latest Soviet tanks, but the recoil is so severe, and the carriage so light, that the entire gun leaps backwards a couple of metres on firing.

After a week of desperate fighting, Zhukov's forces, and the infantry who have so recklessly sortied from Moscow, are virtually wiped out. Zhukov manages to extract remnants of his divisions but hundreds of thousands more go into the cage. Very few Russian tanks are able to escape, and the Red Army is now virtually finished as a major organised military force.

With the hope of immediate relief smashed, the desperate Soviet defenders of Moscow settle down to a grim seige, cut off from the outside world apart from nightly flights by elderly Po-2 biplanes which risk the FlaK and Luftwaffe nightfighters to maintain liaison with the surviving Soviet forces to the East.

The major industrial centres west of the Urals are now all in German hands. The speed of their advance has foiled Stalin's plan to move all tank and gun production facilities far to the East, out of reach of Hitler's legions.

Some plants have been moved just in time, the Tula Arsenal machinery being removed under the noses of the advancing panzers. Mosin-Nagant rifles marked with the Tula stamp have been found with dates of 1942 and 1943, built in the shadow factory several hundred miles east of the Ural Mountains.

There is high drama at the giant tank production factory in Kuibayshev. Brand-new T-34 tanks are being mass-produced and driven straight to the front lines. German reconnaissance aircraft have pinpointed the source of these troublesome tanks, and a column of fast Panzer 38(T)s, with a group of converted French 75 guns in support, is detached to mop up the complex. With Soviet aircraft driven from the skies there is virtually no warning of the German advance, and the first inkling the factory workers have of their imminent doom is the sight of the Panzer 38(T)s breasting a hill some five kilometres from the outskirts of the town. In desperation the tanks able to move under their own power are fuelled up and driven out of the plant, at speed, heading for the illusory safety of the Ural Mountain foothills far to the East. Most will never make it to safety, as the fast Panzers cut them off and swarm all over the defenceless fugitives. There are desperate combats between those T-34s whose novice crews have managed to haul on board a number of shells for their 76.2mm guns before fleeing. Most, however, are unarmed and will be hunted down one by one. The drivers of several turretless T-34s, including some manned by female production line workers, resort to ramming the smaller Panzers head-on at full speed, wrecking both vehicles, and in this way they inflict a significant number of German casualties. Their respite is brief, however, and the devastation is complete. Several T-34s make it as far as the Ural foothills, where they run out of fuel. Their abandoned hulks will be found by the advancing Wehrmacht only a few weeks later, as they move to consolidate their positions on the crests of the Urals before the Russian Winter can break.

Leningrad is cut off on all sides. 15-inch and 11-inch guns landed from the disarmed Kreigsmarine heavy ships smash the resupply route over the ice of Lake Ladoga, and destroy all attempts by the Russians to establish oil pipeline and electricity cable links with the beseiged city. They also completely cut off all traffic on the new road and railway connections built between Novaya Lagoda, Volkhov and Lednovo. There will be no Russian equivalent of the "Voie Sacrée" which saved Verdun, and their own aptly named "Road of Death" becomes just that.

While the Finns make a demonstration against the Northern defences, the final push by the Wehrmacht comes in from Schlüsselburg in the South-East. At the same time Fallschirmjaeger units drop inside the Russian perimeter and seize Ladozhskoye Ozero, for sound tactical reasons but primarily to boost Goering's prestige. The paratroops suffer heavy casualties, but their diversion succeeds and the city falls. Leningrad is renamed 'Petrograd', the first of many Russian cities to lose their recent Soviet names. The Finns claim hegemony over the city, but its political significance is such that Petrograd becomes the headquarters of the Greater Reich in the East, and Heidrich moves into the Winter Palace with his staff, followed by Albert Speer who takes over a complete wing for his economic planning unit.

In the headlong German advance the politically significant city of Stalingrad is cut off and left as an isolated bastion of Soviet power hundreds of miles behind the front, with no hope of resupply or reinforcement. It will finally fall after bloody street fighting and heavy Waffen SS losses, some seven weeks later. The starving Russian defenders know they have been abandoned by the STAVKA but resist until their ammunition finally runs out.

The following week, once all Russian snipers have been hunted down and eliminated, Adolf Hitler flies down to captured Stalingrad in his personal Condor, to tour the city named after his Soviet opponent. He promotes General Von Paulus to Field Marshall on the spot, and renames the city "Tsaritsyn", its former pre-Soviet name.

The scuttled Soviet destroyer Lenin

Further south, Rommel detaches Hoth to sweep down the eastern seaboard of the Black Sea and capture the last remaining Soviet naval bases still holding out. Since the fall of Sebastapol and then Novorossisk, the remnants of the Soviet Black Sea Fleet have been holed up in Batum and Poti, near the Turkish border. These two ports, however, lack the facilities to maintain modern warships, so the fleet has eked out a twilight existence while the rest of the Soviet Empire collapses to the North and East.

Now Hoth's panzers approach the final fleet refuges, leaving the Soviets the option of either sailing their ships into internment in Turkey, or of destroying them. Since the Turks have long been regarded as the mortal enemies of Russia, the Soviet commanders choose the latter option, and the Black Sea fleet ceases to exist.

The larger warships are taken out into deeper water and scuttled. Destroyers and smaller craft are blown up in the port facilities, thereby denying their immediate use by the invader.

The sailors try to join in the precipitate flight of their Red Army counterparts. However, Rommel's major panzer thrust to Baku lies astride their escape route, and the majority of the sailors of the former Black Sea Fleet go into the bag.

Rommel reaches Baku. As predicted the local commisars order the demolition of the oil installations, and the Germans arrive to find the wells ablaze. Rommel's Roumanian oil technicians help advise the Army Engineers on how to extinguish and cap the damaged wells.

The work takes much longer than anticipated, and gigantic black clouds from the burning wells turn day into night for many miles and for several weeks.

A confident Erwin Rommel framed by the flames from the sabotaged Baku oilwells.

However, once the fires are extinguished, repair work can begin immediately. Typical German efficiency swings into action, and only three months after their capture the Baku oilwells begin to pump out their black gold once more, but this time for the invading Germans. Thus one component of their enormous logistical headache is immediately resolved.

Stalin, his terror organisations restricted virtually to the immediate region around his mobile base, is fast losing popular support because of the debacle. He holes up in the town of Saratov on the Volga, to the North-East of Stalingrad. His personal bodyguard have recently been killed in a Stuka attack on his armoured train, and he is now guarded by a squad brought in by one of his recent acolytes, an ambitious Political Officer called Nikita Khrushchev. Impressed by Khrushchev's keenness, Stalin has ordered him to fly into Stalingrad in a Po-2 biplane, take command of the garrison, and fight to the last man. Khrushchev, who is astute enough to know the battle for Stalingrad is already lost, realises the last man will probably be himself. Instead of putting a gun to his own head, he decides on a desperate course of action.

In the early hours of June 3rd 1941, the officer of the watch going about his rounds discovers the two bodyguards who normally stand guard at the foot of Comrade Stalin's bed lounging against the outside of the bedroom door, taking a cigarette break. They assure him all is well, he is simply too fatigued to press the matter, and lets it pass for fear of rousing his wrathful leader.

The next morning Stalin's faithful handservants fail to raise their master from his slumber, and the doctor who is urgently summoned pronounces him dead. Probable cause is pronounced to be heart failure, brought on by the stress of the defeats and continuous forced retreats. An autopsy might have revealed the presence of the poison which has hastened him on his way, but there is no time to have one carried out, and little incentive so to do.

With the approaching Nazi patrols so close, there is precious little time to arrange for Comrade Stalin's lying in state in the small town hall. As the leading Panzers break through the last screen, his entourage panic and throw Stalin's body down a nearby well before fleeing. Thus perishes 'Uncle Joe', the butcher of more than two million of his own countrymen, and the first of the megalomaniac leaders to exit the stage – ironically at the hands of his own people whom he has terrorized for so long.

Khrushchev takes over day-to-day running of what is left of the Soviet apparatus, and leads the Red Army in even more "strategic withdrawals", an euphamism for headlong flight.

Back in Moscow, the city fathers are badly shaken by news of the successive disasters in Leningrad, Stalingrad and Baku. Then comes the news of Stalin's death and the takeover by Khrushchev. The latter's first missive to the beleagured citizens of Moscow is, ironically, a call to them to fight to the last man and woman, and the last bullet, and to never give in to the invader.

Fortunately, saner counsels prevail, and the remnants of the Senate who have not already fled the city make it known to German emissaries that they are prepared to cease fighting and declare Moscow an "open city", much in the same fashion as Paris a year earlier, on the understanding that the Germans will respect the safety and well-being of the millions of citizens, and preserve the city's institutions and monuments.

Facing the need to expose tens of thousands of troops in the attack on the city, with the risk of suffering huge casualties, the Germans agree to the peace proposals. The citizen militias are to be disarmed and their weapons stockpiled for the use of the new Germanic satellite states which are to be created in the East. Many Muscovites will be drafted into the future anti-Soviet units to be raised as the guarantors of Greater Deutschland's Eastern frontier.

But in the meantime Adolf Hitler cannot resist the publicity opportunities offered by the surrender of Moscow. He flies into Hodynskoye Field Airport, some five kilometres from the Kremlin, and proceeds on a tourist trip around his new dominion.

Unlike his predecessor, the new Napoleon does not gaze upon acres of desolation, for most of the city has now been spared destruction. He begins his tour with a visit to view the bare steel skeleton of the Palace of Soviets, a project to construct the world's largest building, at a total height of 415 metres, including a gigantic 100-metre-high statue of Lenin topping what the architect Boris Iofan had planned as a "ladder to the skies". The steelwork will be pulled down and transported back to Germany to turn into Panzers. Hitler views this prospect with especial relish.

One of the highlights laid on for the Führer is a viewing of the 96-metre-tall statue of the founder of modern Russia, Peter the Great, on the Moskva riverbank, which is one of the tallest statues in the world. As a megalomaniac with dreams of grandeur, such sights gladden Hitler's heart.

He then moves on to Saint Basil's Cathedral, with its famous onion-shaped domes. Here Hitler takes the opportunity to publically praise the Orthodox Church, hoping to bring its hierarchy and adherents over to the side of his New World Order, just as he had so successfully done with the Roman Catholic Church back in Germany proper. He also announces that his architect Speer will aid with the reconstruction of the Cathedral of Christ the Saviour, so criminally demolished on Stalin's orders only eight years earlier to free up the site for the Palace of Soviets.

The next stop for the triumphant Führer is the extensive appartments of the Kremlin Palace, still littered with the detritus of a hasty Soviet Government evacuation.

Strutting across Red Square, the German Dictator visits the Mausoleum where Lenin's embalmed body lies on display. Despite the fact that the leader of the Soviets had been secretly transported back into Russia by the Führer's Imperial German antecedants, Hitler makes no secret of his disdain for the corpse of the Bolschevik leader, the antithesis of everything New Germany stands for. Lenin's body is to be removed from the tomb and buried in one of Moscow's graveyards, with little in the way of publicity. In the meantime the tomb itself serves as the Führer's own viewing stand as his victorious army parades down Red Square in a copy of the huge Soviet military parades of the 1930s. The irony is completed by the fact that Lenin's embalmed body remains in situ, and the dead Soviet leader suffers the humiliation of being rocked by the stamp of jackboots of the victorious German legions and the rumble of their panzer tracks.

Hitler's triumphal day is rounded off by a visit to the Bolshoi Ballet, which puts on a special production of *Swan Lake* for its new masters. The Führer's comments on the ballet have gone unrecorded, but every photo of him on this triumphal tour shows a broad grin from ear to ear, thus is his cup overflowing.

Striking far to the East beyond Moscow, the Wehrmacht begins to run out of enemies to fight and cities to assault.

At the end of November 1941 leading Wehrmacht Alpine troops fight their way to the top of several dominating heights in the Ural Mountains, which have long loomed in their sights during their relentless drive eastwards. Russian defenders cling desperately to several mountaintops, but they are remorselessly Stuka-ed and shelled off their tenuous positions.

And then the infamous Russian Winter begins to bite in earnest, bringing all operations to a dead stop.

To keep up the idea of momentum on the Home Front, Leni Reifenstal is sent by Goebbels' Propaganda Ministry to make a film of the legendary Aryan flyer Hauptmann Hans-Joachim Marseille. As the pinnacle of the Nazi meritricious system used with such effect to incentivise the young pilots, he is to be presented with the Diamonds to his Oakleaves with Swords, on achieving his 400th confirmed victory.

Red Air Force wrecks litter the airfield now used by the 109s of Hans Joachim Marseille, the "Young Lion", which are lined up in the background. The disparate collection of wrecks appears to be a graveyard of several different models, collected together by the Germans for scrapping.

Normally such heroes return to Berlin for the Fuehrer to make the presentation in person, but Goering has decided to make the trip to the Eastern Front to be filmed pinning the highest award on his top fighter pilot 'in the field'.

The old flyers' superstition that one should not be photographed before a mission will come to haunt her until her dying day. Reifenstal's last sequence of shots is to be Marseille taking off on yet another mission, and she cuts to the final image of him flying East in his brand-new Bf 109 'Gustav' into the dawn's light.

Just 30 minutes into the mission, Marseille's plane suffers a major mechanical failure, a conrod goes through the crankcase, and the engine bursts into flames. The cockpit fills with smoke, and his desperate wingmen radio Marseille to bale out. Finally he recovers sufficiently to release the canopy hood, and bales out. Tragically, Marseille strikes the tailplane of his 'Gustav', is knocked unconscious and does not pull the ripcord. His distraught comrades can only watch as he plummets to his death on the frozen steppe thousands of feet below.

His unit, JG27, erects a memorial at the spot where he fell. Later, a Russian guerilla band dynamites the monument and it has to be rebuilt, using money donated by Marseille's home district of Berlin-Charlottensburg. The bronze eagle and swastika, however, in the form of a Flugzeugfuehrer badge, has been torn off and lost - until, forty years later, it turns up in an antique dealer's shop in Riga and is restored to the monument.

As the famous film director recalled so tearfully:

I will never forget that day as long as I live. Our brave young lion had been so mischievous the previous evening, both in word and deed, a performance which climaxed in him lashing a rope fastening from my technical director's tent to the fender of his Kubelwagen, and then driving off in the middle of the night, leaving poor Hans staring up at the cold starry night ....

Joachim's Commanding Officer came over to me as I was setting up our cameras to record what would be his last takeoff. He remonstrated with me that in his days in the Great War, it was held to be extremely bad luck for a pilot to be photographed immediately prior to taking off on a combat mission. He had personally seen many brave young men who "went West" immediately after being captured on film in such circumstances.

I smiled condescendingly at him and tried to ignore such superstitious ramblings.

Ah, if only I had known what was to happen just a few brief, tragic minutes later......   I would do anything to have undone that bitter experience, the shock, the feeling of hopeless remorse. Oh, I am sorry, I.... you must go now, I, I cannot go on with this interview.

At this stage, economic and political factors begin to come to the fore and take precedence over purely military and national socialist aims.   From his wing in the Winter Palace, Albert Speer does an inventory of the spoils, and draws up plans for the economic and agrarian future of the eastern provinces of Grosser Deutschland. Like Classicianus arguing against General Agricola's programme of massacre and oppression in Britannia nearly two thousand years before, Speer presents to his master Hitler an argued proposal that massacres and pogroms should stop, simply because the peasants are required to harvest the crops and plant the seeds for the next season. Only in this way can Grosser Deutschland remain independent of the Anglo-Saxon Democracies. As a corollary, thousands of 'gastarbeiter' can be drafted into Germany proper to repair bomb damage, build new communications and civil buildings, and free up thousands of Germans for war production and defence, to prepare for the final showdown with the West.

The German Army copies its Roman predecessor, and establishes a new 'Limes' in the East. Unlike the continuous Roman walls, the Wehrmacht establishes interlocking groups of fire bases across the steppes, backed by two complete railway systems running the length and breadth of the defences.

The Roman analogy is continued in the garrisons, which are recruited from local indigenous peoples who have willingly thrown off the Soviet yoke. In the main they comprise Georgians, Ukrainians, and Don Cossacks.

The German panzer divisions designated to support the line garrisons play the role of their Roman Legionary counterparts, ready to move quickly to any threatened zone of the front.

Partisan groups engage in lightning raids, slipping between the strongpoints and trying to cut the railways, but strong Luftwaffe aerial reconnaissance usually detects them and tracks them remorselessly. Cossack units of the German Army give no quarter when they run these partisans to ground.

Units of the regular Red Army still survive, holed up in remote forest areas. However, they have few heavy weapons, virtually no tanks, and their air support is negligible. They are still a substantial infantry force in being, and as such cannot be ignored.

The Soviets have lost virtually all their tank and aircraft production facilities, overrun by the speed of the initial German advance before the factories could be moved further East. The Western Democracies investigate how they could resupply the Soviets, on the basis that 'My enemy's enemy is my friend'. However, all the ports which might have been used to resupply the Soviets are now far behind German lines. Equally the route from the south via Persia and Iraq has been cut by Rommel's advance. The only way to resupply the remnants of the Red Army is from the Far East and across the Trans-Siberian Railway. This route is under regular air attack by the Luftwaffe but food, medical supplies and small arms ammunition reach the rag-tag army in sufficient quantities to ensure their survival, if not any major offensive capabilities.

In any case, the bulk of American production is earmarked for Britain and French North Africa.

By the time the ferocious Russian Winter arrives and puts a vicious brake on all German military and air activities, Hitler's Third Reich has extended its reach far beyond the ruins of Moscow, and from the heights of the Ural Mountains looks down on the plains stretching as far as the eye can see to the East.

WESTERN STALEMATE

The conquered peoples of the West, the Norwegians, Danes, Poles and Czechoslovaks, are powerless to remove the occupying army, and must wait expectantly, along with the citizens of Metropolitan France, for the promised liberation by the Western Democracies.

In the meantime, they continue to provide slave labour for German defensive works and war factories. At the same time the Underground Resistance movements suffer mixed fortunes. Nazi successes in the East have led to a feeling of despondency, with many defections from the Resistance, especially in Slovakia and Denmark. Local people begin to think that the Thousand Year Reich may be around for a long time, and they feel they must begin to try to come to an accommodation with their occupiers.

In Norway, however, the Resistance movement continues to make strong progress, under the cover of camping organisations, and even succeeds in turning out large numbers of home-made Sten guns in basement workshops. They are test-fired each Sunday morning while the church bells ring.

The neutral Swedes and the Swiss feel even more vulnerable, and following Nazi victories in the East and the virtual elimination of the Russians from the War, citizens of these two states actively press their Governments to openly come out on the side of Germany.

Roosevelt tries to counter these developments by secretly promising economic aid, but the Swedes and Swiss know only too well that the Americans are completely unable to supply military support to them, isolated as they are by the tide of Nazi conquests. The Western Democracies begin to suspect that, despite their secret assurances, both Sweden and Switzerland are actively supplying covert war supplies, including automatic weapons and artillery, to Germany. This is tolerated at the time due to *force majeur*, but the free nations reserve the right to take appropriate action when the War is won.

A serious situation threatens in Czechoslovakia. Himmler's deputy Reinhard Heydrich, ruthless Reichsprotektor of Bohemia and Moravia, has called a halt to terror tactics and, in order to encourage increased war production and reduce sabotage on the production lines, is using a "carrot and stick" approach.

On 27th May 1942, as Heidrich's limousine turns a corner in Prague on his daily route to the office, a group of men standing on a corner suddenly produce automatic weapons and attempt an ambush. Infuriatingly for them, their Sten guns refuse to fire. The SS officer, instead of exiting the scene at speed, foolishly orders his driver to stop and pulls out his pistol to confront the group. One of the assassins throws a bomb, which turns the car into a ball of fire, killing both occupants. Heidrich's SS officers are enraged, and hunt down the assassins, who are traced to the basement of a nearby church and killed. The Nazi riposte is bloody and ruthless. Hitler calls for the immediate execution of 30,000 Czechs. Because a letter found on one of the assassins seems to implicate the nearby village of Lidice, the entire village is razed to the ground, all men and boys over 15 are shot, and the women are sent to concentration camps. A handful of the children chosen as suitable for 'Germanisation' are brought up in Aryan families, but the majority are sent to the gas chambers. Even the dogs and cats are killed. Similar atrocities take place in the Czech villages of Ležáky, Švermovo and Javoricko.

Only, Heidrich was not in the car. It was his Deputy, Sturmbannfuhrer Simon, who was killed. Heidrich has been called to Paris for a conference on how best to promote an increase in French war production for the Reich, down on target because of reluctance and in some cases covert sabotage by the French workers. Back in Prague his faithful deputy has, with typical German punctuality, been keeping to his master's daily schedule and has died in his place.

When he is told of the attack, Heidrich is traumatized. Later reports indicate that the assassination attempt was carried out by renegade Czechs sent by the exiled former Government in London, and Heidrich orders an immediate halt to the killings. He is anxious above all to safeguard the significant contribution the Czechs are making to Germany's war effort. As a further inducement, Foreign Minister Ribbentrop reports back on the worldwide outrage at the news of Lidice. Further reprisals are curtailed, but the Czechs have been given a sharp lesson.

Heidrich has been shaken by the attack, and his close shave with death. However, it only reinforces his belief that the Third Reich, led by the SS, with himself in the forefront, is destined to become the dominant World power. He becomes one of Speer's most ardent supporters in the latter's arguments against continuing the pogroms against former Soviet citizens. In any case, with the remaining few battles going on a thousand miles to the East, it is time to begin re-organising the conquered territories along Germanic lines. The Ukraine, in particular, must become – in the Fuhrer's terms – the breadbasket of Greater Germany.

Chapter Eight
JAPAN MAKES HER MOVE

In the fall of 1941 *Richelieu* is flagship of a powerful French naval force, with *Strasbourg* and *Dunkerque* and their destroyer escorts, sent through the Suez Canal to bolster French resistance in Indo-China.

In the Indian Ocean they rendezvous with the new battleship *Jean Bart* (completed in the USA) and several cruisers, and arrive unannounced off Haiphong (just like the *Surcouf* had earlier turned up at St. Pierre et Miquelon).

Other destroyers and cruisers escort the old French carrier *Béarn* on several ferry trips to Indo-China, where she unloads hundreds of US-built P-38 and P-40 fighters to re-equip local Armee de l'Air squadrons. The obsolescent Moranes which they replace are brought back to the USA by *Béarn* and end their days in the hands of rookie French fighter pilot trainees in the USA.

Some fifty French submarines are also transferred to the French Far East station a flotilla at a time, and they are provisioned and maintained at the new Singapore Naval Base.

To bolster this new Naval Base and support the French Squadron, the *Prince of Wales*, the *Renown* and the rebuilt *Queen Elizabeths* are sent to the Far East. It is planned for *Repulse* to join them, but she runs aground in the West Indies, is badly damaged and is laid up. Her crew is released for reassignment to the new fleet in building.

Faced by nine modern capital ships with their escorts of cruisers and destroyers, not to mention the dozens of Allied submarines, the Japanese are deterred by this show of strength from their plan to seize the French Indo-Chinese airfields.

Forced to revise their battle plans, Malaya and Singapore are deleted off their list of primary targets for the time being. The longer-term Japanese aim of striking through Burma into India is also postponed as a result. In their place, the Dutch East Indies and the vital oilfields are chosen as a softer option for seizure.

Instead of a direct unprovoked assault, the Japanese take a leaf out of their Axis partner's book. Ever since the Netherlands fell beneath the Nazis' jackboot in May 1940, the Dutch East Indies have been seething with unrest as local nationalist groups plot to throw off the colonial yoke of the prostrated mother country.

In Jakarta the Japanese Consul makes contact with a young firebrand named Suharto, and encourages his Freedom Movement with money and clandestine weapons drops. With promises of Japanese support, the nationalists show their hand and rise in open revolt. There are several massacres of Europeans, and many of the native troops refuse to fire on the rebels.

Cunningly, the Japanese wait until the Dutch authorities begin to gain the upper hand and arrest the leading insurrectionists, then they strike.

Japanese "peacekeepers" arrive in the Dutch East Indies

Ostensibly arriving as a 'peace-keeping force', large numbers of Japanese Marines, paratroops and Army units descend on the islands, backed by powerful naval and air support, plus large numbers of tanks.

Faced with such overwhelming force, Dutch resistance is sporadic and short-lived. After three days the Dutch armed forces have been confined to barracks and the entire Dutch East Indies is in Japanese hands.

Outnumbered KNIL soldiers surrender to Japanese "peacekeepers"

Dutch cruisers and destroyers which attempt to head off the Japanese occupation fleet have been sunk or disabled. Several surviving naval units fall back on Australia to regroup, but there they are officially interned and temporarily demilitarized.

The Japanese gamble correctly that neither the USA nor Britain is prepared to go to war at this juncture to support the Dutch, whose homeland is under German occupation. The writing is on the wall, however.

Since British Far Eastern possessions are not to be attacked for the time being, Britain's unofficial ally the USA is also left untouched.

Japanese Naval officers led by Admiral Yamamoto enthusiastically propose an attack on the US Pacific Fleet based at Pearl, but the plan is put on hold for the present, while Japan builds up her naval strength.

Japan is a nominal ally of Nazi Germany, and the Americans recognises that ultimately they will have to face up to, and curtail the expansion of, both these military dictatorships. However, for the present the USA does not yet come into the war against Germany.

With the German surface fleet eliminated as a valid threat, the Battle of the Atlantic won, and German attention focused deep inside Russia, Britain concentrates on building up her fleet, laying up more of her older warships to free crews for *Temeraire*, the first of the Lion Class battleships, plus the *Vanguard*, and also for increasing the number of armoured-deck carriers, two of which will be French-manned and officered. Their aircraft complement of Wildcats and Dauntlesses is provided by the USA, which once again takes on the role of industrial powerhouse for the Western Democracies although not yet involved in the actual fighting.

With the Dutch oilfields in their possession, the Japanese concentrate on completing all three of their monster battleships (including the *Shinano*) before daring to go head-to-head with the combined Navies of the US, Britain and France.

While still at peace with Japan, the Western Allies are able to obtain basic details of the monster trio, the first of which is unwisely exposed during propaganda cruises to overawe potential Japanese targets.

A NASTY SURPRISE

The drubbing handed out by the French light cruiser *Lamotte-Picquet*, when she sank both of Siam's Japanese-built "pocket heavy cruisers", the *Ayuthia* and *Dhonburi*, has led to significant loss of face for Japanese warship constructors. To counter this negative situation, the Imperial Japanese Navy decides to throw caution to the wind and stage an impressive publicity stunt.

Despite building the *Yamato* Class super-battleships in conditions of paranoid secrecy, even screening off their building slips with gigantic curtains of sisal rope, the name ship of the Class is now to be demonstrated to the Siamese – and to the world at large – in an attempt to rebuild confidence in Japan's naval capabilities. Now the *Yamato* is in commission, her sister *Musashi* is about to run trials, and the launch of *Shinano* is imminent, the IJN feels it has nothing to fear from the competition. Designing and building comparable ships will take the US Navy several years, and in the meantime they can earn their colossal building cost by performing as ambassadors of Japanese power and influence.

And perform the *Yamato* does. The Japanese naval squadron which sails into the Andaman Sea, and anchors off Phuket, is impressive in the number and size of its latest destroyers and heavy cruisers. Large and powerful as the cruisers are, the sheer size and presence of *Yamato* dwarfs all her consorts. The Thais are suitably impressed, and discrete foreign naval observers are shocked. Soon the wires hum with ultra-urgent coded messages.

The foreign naval observers make educated guesses at the size of the new monster dreadnoughts, but no-one has any idea that they mount 18.1-inch guns – which are only discovered long after the War when a proof barrel and projectiles are discovered at Nakajima..... Instead they identify the armament as the standard Japanese 16-inch as mounted in *Nagato* and *Mutsu*, little guessing that the next generation of "*Super-Yamatos*" is to be armed with a 20-inch gun.....

ALLIED RIPOSTE

In response to the dramatic appearance of *Yamato*, the US Navy frantically up-armours their four new Iowa Class battleships, sacrificing four knots speed for two more inches of armour on the belt and two more inches on their decks. A further penalty is lowered freeboard, but paradoxically this has the trade-off of making them better sea boats by reducing their roll angles in heavy weather.

The Royal Navy also builds more armour into the *Temeraire* and *Vanguard*, and into the last of the KGVs, *Anson* and *Howe*, which are redesigned to carry nine 16in guns. The actual gun barrels for three of these ships are supplied by the USA and are identical to the guns used in their own battleships. *Vanguard* is completed using the spare 15in turrets kept in store ever since *Courageous* and *Glorious* were converted to aircraft carriers.

The three completed vessels of the King George V Class, namely *KGV* herself, *Prince of Wales* and *Duke of York*, have an extra two inches of armour plate worked in over the six inches covering their magazine spaces, which tests following 1919 have indicated as the minimum total thickness to give protection against a 16-inch shell. Ironically, the same tests had shown that this thickness should resist even the 18-inch APC shell fired by the largest British gun mounted afloat in 1918. The machinery spaces, however, will have to make do with the original five inch armour thickness, and there is always the chance of an unlucky hit below the armour belt itself, as *Prince of Wales* had suffered in the action with *Bismarck*.

HMS Anson as completed with triple 16-inch gun turrets

To compensate for the up-armouring, all of the KGVs are fitted with additional external bulges, which increase their resistance to torpedoes but demand a speed penalty of at least a knot.

MONSTER BOMBS

The RAF is asked to take on a specific anti-ship role, and casts around for a way to counter these monster battleships. The aircraft designer Barnes Wallace of Vickers thinks he may have the germ of an idea in his new super-heavy bomb, codenamed the 'Tallboy'. In a happy coincidence, at the same time the Avro Manchester bomber, having been dubbed a failure through use of the fragile Rolls-Royce Vulture engines, is re-engined with four Merlins and becomes the famous Lancaster. With minor modifications, the new Lancaster will prove ideal for carrying Barnes-Wallis' enormous new bomb.

Between the Wars the Royal Air Force has had little success in hitting ships with high level bombs, even the slow radio-controlled ex-battleship HMS *Centurion*. A team is therefore assembled which includes bombing experts, and several naval officers who have already been at the receiving end of aircraft bombs, from either high-level or dive bombers.

It has been noted that high-level bombing is extremely difficult if the target was under way. Dive-bombing was felt to give the best results, but no-one can envisage a dive bomber of the day big enough to carry the kind of bomb which would hurt a *Yamato* Class battleship.

The best results noted were by the Luftwaffe's special anti-shipping Stuka units, which had evolved a particularly effective attack formation. Typically, a Stuka formation approaching a fast-moving naval vessel would divide up as follows: The leader would be flanked by two wingmen. Some distance behind would follow a second flight of three aircraft, but with the wingmen spaced further out to one side of the central plane. A third, and sometimes a fourth flight would follow, and again the wingmen of each flight would be spaced further out again to the side.

Thus, if the target was moving and manoeuvring at high speed, the leader of the first flight would aim his Stuka directly at the target ship. If the vessel's captain threw his ship in a sharp evasive turn to, say, starboard, the Stuka on the right of the leader would pick him up.

Conversely, if the ship evaded to port, the left-hand wingman would be on him.

Depending on the success with which the captain conned his ship, if he survived the first wave, the second wave would be spread further apart and would have a better chance of hitting the ship, and so on with succeeding waves.

An additional feature suggested by one of the French aviators present is the presence of at least one "command aircraft". This aircraft, while retaining its own bomb load, would not immediately commit itself to an attack, but would circle the target, relaying instructions to the incoming attack waves, in much the same way as the French multi-place Potez twin-engined fighters had sought to control their squadron of single-engined fighters in an aerial combat. This had not often worked as well as intended, because of the modest performance of the Potez and the speed and confusion of aerial dogfights. With anti-ship attacks, however, it holds out great promise. The command aircraft could, when all other planes have attacked, also come in and bomb the target, adding its bombload if all others have missed, or administering the *coup de grâce* to a crippled opponent.

The elements of this special team are slowly forged together, and two squadrons of modified Lancasters established – No. 617 Squadron drawn from RAF crews, and Flotille 25F made up of experienced French crews. After working up on their new aircraft, both squadrons enter into a phase of intensive anti-ship training.

They soon discover that it is relatively simple to place their training bombs, designed to mimic the aerodynamic properties of a full-sized "Tallboy", alongside or on the decks of the slow, cumbersome *Centurion*. A faster target is needed, so the large old cruiser *Hawkins*, still capable of around 29 knots, is converted to radio-control and used as a high speed target ship on which to practice.

Several RAF and Armée de l'Air officers have raised concerns that the heavily loaded Lancasters, with the mid-upper turret removed, will be extremely vulnerable to fighter attack. One answer is to build up the number of long-range escort fighters, basically the Bristol Beaufighter with its four 20mm Hispano cannon.

Naval officers are keen to have their own air component closer at hand, and it is recalled that, at the height of the Norway Campaign, a Spitfire was fitted with a pair of floats from a Roc. The project is updated, using first the Spitfire V and then the latest Mark IX, producing the fastest floatplane to be used by any of the adversaries. Training is especially problematical. The pilots for these floatplane Spitfires need the reflexes of the fighter pilot, the navigational skills of the Naval officer, and the ability to safely land these small floatplanes in the open sea. Accidents are frequent and sometimes fatal, but slowly a core of dedicated "fleet protection" fighters is built up, ready to be sent to the Far East.

In the meantime, the Japanese have built up their Carrier fleet, and because they have not been risked in direct conflict, all six large fleet carriers are operational, plus the smaller *Ryujo,* and the *Zuiho* which had been converted from a submarine support ship.

This has allowed the Imperial Japanese Navy to concentrated on building up its heavy armoured might, by completing *Shinano* as a super-battleship - as originally envisaged.

Shinano joins her sisters. A poor-quality photo, taken by a foreign naval attaché in secret at long range, at dusk, but the only one showing the three super-dreadnoughts together, for the first and last time.

Chapter Nine
SHOWDOWN IN THE EAST

In retaliation for the seizure of the Dutch East Indies, the Allies step up action to hit Japan where it will hurt the most, in China. Massive quantities of American food and war materials flow unhindered through India and North Burma, bolstering the Kuomintan in their struggle to evict the Japanese invaders.

Stung by this, the Japanese Navy plans to gain the kudos of relieving pressure on the Army, by a direct attack on the head of the China resupply line. In late 1942 they draw up an ambitious plan to strike through the Indian Ocean at Eastern India itself, destroying convoys of materials bound for China.

In case a suitable opportunity presents itself, a full-blown invasion fleet accompanies the force and will effect a landing in Burma, Malaya or Thailand, allowing the Army to strike north and sever the link with China for good.

The crucial naval clash planned by the Japanese takes place in the Indian Ocean in early 1943, in what will become known as "Second Jutland" – because of the losses inflicted on both sides, and also the final outcome which, as for Germany in 1916, will spell the end of Japanese Naval ambitions.

The Japanese suffer one unexpected loss when the super-dreadnought *Mutsu*, ammunitioning for the sortie in Tokyo Bay, suddenly explodes and sinks. She is the fourth major Japanese warship to be destroyed by a magazine explosion, and Western naval experts could only conclude that the Japanese had not yet come to terms with the problems of handling cordite in hot climates – a serious situation which claimed thousands of lives in the navies of Britain, France, Germany, Italy and Russia before and during World War One.

Another less charitable conclusion is that the rapid expansion of the Japanese armed forces has resulted in raw inexperienced naval conscripts, who brought about the disaster by failing to carry out proper fuzing procedures on the *Mutsu*'s 16in shells *(9)*.

The over-confident Japanese fatally divide their forces.

Six large aircraft carriers, *Kaga, Akagi, Hiryu, Soryu, Shokaku* and *Zuikaku* together with the smaller *Ryujo*, and escorted by heavy cruisers form the punch of a powerful striking force which is aimed at Ceylon, Southern and Eastern India.

The covering battleships are divided into three strong squadrons, intended to operate independently in support of the carrier fleet. The four modernised battlecruisers, *Kongo, Hiei, Haruna* and *Kirishima* form the homogenous Fast Scouting Division.

Backing them at a range of forty miles is the Support Division, comprising *Nagato, Ise, Hyuga, Fuso* and *Yamashiro*. A further forty miles to the rear is the Main Body, formed of the super-battleships *Yamato, Musashi* and the newly-completed *Shinano*, with a strong destroyer escort.

---

9 *The British losses were: the pre-dreadnought battleship Bulwark while taking on ammunition at Sheerness in 1914; the large armoured cruiser Natal which blew up in 1915, taking with her not only her entire crew but tragically groups of Sunday School children on a guided tour; the dreadnought Vanguard which blew up in Scapa Flow one night in 1917.*

The French had lost the pre-dreadnoughts Jéna which had exploded and burned while in dry dock at Toulon in 1907, and the Liberté which exploded at anchor in 1911.

The German light cruiser Karlsruhe was destroyed by an internal explosion east of Trinidad in 1914.

Italy had lost the dreadnought Leonardo da Vinci in 1916, which at the time was blamed on Austro-Hungarian saboteurs.

In the same year the Russian dreadnought Imperatritsa Maria blew up and capsized in the Black Sea.

Japan had previously lost Admiral Togo's famous flagship the Mikasa in 1905 (although she was to be salvaged and preserved as a museum ship), the battlecruiser Tsukuba destroyed in Yokosuka Bay in 1917, and the Kawachi, which exploded in Tokuyama Bay in 1918.

Of the major naval powers, only the USA avoided this major problem through careful ammunition storage and inspection procedures - although the infamous destruction of the Maine in Havana harbour may have been the Americans' lesson in this deadly game.

Against this formidable armada the Allies manage to concentrate the following ships:

The Battlecruiser Squadron: *Hood* (flagship), *Renown*, *Strasbourg* and *Dunkerque*.

The Battle Fleet: *King George V, Prince of Wales, Duke of York, Anson, Howe, Rodney, Nelson, Temeraire, Vanguard, Richelieu* and *Jean Bart*.

The Carrier Strike Force: *Ark Royal,* and the armoured carriers *Illustrious, Victorious, Formidable, Indomitable, Unicorn,* the French-manned *Foch* and *Clemenceau*.

They receive an unexpected and decisive reinforcement in the shape of the US Pacific Fleet, which Roosevelt has sortied from Pearl. He orders them into the Indian Ocean to stand by the Allied armada, but at a diplomatic distance of 100 nautical miles. Ironically it is the US Navy ships which are first found by Japanese cruiser-launched scout planes.

Mistaking them for Allied ships the Japanese launch a furious aerial assault on the Americans. They seriously damage *Hornet* and slightly damage *Yorktown*. Then, just as suddenly, the Japanese assaults peter out - they have realised the magnitude of their mistake when the main Allied fleet is detected by flying boats, and the Kates and Vals are hurriedly recalled and re-armed.

By the frenzied efforts of their damage control parties, *Yorktown*'s fires are brought under control and her flight deck is patched up. *Hornet* is more seriously damaged, however, and her aircraft aloft are gathered in on the decks of *Saratoga* and *Lexington*. Admiral Spruance breaks radio silence to inform the President, who orders him to concentrate his battleship force, comprising *Iowa, New Jersey, Washington, North Carolina, South Dakota, Alabama, Indiana,* and *Massachusets*, on the main Allied Battle Fleet.

Like Blücher at Waterloo, they will arrive in time for the final, cataclysmic clash, here with the three great Super-dreadnoughts.

The large fleet carriers *Lexington*, *Saratoga*, *Enterprise*, *Yorktown* and the damaged *Hornet* will add their air arms to the Allied carrier force, and tip the air balance decisively in the Allies' favour.

Roosevelt had sent these major units of the American Fleet to help face off anticipated Japanese aggression. Through the failure of the Japanese scouting planes, the might of the United States is drawn into the shooting war on the side of the fighting Democracies. The USA is now officially at war with Japan.

In a re-run of First Jutland the battlecruisers clash first, with the *Hood*, hit by a full broadside of 14in shells from *Hiei*, exploding and sinking within the first few minutes, taking all but a handful of her crew to the bottom with her. The lightly protected *Renown* is badly damaged and left dead in the water, engulfed in the smoke from a dozen fires, and the two French ships take heavy hits from the *Kongos'* 14in guns.

In return, *Kongo* herself is hit hard and brought to a stop, and the French battlecruisers fall back on the Battle Fleet. *Kongo*'s crew get their vessel under way again, but during the night action she is torpedoed by a Dutch submarine, the *K XIV*. *Kongo*'s commander keeps her running at high speed to escape further submarine attack, but slowly she floods, capsizes and sinks with heavy loss of life. Before she sinks, her damage control officer commits hara-kiri.

The three surviving *Kongos* pursue *Dunkerque* and *Strasbourg*, backed by the Support Division which arrives on the scene just in time to be confronted by the fearsome sight of the horizon ringed by the gun flashes from the massed Allied 13, 14, 15 and 16 inch guns.

The Japanese attack with reckless bravery, but are defeated in detail, the battered survivors being temporarily reprieved by the arrival of the super-battleships.

The following first-hand account is by the Gunnery Officer of *Duke of York*:

We were steaming at full speed in pursuit of the Battle Cruisers scouting several miles ahead of the main Fleet, but of course they had pulled far ahead of us with their superior speed. The C.O.s of both *Richelieu* and *Jean Bart* were champing at the bit, for their ships were at least a couple of knots faster than us, but we were under strict orders to keep together and concentrate our force.

Then at 0940 we spotted a large mass of smoke on the horizon just off the starboard bow. The flagship *Temeraire* ordered a change of course to bring the smoke dead ahead. Radar began to pick up two groups of blips, closing our position at a combined speed of almost sixty knots. There were two large vessels in the first group, and three following some six to eight miles behind them.

I obtained the ranges of the first group from our Type 284 gunnery radar set mounted on the director, and gave the order to load with armour piercing shells. The range came down rapidly, and my spotting numbers were reading out the falling distances, my assistants were feeding the data into the Fire Control Table deep in the bowels of the ship, and I had my fist clenched on the firing handle, my index finger itching to press the trigger and send our first salvo of "bricks" howling out at what we took to be the long-awaited enemy.

As the images in our rangefinders became clearer, we noticed that the two leading ships were making large quantities of smoke, or indeed were on fire in several places, as they were under heavy shelling, and zig-zagging wildly. Great gouts of shellburst shot skywards at regular intervals, and I estimated from the frequency and the number that they were being fired on by at least three other vessels... but by whom?

Suddenly the Captain's voice rang clear in my headphones, "Leading vessels are *Dunkerque* and *Strasbourg*" then "Hold fire until enemy targets identified".

I relaxed my grip on the trigger. Several more minutes passed, each one bringing the separate groups of ironclad monsters hurtling more than a nautical mile nearer together.......

Then my Number Two yelled "Japanese battleships bearing green two-oh!". They are firing on the French ships." "Three fast battleships of the rebuilt *Kongo* Class, estimate speed at 31 knots – three-one knots - from the radar plot".

I gave the order to switch target to the rapidly closing *Kongos*. Fast they might be, with guns of equal calibre to our own, but their armour protection was half that of our modern *Duke of York*, so just let them keep on coming into our web, as the spider said to the fly....

"Radar gives twenty-eight-oh-oh-oh yards to the leading *Kongo*". The main DCT rangefinder gives a hundred yards less, I average the two and tell the C.O we are ready to open fire. The green lights show all turrets and all heavy guns are ready. I am itching to be the first to open fire on these unseen opponents. The Old Man concurs, I select a series of two-gun salvos, calmly intone "Shoot" and press my master trigger. There is a sudden crash and the deck leaps momentarily beneath our seats. Huge yellow-orange globes burst from the first two guns to fire, followed by a monstrous belch of brown-black smoke, which we rapidly leave astern. *Duke of York* heels, but just imperceptibly. Our directors compensate for the heel, and in rapid succession I fire off the following two-gun salvos of our sighting ladder........

All the while, the guns which have fired are dropping back down to reload, the air blasts purging them of the last embers of burning powder and smoke, then elevating back up towards the enemy, and the green lights wink back at me on my ready board.

Hundreds of well-trained men working as the cogs of our gigantic machine, paying back all those months and years of practice, for this is the be-all and the end-all of our existence.

But where are our shots landing? Ah, the fourth salvo is a straddle, but then all hell seems to break out around the ship we are firing at, as at least half a dozen other battleships bring her under fire. I order the director to switch target to the last ship in the enemy line, which so far seems to be completely undisturbed. One cannot allow one enemy ship to have all the time in the world to calmly fix the range and adjust his fall of shot. I am going to spoil his day for him.

Again we fire a ladder, and the third salvo bursts on either side of our opponent, a "straddle". Ranging on that shot, I continue to send two-gun salvos in his direction at frighteningly regular intervals. Our twelfth salvo brings only one splash, an "Over", and my Number Two who is relating the progress of our gunnery in an otherwise calm manner suddenly shouts "Hit". He settles back down to his deadly monologue, and the word "Hit" comes more and more frequently. I wonder to myself how long this old Great War veteran can stand the kind of punishment we are dishing out, when suddenly the spotter on my right jumps in his seat and shouts "My God, look at her go". Squinting into my lenses I catch the moment of the enemy's death....... A gigantic orange fireball is climbing into the sky beside his mainmast. A mushroom cloud follows and spirals upwards hundreds of feet in the air. I swear I can see large pieces of ship flying through the air in and around this cloud – including what I take to be a main gun turret…….. Then the bows and stern jacknife in that horrifyingly familiar picture from the German Jutland, and she is gone.

No time to reflect on the fact that I have just killed a thousand men. We switch targets to the next ahead, and continue our litany of destruction. "Up 200" - "Shoot" - "Straddle" - "Up 100" - "Shoot" - "Under" – "Hit" – "Hit"…

Our current target turns away, making smoke, but our radar continues to give us her exact range and course. She can not escape us that easily.

I take advantage of the momentary pause to appraise myself of the situation of our accompanying ships and the enemy formation. It seems that our fleet is now engaging not only the remnants of the opposing *Kongo*s, but also enemy battlewagons, of the *Fuso*, *Ise* and *Mutsu* classes. They are, it seems, doing very badly, and several have already sunk or been smashed into immobility.

Suddenly the radar rating calls my attention…… "Sir, three very large echos beyond the enemy's position, closing at – estimate 27, that's two-seven – knots. I say again, three VERY LARGE echoes".

I feel the hair start to creep up on the back of my neck, and a cold, clammy sensation comes over me despite the stifling heat inside the director tower. So, are these the new Japanese monster dreadnoughts our intelligence had warned us about? The reason why our newer sisters *Anson* and *Howe* had been frantically up-gunned to sixteen-inch calibre? And for the working in of an extra two inches of armour over our magazines, which had forced the dockyard to give us external bulges to compensate for all that topweight, knocking at least a knot off our top speed. Would it all be worthwhile, would it work and protect us? The answers came all too suddenly, and at an amazing range.

Two absolutely gigantic columns of yellow-tinged water erupted three hundred yards off our starboard bow. I called for the range to the latest enemy arrivals. "At least forty thousand yards, that's four-oh, -oh-oh-oh." I asked for the range again, and was not pleased to have this confirmed by radar. And to be picked out by our radar at that enormous range, these enemy ships had to be big, very big indeed. I tried to swallow, but my throat had long gone dry.

"Switch targets!" "Prepare to engage second enemy group when in range". And just how long would we have to run the gauntlet of their fire before I could shoot back?

The *Queen Elizabeth* and *Valiant*, modernised lightweights in this titanic battle, have been wisely retained on the disengaged side of the Allied battle line – ready to move in and administer the *coup de grâce* to any disabled opponents. They are carrying two Walrus observation seaplanes apiece, for spotting fire, but also two each of the latest floatplane Spitfire fighters. Two Walruses and two Spitfires are catapulted off, and circle to await developments. Unfortunately, one of the Walrus pilots strays too close to the dozens of "bricks" curving between the opposing battle lines, and the passing of a sixteen-inch shell – from which side will never be known – crumples his frail craft like a paper butterfly swatted down by a playful cat.

One of the two Spitfire pilots, on the other hand, wisely skirts the immediate battle area, and is rewarded by the sight of a Japanese Pete, a floatplane flown off from the *Musashi*, which is spotting for its parent ship. Curving round to take the floatplane from behind and below in the classic fighter stalking manoeuvre, the Spitfire pilot pumps a dozen 20mm shells into the Pete, which breaks up in the air and falls into the sea in several pieces.

Unbeknown to the Spitfire pilot, he has deprived the *Musashi*'s Gunnery Officer of his long-range eyes, and probably saved the *Duke of York* from a ferocious battering as her crew anxiously wait for the range to close to the point where her own fourteen-inchers can respond.

The Allies realise the magnitude of the task they have taken on, and concentrate the fire from almost 200 heavy guns on the Japanese trio. A salvo of 18.1-inch shells from *Shinano* strikes *Prince of Wales*, which continues in line for a few agonising seconds before blowing up and capsizing. A similar fate befalls the *Washington*, this time at the hands of the *Yamato*, and *Nelson* is badly mauled by *Musashi* but survives, dead in the water. Gradually, however, the Allied superiority in firepower and radar control takes effect. The three super-battleships cannot be sunk by direct gunfire of any of the ships opposing them, but the literal hail of one-ton projectiles begins to smash their superstructures and control facilities. One by one they are reduced to virtually impotent floating citadels, their speed cut to a crawl.

At this stage the Japanese, facing annihilation, desperately recall their Carrier Strike Force to save the day. This force, however, is about to fall foul of the combined naval airforces flown off by the 13 Allied carriers, outnumbering them more than two to one in ships and more than three to one in planes.

In addition, they run into the ambush line established by two dozen British, French and Dutch submarines. *Kaga* takes a torpedo hit in the bows which will seriously reduce her speed. *Ryujo* is hit by first two, then a third tinfish and capsizes.

Then the carrier-borne airforces clash. Many of the Japanese pilots have combat experience over China, against the obsolescent aircraft of the Chinese Air Force. Many French and British pilots also have previous combat experience, and the some of the Americans have served in the 'Eagle' and 'Lafayette' squadrons as volunteers. At the end of the day, however, the superior numbers of the Allies and the ruggedness of their American-built Wildcat fighters and Dauntless dive bombers bring Allied victory.

In the mutual orgy of destruction no less than four of the Japanese carriers go down in flames, a fate shared on the Allied side by the *Ark Royal* and two American vessels *(Lexington* and, finally, the *Hornet*) - basically due to bomb hits through their unarmoured decks starting uncontrollable ammunition and petrol fires - although *Ark Royal* is also hit by one aerial torpedo which, it is thought, hastens her end. The armoured deck Royal Navy ships, though badly battered, fight through and survive, including the two French-crewed ships, the *Foch* and *Clemenceau*. In the closing stages of the air battle, many Japanese pilots who know their carriers are badly damaged or sinking, and with no hope of survival, selflessly fling their aircraft in suicide dives against the enemy carriers, hoping not to die in vain.   The armoured decks of the British-built ships again save them from serious damage, and except for *Formidable*, they are soon able to fly on aircraft again. US Navy pilots unable to land on their remaining two carriers fly on board their Allies' vessels.

The two surviving Japanese carriers *Shokaku* and *Zuikaku* flee the scene badly damaged and on fire, their flight decks a mass of twisted steel and timber. They do not get far, as *Shokaku* crosses the path of the British submarine *Tally-Ho*, which puts three torpedoes into her blazing wreck, and *Zuikaku* suffers the indignity of being shelled to destruction by French and US heavy cruisers. Worst of all the highly trained Japanese air crews have suffered disastrous losses, and only a handful of pilots successfully ditch their planes beside Japanese cruisers and destroyers to be picked up.

As dusk falls, the Japanese fleet is outlined in the flames from their ships' blazing superstructures, and   cripples are hunted down and sunk in the course of a nightmare battle in the moonlight, reminiscent not only of First Jutland but also of that previous Japanese triumph, the Battle of Tsushima. The 'Morning Glory' which was the Imperial Japanese Navy is utterly destroyed, never to rise again.

Duke of York's Gunnery Officer takes up the tale again:

With nightfall, the C.O. gave the order to cease fire. Our radar continued to give us the ranges to a succession of ships surrounding us, but in the dark we could not clearly identify friend from foe. The flash of our remaining guns would draw enemy fire to us, and we could so easily run down friend as well as foe.

Intelligence reports I had read stressed the Japanese proficiency in night fighting, and we were not prepared to hand them an advantage at this late stage of the game.

And we had taken grievous hits. I glanced forrard to the smoking ruin of "B" Turret, its guns pointing out to starboard at an impossible angle. There is a gaping hole in the turret front face, and the complete back has been blown out. One of my best friends was turret commander of 'B'. But for the bravery of whoever flooded the magazine – proably the last thing he ever did in this life – we would have followed our first victims in an exploding fireball of sudden, final, oblivion.

"Sir, you're bleeding." And so I was, but just a slight cut to my right temple, a mere scratch – and that was not said from bravado – compared to the hurtling piece of razor steel shrapnel which had entered the DCT from starboard to port, cutting two of my ratings clean in half and decapitating my faithful Number Two.........

Although our main guns are silent, I keep what is left of our secondary turrets on high alert, the guns loaded with semi-armour piercing shells, ready to fend off a sudden lunge by torpedo craft.

But they never come, and our numbed continued existence is punctuated by far-off gunfire, explosions and cataclysms of flame, as our own destroyers hunt down crippled Japanese battleships seeking to crawl painfully away from the holocaust which has engulfed their force. This dazzling firework display, a pyrotechnic delight for our tired eyes, and a funeral pyre for hundreds. I suddenly feel immensely tired, and sad. These were fine ships, and fine men, and we have slain them in large numbers. Moist-eyed girls and kimonoed ladies will swait at the dockside for these ships which will never more sail into port, grim-faced young boys will stare at fading photos of lost fathers and brothers and uncles...... But, thankfully, tomorrrow at least, it will not be the turn of our loved ones.

Allied losses are grievous, and if not for the ready succour of Trincomalee would reach catastrophic proportions, but of the many battered ships which limp into port, a third are reporting ready for action three days later. But Japan's dreams are gone forever.

Suzuki Toro was an anti-aircraft gunner on *Shinano*. On the morning after the cataclysmic clash, he was found clinging to an overturned life raft by a patrolling American destroyer. This is his story of *Shinano*'s last hours:

A car mechanic by trade, I was plucked from the Daihatsu plant and drafted into the Imperial Japanese Navy in April 1942. After training on the Hotchkiss gun, I embarked in a transport for Truk, where I came on board the brand-new battlewagon *Shinano* just two weeks before our sortie to drive the Allies from the Indian Ocean. My battle station was on the No. 3 Portside 25mm triple anti-aircraft mounting. I was the gunlayer in the left-hand seat, responsible for pointing the complete mounting.

En route to the battle we had been ordered to train our guns on an enemy Catalina flying boat, which however refused to close within range of the 25s, but instead circled us obviously reporting our position. Our heavy Ack-Ack boys had a go, and the enemy pilot sheered away from the shell bursts which were creeping closer and closer to his plane. Just then one of our Type Zero observation floatplanes passed directly overhead and put in an attack on the enemy flying boat. Our Gunnery Lieutenant told us she had been catapulted off our own ship just before the Catalina appeared. The floatplane made several passes at the lumbering enemy plane, we were cheered to see one engine of the Catalina catch fire, but then the observation floatplane suddenly seemed to stagger, and it fell into the sea and exploded. The Catalina flew slowly out of sight on its remaining engine, gradually losing height, until it disappeared from our view.

We were saddened by the sight but had no time to dwell on this little tragedy. Our Lieutenant told us over the message tube that we were steaming at high speed to support the ships of the first two Divisions, who were already heavily engaged with the enemy. From our high vantage point we would have a grandstand view of what happened next.

The first sight of the battle was confused, but soon we could tell that our ships had suffered badly. We steamed past the shattered bows of a dreadnought emerging from the sea at a steep angle. As we turned to manoeuvre around this pathetic wreck of a once-proud ship, I was stunned to see the bow bore an Imperial chrysanthemum, so this had been a Japanese battleship. One of the loaders ventured the guess that this had been one of the Kongos, but the rest of us were too shocked to dispute or confirm this.

Suddenly an enemy heavy calibre salvo burst in the water immediately alongside our port beam. Geysers of water rose hundreds of feet out of the sea, and the air was filled with thousands of whistling fragments. One jagged piece of metal sliced a chunk off the top of our gun shield, and ricocheted off somewhere. We all instinctively ducked, then each member of the team called out to reassure the others that they were untouched and still capable of action. It had been close - Ito pointed to my head, I took off my helmet, and stared at the bright silver scar which streaked the side of it! A narrow shave for me!

Much worse was to follow immediately after........ Our lieutenant in the director overhead ordered us to crouch down behind our shield as far as possible, for our own main battery rear turret was to engage the enemy ships. I looked out astern over the shield before crouching down behind its illusory protection, and saw the three muzzles of our enormous

18.1 inch guns swinging round to point in the enemy's direction. Then came the three monstrous tongues of flame which seemed to take our breath away. More dramatic in its effect, however, was the blast wave which picked up the whole of our gun team, ripping me and my opposite elevating number from our seats and depositing us in a jumble at the back of our small platform.

For several seconds I was deafened. When my ears stopped pounding and I could begin to hear some muted sounds again, I heard Ito screaming like a wounded animal. Through a haze of blood I vaguely saw him lying at a drunken angle, his broken leg folded under his body. And this from the fire of our own guns!

Our rear turret fired three more salvoes at the same angle, the concussion beating us back breathless against the side wall of the superstructure, until the turret trained around to the starboard side and we obtained some relief. And what a desperate sight our gun team presented .... At that moment I could not care how many enemy planes had come down in power dives to release bombs against us.

Painfully I hauled myself up to see over the top of the battered gunshield, and the view that met my straining eyes was fantastic. For as far as the naked eye could see, the horizon ahead of us, from left to right, was lined with dimly-seen silhouettes of ships. I knew they were warships, and enemy ones at that, because at regular intervals each small silhouette would erupt in a sheet of orange flame as she fired her guns at, well, at us.

Then the heavy hits started to come in, singly at first, and then in groups. I looked down at the sea and saw in dismay that we seemed to be slowing. Looking up it was not difficult to see why - above us the funnel casing had been punctured in dozens of places, and smoke streamed through the holes. I heard afterwards that several shells striking the uptakes in close succession had succeeded in extinguishing many of our boiler fires....

And always the rushing sound of a huge passenger steam engine when you stood, like I had done as a boy, next to the railway line. Sometimes we heard the sound of the strike, but more often we FELT it. I would never have said that a seventy thousand ton ship would shake to shell hits, but these bricks were weighing over a ton each and arrived at huge speed. The impact alone, never mind the explosion, was bound to rock us.

Once I was straining to catch a glimpse of the battle when a blinding flash came from up ahead. I involuntarily ducked as a huge black shape flew almost directly overhead, bounced once on the deck edge, and plunged into the sea where it immediately sank. It was only several seconds later that I realised what I had seen was the No. 2 Port twin 5 inch anti-aircraft mounting, which had been plucked from its platform as if by some giant seagull, and flung overboard.

Sitting at my seat, half deafened and more than half-stunned, I lost count of all idea of time, and only slowly became aware of the fall of night, coming down to spread its blessed curtain over the scene. If I had hoped that darkness would cloak us from further damage I was cruelly disillusioned. The relentless enemy shelling mostly ceased, though one determined battleship kept her guns firing at us for a long time, but other threats stalked us in the night.

By this time, we could see that large parts of the ship's superstructure had been smashed into tangled ruin. Our own gun mounting seemed to lead a charmed life, perched on its little platform half-way up the port-side superstructure. At around 2300 hours, however, it became clear that our mounting was to be threatened by another peril. Flames and smoke billowing from several shell hits below and behind us threatened to fry us alive, and the order came to evacuate our position and make our way as best we could down to the main deck.

Here we huddled in the lee of the rear main armament turret, which luckily was trained away from us still. Occasionally it came to life and fired a desultory salvo, but I could see that the turret's own portside rangefinder hood was hanging down brokenly. I could only guess at the punishment that had been taken by the delicate rangefinder and director equipment mounted much higher up.

The hell that was the deck of *Shinano* continued on into the night. At around 0300 we heard that two groups of enemy destroyers were stalking our ship from both sides. My hair stood on end - as a boy I was enthralled by the stories of Japanese seamen at the Battle of Tsushima only thirty eight years earlier. The Russian ships had been battered all through the daylight battle only to be picked off one by one during a running night action with our destroyers. Now the tables were turned and we were the prey!

With very little gunpower left to resist - I heard only the triple 6.1s above our heads fire back - we were a virtual sitting target. I thought of climbing back to our triple 25mm mounting to fight back – the platform and mounting were still there, but since we had vacated our isolated erie all the communicating ladders had been blown into tangled scrapiron.

We stayed put. The ship still had way on her, but *Shinano* was handling sluggishly, and to avoid torpedo attack even I knew you needed full speed and a handy response to the helm. We had neither, and one by one the enemy destroyers put their 'tin fish' into our massive sides. The explosion of each torpedo caused the hull to whip, and we were thrown bodily in the air, only to crash back down on the deck planking – until, the next torpedo found its mark and our crazy gyrations were repeated. Because the hits came in on both beams, the flooding cancelled itself out for a while, and we stayed on an even keel. Slowly, however, our bows came down level with the surface of the sea, and we knew the end was close. When it came, *Shinano* gave a quiet sigh, as if from an exhausted deer, and simply slipped beneath the waves from under us.

I was swept off the deck with my brave shipmates, but we were separated in the water. I never wished for death to come and claim me as fervently as I wished at that dark moment, but suddenly I felt the tug of a grappling hook in my life preserver, and I was hauled aboard an American cutter. Looking back over her gunwale I was shocked to see no sign of our mighty *Shinano*, no sign except for wave after wave of heads bobbing in the swell.

Toro ended up in a prisoner of war camp in Oregon, and after the War he settled down in the region, eventually opening his own garage.

Musashi also, does not survive the night. Her Captain realises that the coming of dawn might see enemy ships attempting to board and seize his ship. Calling for destroyers to take off the survivors of his crew, her Captain and those senior officers still alive go below and scuttle the ship. At 0530 she slowly turns turtle and takes all those brave men down with her.

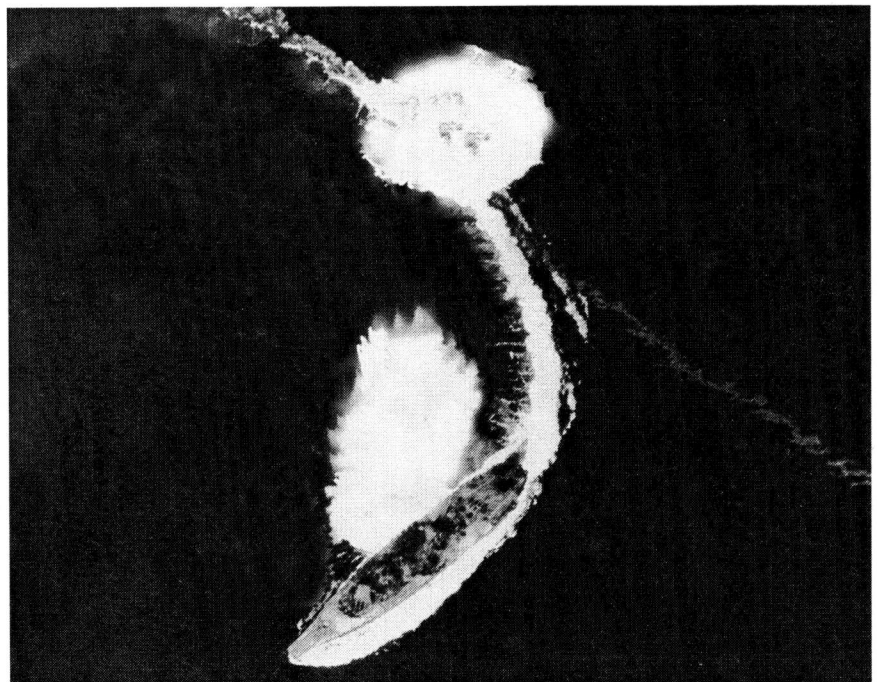

Yamato at high speed, under attack by Tallboy bombs.

Yamato's end is much more spectacular, and in full view of all the surviving vessels still afloat at dawn. Captain Aruga and his devoted crew have shored up damaged bulkheads, counter-flooded to bring her back onto an even keel, and have raised steam for 20 knots. She is building up speed, and making good her escape to fight another day when, at 0720 a formation of large four-engined planes come over the horizon from the North, heading straight for *Yamato*. These are 617 Squadron of the RAF, plus Escadrille 25F with their French-crewed Lancasters, which have staged through Ceylon from Southern India with the express role of anti-battleship strikes. Each specially-modified aircraft carries just one bomb, Barnes Wallis' enormous 12,000 lb 'Tallboy'.

According to their well-practised plan, the first nine planes, from 617 Squadron, split up into their staggered flights of three, each wingman spaced further out depending on the flight's place in the bomb run in. Three Lancasters, the attack co-ordinator and his two deputies, begin their ominous circle above the *Yamato*, keeping just out of range of her remaining 5-inch AA guns.

As each flight is directed into the attack, Captain Aruga begins desperately to throw the *Yamato* into a frantic series of S-turns, depending on the warnings given by his lookouts. She is now making over 25 knots, and turning like a destroyer.

The single bombs launched by each plane of the first two flights, in their 10,000 foot fall from the Lancaster, take so long to fall, that *Yamato* – by some seeming miracle – manages to avoid all of them. The aircraft of the third flight, however, close up together on the orders of the co-ordinator, and the Tallboys from the centre and starboard aircraft burst in the sea to port and starboard of the giant target, bracketing her in monstruous columns of water. The starboard bomb goes off only fifty feet from the hull. The tremendous shock waves effectively caves in the *Yamato*'s outer hull on both sides, and thousands of gallons of water flood into her hull. Her inner torpedo bulkheads still hold, however, and she limps on, several feet down by the head.

Her respite is not long, as immediately the last 617 flight clear the scene, the co-ordinator is vectoring in the first triple flight of dark blue Lancasters from Escadrille 25F. *Yamato*, manoeuvring more sluggishly and slowing down, manages to avoid both 'Tallboys' from the centre and starboard aircraft, but the third bomb, dropped by the Lancaster flown by Adjutant Muselier, succeeds in scoring a direct hit. The 'Tallboy' seems to have struck the roof of the forward triple 6.1in secondary turret and burst deep within the hull. There is the agonising wait of several seconds while nothing seems to happen. All at once an enormous jet of flame, smoke and debris erupts from *Yamato*'s forward main magazines, completely shrouding the stricken ship. The huge plume of smoke rises to several thousand feet, and the flash of the explosion is seen as far away as Rangoon. When the cloud begins to disperse, the giant ship has capsized and sunk, taking

Vice Admiral Ito, Captain Aruga and more 3,000 of her crew to the bottom with her.

Yamato explodes, while the last of her attackers fly away

The final death toll is over 20,000 Japanese sailors killed or missing – the greatest disaster ever to befall a fleet since the great Kamikaze wind destroyed Kublai Khan's invasion fleet on its way to Japan.

Allied losses are also grievous ......Only seventeen men survive from *Prince of Wales*, from her entire ship's complement of more than 1,600 officers and men. In *Hood* the loss is almost as great, with only three survivors plucked from the sea out of a crew numbering 1,417. *Washington*'s crew is slightly more fortunate: some 300 of her crew of almost 2,000 are rescued by friendly destroyers. *Nelson* suffers 423 killed and more than 300 wounded, some seriously. *Renown*'s losses are 281 dead and only 56 wounded. She later founders while under tow, with the loss of a further 42 men. *Nelson* was much tougher and, although virtually awash, is safely beached in the Andaman Islands. A total of almost 5,500 men were killed for these five ships alone.

Casualties among the rest of the Allied Fleet are not on the same scale per ship, but the total of dead reaches almost 8,000, with twice that number wounded.

The damaged *Yorktown* is limping away from the battle to safety when, the next morning, she is torpedoed together with the destroyer *Hammant* which is standing by alongside, by the Japanese submarine *I-168* and has to be abandoned and sunk by her own side.

Surprisingly, three heavy Japanese ships survive the battle, in various states of seaworthiness. They are the sister battleships *Ise* and *Hyuga*, plus the battlecruiser *Haruna*, sole survivor of the Fast Scouting Division.

The Imperial Japanese Navy will rush more carrier conversions into service following the disaster in the Indian Ocean, including the *Ise* and *Hyuga* changed into hermaphrodite half-carriers, half-battleships, the *Ryuho* and *Shoho*, and the ex-liners *Hiyo* and *Junyo*.

In addition, several of the *Amagi* class and the armoured-deck *Taiho* will be launched, but none of these units will be completed before the war ends.

All thoughts of trying to restore their battleship force will be quietly forgotten.

After this stunning setback, the Japanese turn to China to try to compensate for their losses.

Major battles are fought around the cities of Changsha and Hengyang.

These involve hundreds of thousands of men on each side, and the carnage is appalling. Rivers run red with the blood of the slain.

Second Lieutenant Hito Watanabe of the 58th Division was a participant in these battles, now living in Saigon. His experiences left him with permanent mental scars, and he still has trouble sleeping, many decades after the events he witnessed.

Born in Nagasaki, my parents raised me in the Christian faith. I was lucky to travel overseas as a teenager, spending several months in Europe. My favourite city was Paris, where I picked up enough French to take up my present job with a computer firm in Vietnam.

On entering the Army Academy at the age of nineteen, I was immersed in the cult of Emperor worship. Since to worship a living human being went completely against my religious upbringing, I was forced to come to terms with how I would handle my required adoration of Emperor Hirohito. Personally I justified this double standard by deciding to swear my personal oath of loyalty to his Imperial Majesty as my earthly leader and supreme commander. In this way I was able to accommodate both my religious and secular lives and devote my life to a successful military career. And make no mistake about it, I was prepared to sacrifice my wellbeing and my very life in the service of my Emperor, as all young men of my generation and our forefathers were.

My visits to Paris had convinced me that the French were a decadent military power. They had fought the German Army to a standstill in the Great War, but at such a tremendous cost in dead and mutilated survivors that the very fighting spirit seemed to have gone out of the country. As an ambitious young man who was destined from birth to follow my father and my grandfather in the service of my Emperor and our country, I personally felt a strong distaste for this negative, defeatist attitude.

Imagine my disgust when it was the French who thwarted our necessary expansion in what they called the "Far East" and we looked on as our potential Asian Co-prosperity Zone. The Imperial Navy had soaked up millions of yen, and had dramatically failed our country and the Emperor. We young Army officers felt it was our turn to try to save face, to wash the stain of defeat from our flag. We literally bayed for blood, and whose it was did not matter so long as it was *gaijin*.

For decades we had enviously eyed the vast, underdeveloped territories of our close neighbour China. This vast land had wallowed in decadent decline for centuries. In Japan we had felt that, if the Chinese could not properly run their rich country, then we should take over. And so for years our Army had been encroaching on the ancient Manchu lands, bringing the benefits of modern civilisation to this backward place.

When our commander brought us the news that we were going over to the offensive on a massive scale, we gave a *Banzai!* cheer that could have been heard halfway across the province. Certainly it must have struck fear into the craven Chinese soldiery crouched in their front lines just a few kilometres away.

The intervening years have drawn a veil of obscurity across the series of individual events that happened next. I am left with a jumble of disconnected memories which come back to me when the spirit is at its lowest ebb, in the sleepless hours preceding dawn. My Christian upbringing has left me with the ability to feel overwhelming guilt, and thus I do not sleep well.

The Imperial Japanese Army was a brutal affair. We officers were even expected to instill discipline in the ranks by administering physical beatings to the common soldiery. Our only other principal attributes were absolute obedience to orders, and a fanatical desire to dominate the enemy. Of course, in purely military matters we took a great deal of pride in our trade of soldier, and our theoretical and practical training was of a very high standard indeed. In order to first equal, and then master the foreign armies which oppposed us, we Japanese had quickly absorbed all the required disciplines.

But the old traditional streak of what I can only, in retrospect, describe as cruelty always came to the top. In our view, if a soldier surrendered, he ceased to be worthy of our respect, and deserved any punishment, even death, which we might inflict on him. Similarly, any civilian who had not enlisted in his country's armed forces merited no respect from us in any way. While this kind of attitude encouraged a certain blood lust in our armed forces, in retrospect I have to wonder if it was not self-defeating?

The kinds of things which keep me awake at night are remembering the times our men used live prisoners for bayonet practice, tied to stakes. This custom dated from our distant past, when new or resharpened samurai swords would be tested on the bodies of condemned criminals. In our eyes, anyone who opposed our glorious advance would suffer the same fate as criminals.

Then there were the many rapes which we carried out. By that I mean, not me personally, but the men in my unit. We had been indoctrinated with the notion that the Chinese were somehow inferior beings to ourselves, and once that idea had sunk in, then any brutish kind of treatment we cared to inflict was somehow sanctioned. In any case, the Army kept our soldiers supplied with plenty of Korean women to use as sex slaves. It is difficult to discuss this aspect from a traditionally Western mind set.

The worst excesses of our High Command we discovered by accident, when one of their most lethal experiments backfired. We had bivouacked in the outskirts of Hengyang, prior to making the final push to capture the city, when several of my men reported sick with huge black boils on their faces and skin. As this ailment spread rapidly through the ranks, panic began to set in. Our doctor was at first puzzled, but after several long radio exchanges with his superiors he announced that the men were suffering from a variety of bubonic plague, which was more familiar in Europe under the name of the Black Death. It seems that our Air Force had been dropping bombs laden with bubonic bacilli, to infect the local population with this deadly, and usually incurable, disease. Because of the top secret nature of this experiment, and our rapid advance, we had stumbled into the plague contaminated area by mistake. But for this unfortunate coincidence I would classify the experiment as a relative success, for the area in which the plague bombs had been dropped was completely clear of all enemy combatants and civilians when we moved in, so effective was the bacillus. It was only much later that I came to realise the kind of reaction this type of warfare elicited from our Western opponents. Their civilisations had been almost wiped out by the Black Death in past centuries, so they looked upon such experiments as barbarous. Whereas to blow people into pieces with bombs and high explosive shells, or to massacre them in large numbers with machine guns, appeared much more acceptable to them.......

In addition, the Japanese seek revenge for their naval setback by attacking the Americans, in the Philippines, and the British in Hong Kong, on the same day, 1st April 1943.

The isolated Hong Kong garrison puts up a brave token resistance, but the overwhelming Japanese Army and Air Force units attacking from China force the British to surrender after just three days, to avoid needless bloodshed among the native population. Hong Kong will remain in Japanese hands until the end of the war.

In the Philippines, the Japanese land on 1st April, and against all expectations, by 16th April they are laying siege to the surviving American garrison which has been driven into Bataan.

Just two weeks later, however, a powerful Allied relief fleet arrives off Manila Bay. The forts in the Bay - including the 'Concrete Battleship' (Fort Drum) which have remained in American hands cover landings by Allied troops.

On 7th May the siege of Bataan is lifted after desperate ground combats - without carrier air support the Japanese have lost control of the skies over the Philippines, and this is the major factor in allowing the Americans to drive them back.

Japanese forces retreat into central Luzon and to the smaller outlying islands, where they conduct guerilla warfare which continues right up to the end of the Pacific War.

In the meantime Admiral Yamamoto meets his death. The Allies do not see him principally as the arch enemy - this dubious honour is reserved for Tojo - but the temptation to act on an Ultra intercept and assassinate the head of the Imperial Japanese Navy proves irresistible. His Betty is intercepted over Bougainville on the morning of 18th April 1943 by P-38s from Rabaul, and Yamamoto dies in the burning wreckage.

The surviving battlecruiser *Haruna* is despatched to bring the urn containing his ashes back to Japan. The remains of his Betty can still be seen in the jungle even today, and the crash site is a popular Japanese tourist stop where old Navy men silently pay their respects.

Chapter Ten
DE GAULLE REBUILDS THE ARMOURED DIVISIONS

Meanwhile, back in North Africa, the Allies have been planning for the long-promised liberation of France. General De Gaulle had been one of the unsung prophets of armoured forces throughout the Thirties, and had briefly commanded the Fourth Armoured Division during the closing days of the Battle of France. In late 1941 the War Council of the Fourth Republic ask him to take charge of the rearmament and reorganisation of the French armoured units based in North Africa, with the aim of ultimately invading the South of France, and driving north to liberate the whole country. He moves to Algeria and obtains large numbers of British Cruiser and Infantry tanks, including the latest Crusader and Valentine models. With these De Gaulle embarks on a programme of rapid expansion of the Free French Armoured Forces, drilling them in his own brand of 'blitzkreig' tactics.

By mid 1942 De Gaulle's troops are ready for action, but he has long since realised that they will need far more firepower than the weak British Two-Pounder and the newer Six-Pounder tank guns if they are to successfully mix it with the latest panzers. In addition, his tank units are continually plagued with maintenance problems caused by the chronic unreliability of the Crusaders. During any large-scale exercise at least twenty per cent of his tanks would be out of action for one reason or another.

De Gaulle is only too aware that the Allies could not hope to fight off the full might of the Panzer Divisions in France, if the latter are released from the Eastern Front by the buffer states taking on responsibility for border security. The Allies therefore need an 'edge'.

He therefore takes over as head of the French tank design mission, which had been set up in Washington at the end of 1941.

The Americans know they can out-build the Axis in all weapons systems. They had therefore planned to flood the battlefield with large numbers of M4 Medium tanks, which will become the Sherman.

However, the Sherman cannot hope to compete against the large numbers of Panthers and Tiger I tanks which they will confront in any invasion of the European mainland.

De Gaulle is horrified by the American plan to use three Shermans to stalk each Tiger, and he knows they will likely lose two out of the three. He knows just how many tanks the Panzer Divisions can muster against the Allies in the West, and he is determined at all costs to avoid such potential waste in trained tank crews and their equipment.

Drawing on their experience of the Blitzkreig, when one of the few effective instruments of defence against the onrushing panzers was the extempore mounting of a long 47mm anti-tank gun on the back of an armoured Laffley 4x4 Tank Hunter, De Gaulle and his team are instrumental in persuading the American Army that they will need to stiffen the ranks of M4 Medium tanks – soon to become famous as the Sherman - with large numbers of Tank Destroyers armed with a more powerful anti-tank weapon. The result would be the M10, armed with the long 76mm derived from the 3-inch anti-aircraft gun. De Gaulle ensures that this effective vehicle will form the majority of the new American armour supplied to his men.

As the backbone of his own French armoured divisions De Gaulle is looking for a heavily armed and armoured Main Battle Tank similar to the old French Char B1Bis – but avoiding the notorious tactical drawbacks of the latter (one-man turret, main gun mounted low in the hull and aimed by the driver skewing the whole tank, derisory radius of action, mechanically fragile, vulnerable radiator cooling grilles).

*A prototype of the M6 Heavy Tank, armed initially
with a 3-inch gun and a co-axial 37mm.*

The Americans already have a suitable prototype on trials – the 57-tonne M6 Heavy Tank. They have designed the M6 as a result of collaboration with the earlier Molinié technical mission, sent over by the French in 1939 to discuss the possibility of the USA building 'G'-class main battle tanks for the French Army. The M6 displays many of the design and construction features of the stillborn prototype Renault G1R.

The Americans assume that they will have to join in the rescue of the occupied European nations by using the United Kingdom as a springboard into Europe.

The Americans have been reluctant to build the M6 because they can ship three M4 Mediums in the same space as two M6 Heavy Tanks. Assuming that the U-boats will take a heavy toll of shipping, the more tanks that can be crammed into each cargo hold the more tanks will arrive safely in the European theatre of operations.

Also, a further technical difficulty has arisen over the means of land transportation. Long-distance transport of heavy armoured vehicles such as tanks has to be carried out by rail. To drive the tanks on their own tracks would incur considerable wear on the running gear. To carry them on transporters would require larger roads than usually found in the Great Britain, and the strengthening of large numbers of road bridges. So, American tanks have to be suitable for carriage by rail across Great Britain.

Unfortunately Great Britain, as the pioneering railway building nation in the whole industrialised world, has serious problems with the railway loading gauge. The earliest railways were established by individual entrepreneurs, who sought profit in connecting individual towns together or joining a port to its industrial hinterland, without much, if any, consideration to the construction of a national network. Some companies built to a generous loading gauge, but the more impecunious built to more limited dimensions, meaning that the rolling stock from other companies would then strike platform edges, tunnel sides and railside equipment.

This situation means that tanks have to be small enough to fit within the standard British loading gauge. But the size, and more especially, the width of the tank, determines the size of turret and therefore the maximum size of main armament carried in that turret.

In Germany and France, the early railways were planned and built by the state, to a much more generous loading gauge. Accordingly, German tanks can be much wider than their British counterparts, and carry a wider turret, with consequently a much bigger main gun. The M4 medium – to be named the Sherman - will fit inside the British railway loading gauge, the M6 heavy tank will not.

This seeming disadvantage is cancelled out if the M6 is to be used by the French armies in North Africa for an invasion of the South of France. The North African rail network has been built to the same generous proportions as the railways of Metropolitan France itself. Again, once the Allies are established in Provence and repair the rail lines which the retreating German army is certain to sabotage, M6 heavy tanks can be easily transported up to the front line by rail.

In 1942, the complete Allied dominance of the Atlantic allows the Americans to plan for transporting large numbers of M6 Tanks to Europe. It will still need modifications, if it is to survive on the battlefields of France.

De Gaulle at Aberdeen Proving Ground compares an M6 prototype modified to his specifications with the first model armed with two coaxial cannons. The modified M6 is seen here seen behind the General: the main gun has been upgraded to 90mm, and the co-axial 37mm has been replaced with a .30 cal machine gun. In order to make space for the recoiling breech of the larger cannon, the rear turret machine gun has been removed, and the radio has been moved from inside the turret to an armoured box welded on the turret rear. The General has donned his old tanker uniform to ride inside the M6, and his white gloves prove the inside of these prototypes had been cleaned to a high degree for the occasion.

Inspired by the French 1940 Char F1 design with a large anti-aircraft cannon, originally designed to punch a hole through the Seigfried Line, the M6 is up-gunned with the American M3 gyro-stabilised 90mm gun.

In line with Char F1 *(10)*, the frontal armour of the M6 is increased from 76mm to 100mm. To help counter these weight increases, the co-axial 37mm is dropped along with the extra crewman to aim this weapon, but the all-up weight increases past 60 tonnes and maximum road speed falls to 20 mph. However, with French encouragement it is put into mass production as the M6A1 with all-welded armour hull and turret, (or as the M6A2 with a cast hull and turret), and is therefore available in sufficient numbers to confront the Tigers and Panthers.

In view of its intended rôle, the M6 is officially christened the "Liberty", after the prototypes built at the end of the Great War for the massive Allied offensive planned for the Spring of 1919. In French use the name translates appropriately into the "Liberté".

One critical tactical feature is the excellent radio communication equipment fitted in the M6A1 Liberty and, indeed, every other US-built tank.

Gun	Ammunition	600 yards	1000 yards	1600 yards	2000 yards
75mm US M3 (Sherman)	A P Capped	69mm	62mm	55mm	50mm
3-inch US (M6 Prototypes)	A P Capped	97mm	90mm	80mm	74mm
90mm US (M6 production)	A P Capped	111mm	103mm	93mm	86mm
8.8cm KwK 36 (Tiger I)	A P Capped Ballistic Capped	108mm	102mm	94mm	86mm

The penetration of homogenous armour plate at 30 degrees to the vertical by various gun calibers of the period

---

10   The Char F1 or Fortresse Tank was to weigh 143 tonnes, with 100mm armour, solid armour "boat" tracks, twin V-12 engines, fore and aft turrets with a long 75 and a 90mm gun respectively, a 25mm in each flank and several MGs. Only a wooden mockup had been built, but ten production models were ordered at the end of April 1940, just a fortnight before the Blitzkreig struck.

De Gaulle's French technicians also help the Americans perfect the Brandt APDS anti-tank round – first tested in action in France in June 1940 - and armed with this, even the 75mm-armed US Army Medium Tanks have a fighting chance vis-à-vis their Panzer opponents.

The reaction of some of the French tanker veterans is best summed up in the memories of Sergent Chef Maurice Duval of the famous Chasseurs d'Afrique, who took charge of a section of M6A1 heavy tanks:

We had been quite proud of our cavalry Hotchkiss tanks with which we were equipped in North Africa. Then the Germans allowed us to send a squadron of the heavier Somua S-35 battle tanks to reinforce our North African possessions, lest the British came to try to turn us to their side!

After everything changed, we re-equipped with British Crusader and Valentine tanks, since we had been cut off from our homeland and its source of spares for our old mounts. But what an exchange! The Crusader certainly looked the part, with its advanced Christie suspension and sharply sloped armour. From the outside, at least. Inside, we were shocked to find out just how thin their armour was. The main gun turned out to be a puny 4cm, or Two-Pounder, the same size as in our latest Hotchkiss H-39s but no match for our own 4,7cm gun in the Somua, let alone the latest German Panzers with their 5cm and 7,5cm main guns. But the worst aspect of the Crusader was one brought on by its sole advantage, its very high speed. For they were, to say the least, mechanically fragile. Any attempt to run a squadron at speed for more than a few minutes would result in two, three or sometimes more tanks grinding to a halt with all sorts of breakdowns. And the British did like their high-speed charges, in line abreast over the open desert terrain. I suppose if you have a small turret gun and paper thin armour, you have to close the enemy as quickly as possible to have any chance at all.

I had been brought up in the heroic French military tradition, and I knew very well the likely cost of charging a well-prepared enemy position, just like our earlier Chasseurs had done at Sedan.

So I was quite interested in the alternative British tank we trained alongside, the Valentine. It too mounted the feeble Two-Pounder, but it had much thicker armour. But its top speed! Barely 25 kilometres an hour, as she was designed as one of the heavily armoured "Infantry" models, to accompany the ground troops in the assault, rather than trying to go head-to-head with enemy armour. Such was our need for "Cruiser" tanks, as the British called their fast attack vehicles, that we were forced to press Valentines into service in a rôle for which they were clearly unsuitable.

However, these new tanks did allow us to carry out a great deal of training in all kinds of "blitzkreig" manoeuvres, in preparation for the day when we would turn the Germans' tactics against them and reclaim our homeland.

The best features of these obsolescent British tank designs was their three-man turrets, which came as a complete revelation to us. No longer did I, as the chef de char, have to crouch alone in my turret, not only directing my driver, giving and receiving messages via our radio man, but also choosing targets and, finally, loading and firing not only our main anti-tank weapon but also the co-axial machine gun as well. The British turrets were fairly cramped, but I ignored that small penalty as I was now able to concentrate on my main functions of directing my crew, who carried out all the other functions of driving, loading and firing without any physical intervention from yours truly. A revelation, and I now appreciated how easy it had been for the Panzers to overrun and outfight our technically and numerically superior tank force, in the grim days of May and June 1940. Having a radio in each tank, even if it only worked part of the time travelling over the bone-crunching desert terrain, was a distinct luxury as well.

Imagine our delight, then, when we were first let loose to clamber over our brand-new American M6A1 heavy tanks! They may not have been built by Cadillac, but that's what they appeared to us...... Crew comfort and general habitability had been high on the list of American priorities – it was only later that I discovered our own General de Gaulle's rôle in getting these monsters into production and into our hands in North Africa – and the only thing missing seemed to be an icecream maker. Someone had told me that the US Navy had installed these in all their new fleet submarines and, dizzy with delight on examining my new M6, I giddily got it into my head that perhaps one of these gadgets we were pawing over so eagerly might be the icecream maker! No ice cream, but I was absolutely not disappointed.

Our raison d'être, the main gun, was a huge 90mm, the same calibre as the old French anti-aircraft gun of 1939, and from a similar background. At last, something to shoot back at the German 88s with! The armour plating was a hefty 100mm on the front glacis plate and turret mantlet and face, which filled me with a great deal of confidence. Our engine, a huge diesel V8, which never missed a beat.

But the comfort, the padded seats, the spacious interior, the tank-to-tank radios, the crew intercom system, the well-laid-out controls. My head was in a whirl. Here at last was what we had craved for so long. No more the short range of the old Renault B1bis, leaving it so vulnerable during frequent refuelling stops. Gone was the dangerous side ventilation grille which had collected many a German PaK shell in Northern France. Speed was fair, but our mobile bunker's most endearing feature was the sheer build quality, the ease of maintenance and the reliability which is a tanker's waking dream.

And the name, the "Liberté"! How very appropriate……

Chapter Eleven
SECOND BATTLE OF FRANCE

Just four months after "Second Jutland", with Allied possessions in the Far East secured, a huge armada covers *Operation Aphrodite*.

The Italians have been out of the War for some time now, although Italian Blackshirt "volunteer" units have fought alongside the Wehrmacht in Russia in its crusade against Bolshevism. Hitler has long harboured plans to rescue his fellow dictator Mussolini, and now that Luftwaffe reconnaissance flights confirm a huge Allied buildup in North Africa, and Admiral Canaris' spies report back on the rearming and retraining of the huge French Army of North Africa, Hitler decides it is time he took care of the Italian problem. In a typically Hitlerian move, he orders the Wehrmacht to cross the Italian frontier and seize strategic locations the length and breadth of Italy. The Luftwaffe is crucial in airtransporting troops to the vulnerable south of the peninsula. One of Hitler's most dangerous adventurers, Otto Skorzeny, is tasked with rescuing Il Duce from his prison in a hotel on Monte Grosso. Baulked from using the immobilised cable car, Skorzeny parachutes onto the mountain with a band of picked Falschirmjagers, and overpowers the guards. Mussolini is flown to safety in a Fiesler Storch plane, accompanied by his heroic rescuer. The tiny ledge on which the plane has managed to land is too short to allow a normal takeoff run with its burly passengers, so Skorzeny typically orders the pilot to taxi over the side of the ledge, the falling plane quickly gaining flying speed. What Mussolini thinks of this escapade is not recorded.

With the Italian peninsula occupied by hundreds of thousands of German troops, the Allies carry out an elaborate electronic spoof, and feint as if to invade Sicily and the Mainland, obliging Hitler to send large reinforcements to possible landing sites. His basic worry is to ultimately protect Austria from invasion via the South. These troops will thereby be unavailable to act decisively in France.

Churchill has argued long and hard for an Allied invasion of Italy, up into the "soft underbelly of Europe", as he fondly imagines, ignoring the hostile topography facing any army attempting to fight its way up the Italian peninsula. Fortunately, the French vigorously press for the liberation of their homeland. The Navy dreams of returning to their great naval base of Toulon. Since the French will be supplying the bulk of the invasion forces and all the armour, they have their way, and Italy is abandoned in favour of Provence.

Reconnaissance missions over the potential landing sites are carried out by the famous aviator and author Antoine de St-Exupéry. He fails to return from his last mission over the potential landing sites, and wreckage from his P-38 Lightning is not found until more than 60 years later. The Germans claim that a pre-production Focke-Wulf 190 Dora has shot down St Ex's Lightning. However, detailed examination of the wreckage fails to find any combat damage. It is clear from the state of the wreck that his Lightning has entered the water in a vertical dive at high speed. Sadly it is possible that the great aviator may have blacked out due to oxygen failure at the extreme height the missions were normally flown. Alternatively, he may have attempted to lose the intercepting Fw190D in a power dive from which he was unable to recover. We will never know the truth about this tragic loss of a pioneer aviator and a great author.

SAS Units land by glider to bolster the firepower of French paratroops. One Six-Pounder gun manned by 4 Group takes out a troublesome machine gun post in the church tower in the town of Le Muy, which had been holding up the paratroops' advance. A Foreign Legion lieutenant describes how he saw the gun team pierce the fortified top of the tower with several armour piercing shot, in a vertical string. Their next round was high explosive, and it simply opened up the sides of the tower top "just like peeling a banana".

*Operation Aphrodite – the Invasion of Southern France – a production M6 christened
"Verdun" with 90mm gun comes ashore from an LST. Note this early model still
carries the cumbersome twin MG mount in the hull front. In later models this will be
replaced with the simplified hull MG ball mount copied from the Sherman.*

Following up the aerial assault, the British 8th Army and the
French Army of North Africa land in two separate zones and carry
out co-ordinated but separate 'blitzkreig' style advances – the French
straight up the Rhone Valley and the 8th Army covering their flank and
diverting north-west to secure Bordeaux, before turning north-east.

Finally the Allies are able to deploy their own version of the
"blitzkreig". The armoured divisions take full advantage of the tactics
discussed by De Gaulle in his Pre-War writings and perfected by him
in North Africa.

Sergent Chef Duval takes up the story again:

Once the initial landings between Cannes and Cape Camarat had gone
in, with airborne support, and our bridgehead had been stabilised, we
were sent in with our M6 heavy breakthrough tanks, to do just that. Under
cover of a devastating bombardment by 155mm long-range artillery and
all kinds of smaller guns, we launched our assault on the dug-in Germans
near Fréjus.

Using our excellent tank-to-tank radio sets, I carefully co-ordinated
our section attack on a particularly nasty anti-tank nest. Luckily it
contained none of the highly effective, and highly feared, 88s, but their
5cm and 7,5cm PaK guns demanded respect.

When our first tank was brought to a halt by a 7,5cm round through its side armour at close range, I swung the remaining tanks into line abreast, facing the offending gun which had so obligingly unmasked its position, and while the crew of the stricken M6 baled out, we laid down a blistering fire from our heavy 90s, which blew away the remainder of the anti-tank nest's camouflage cover. In the storm of high explosive one of the PaKs sent a couple of shot in my direction. We heard the impacts on our frontal armour in between the reports of our own gun. Inspection afterwards revealed two finely sculpted grooves in our armour plate, but the 100mm of protection had in no way been compromised. God Bless our American friends!

Several of the sections in our Division were equipped with M6s which had the older design of hull armour cast in large pieces, just like our old Hotchkiss and Renault light tanks of 1940. These certainly did not stand up to enemy fire so well as our welded flat plates, and I remember examining one sad example on which three 7,5cm PaK shot had caused the whole nose plate to crack from top to bottom. The crew had been very lucky to survive relatively unscathed. The radio operator told me that after the third deafening crash against their armour, he had looked down in amazement at an extremely hot 7,5cm AP shot lying in his lap, having expended most of its energy in penetrating the plate directly in front of him. He evacuated his seat, and then the tank, in record time, as did the other members of his crew.......

To deal with heavy enemy armour, we developed a new technique designed to lure them out of their lairs. We would generally go straight in to the attack on any Panzers we spotted, using our 90s to smash up their lighter tanks such as the Mark IV and the StuGs. Then we would deliberately throw our M6s in reverse and seemingly retreat from the field of burning tanks. Time and again this bravado followed by seeming timidness would entice their heavy Tiger tanks out of concealment and in pursuit of our "fleeing" forces. We would then endeavour to lead them across a screen of Tank Destroyers who would take these monsters in the flank. Sometimes it worked, and sometimes it failed. But when we heard Tiger engines starting up in the distance ahead – and everyone who has heard that sound will never forget it as long as they live – I was always glad when we put into operation our "strategic withdrawal" manoeuvre.

Tank for tank our losses about equalled those we inflicted on the Panzers. They, however, were a wasting resource, for our Jabos kept up such a continuous assault on their rear areas that for the Germans, resupply was a nightmare. We ourselves were kept continually resupplied by our American "observers" and their excellent logistical organisation. As soon as one M6 was put out of action, a replacement was on its way from the distribution pool. And since we were advancing, damaged and disabled tanks on our side were quickly recovered for repair or despatch to the rear areas. German Panzers which were shot up or broke down, or – as began to happen more and more frequently – had simply run out of fuel or ammunition, were usually recovered by our side and denied to the enemy.

The advancing French troops are delighted to find that the Germans' hasty withdrawal from Provence has left them with precious litle time for major demolitions and sabotage in the CORF defences facing Italy. Here and there a gun breech block has been thrown over the edge of a precipitous drop, only to be replaced from hidden French stores, a couple of the lookout "cloches" have been dynamited and been forced upwards out of their surrounding blocks, and the Italian Army has made off with a complete set of special 75mm fortress gun mountings of the latest type, but in most cases the defences – thanks to Hitler's order in the Summer of 1940, have been maintained in excellent condition.

French commanders recall how the outnumbered R.I.F. units in June 1940 successfully fought off overwhelming numbers of Italian troops, some of whom, unlike their Wehrmacht allies further North, actually succeeded in fighting their way onto the superstructure of a Maginot artillery work, before being driven off (something the Germans never achieved).

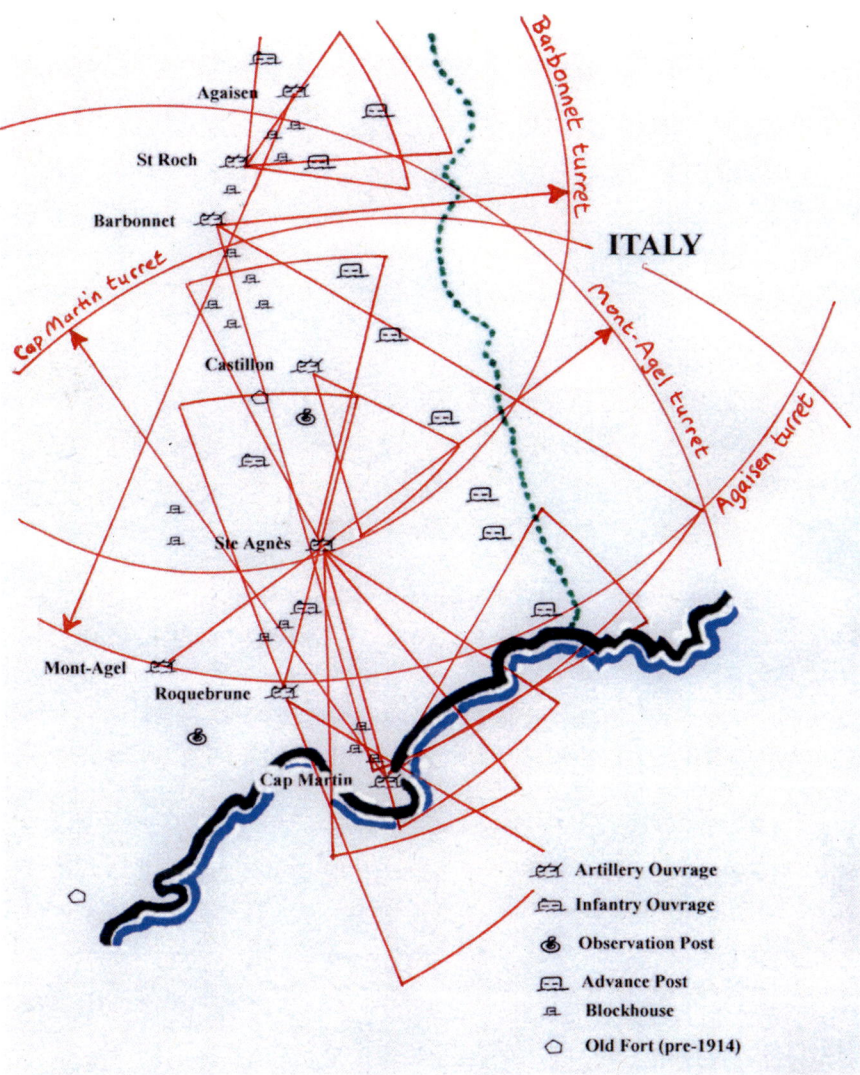

Map of the re-activated CORF defence lines at the Mediterranean end of the Alps,
showing how the interlocking fields of fire from the Ouvrages cover each other
and also the advance posts and blockhouses.

They therefore re- activate the surviving 1940s defence line, and
station sufficient troops and armour on the Alpine and Coastal Fronts

to block any advance by the Germans in Northern Italy. The large forces Hitler has committed to Italy are effectively bypassed and left impotent. Hitler dares not pull them back for fear the Allies will surge through Italy and take his home city Vienna.

The Americans follow in the wake of the fighting Allied spearheads. The USA is still nominally at peace with Nazi Germany, but her troops are used to guard Wehrmacht prisoners, rebuild damaged road and rail communications links, and guard stockpiles of military stores. The vast American transport fleet of C-46, C-47 and C-54 airplanes is put at the disposal of the Allies, together with thousands of supply trucks.

At the same time, several hundred American combat aircraft are flown into Britain, ready to back up the invasion. The US 8th Air Force takes over the role of local air defence, freeing virtually all the RAF to throw its weight behind the Allied advance.

American units in Allied uniforms actively join in the fighting as "observers", gaining valuable combat experience. Officially, tank crews are stationed 'near' the front lines to report back on the combat effectiveness of American arms. When, inevitably, the Germans capture several Americans and protest to the United States, they are dismissed by Washington as 'volunteers' similar to those brave men who fought Fascism in the Spanish Civil War.

Hitler orders the armoured riposte. He must leave sufficient SS Panzers in the firebases of the Eastern 'Limes' to support his as-yet inexperienced and shaky client states. Also, the East has become the private province of Himmler's SS and they are reluctant to be diverted from their 'crusade'. Therefore, Hitler orders virtually all his Wehrmacht Panzer and Panzer Grenadier Divisions westward to confront the British and French and their American ''observers'.

They are moving into blocking positions from the Loire to Belfort when the Allies spring their masterstroke, *Operation Overlord*.

At this juncture Roosevelt officially commits his forces to the fight against the abomination which is the Thousand Year Reich. The USA declares war on Germany, and the Allies attack across the Channel with the full force of the huge American Army stationed in the South of England. They land in Normandy, outflanking the most massive parts of the Atlantic Wall, and fall on the rear of the German Divisions which are caught having to fight back-to-back on two fronts.

Hundreds of Allied tactical aircraft, including tank-busting Typhoons, support the ground forces. The entire Allied heavy bomber fleet is thrown into the equation, carrying out saturation bombing of enemy troop and tank concentrations, supply dumps and marshalling yards. The bombers are escorted by hundreds of fighters, P-51s, P-47s, P-38s and Spitfires, and they are met by hundreds of Luftwaffe fighters. The largest dogfights of the War take place over Northern France, with heavy losses on both sides.

Pockets of German resistance harden around the ports of La Rochelle, Brest, Cherbourg, Le Havre, Dieppe, Boulogne, Calais and Dunkerque. These 'hedgehogs' are aimed at denying the Allies the ability to bring in supplies through conventional ports, especially across the shorter Channel route.

To circumvent this the Allies resort to massive air resupply, and land a pre-fabricated Mulberry harbour on the Normandy coast, parts of which can still be seen on the beach today. They also put in place the PLUTO ("Pipeline Under The Ocean") to pump fuel oil across the Channel.

Slowly and deliberately, the remaining Wehrmacht forces carry out a fighting retreat to the Westwall and prepare to defend their homeland.

The Germany XIXth Army under the command of General Blaskowitz is forced by General de Lattre de Tassigny against the Swiss border.

General de Lattre de Tassigny with Swiss soldiers

De Lattre meets with his Swiss opposite number General Guisan to co-ordinate joint action in the event the German forces attempt to escape back into Germany by violating Swiss territory.

The Wehrmacht units attempt an incursion but are held by the powerful Swiss border defences.

Typical Swiss "Toblerone" anti-tank defences

StuGs are sent to force a passage through the valley, and come up against the "dragons teeth" defences, known to the Swiss as "toblerones". Unbeknown to the Germans, the concrete "toblerones" are completely resistant to being charged down by even the heaviest tanks, because all the lines are cross-connected underground into one complete unit, by metre-square reinforced concrete sections.

Frustrated, the armoured vehicles concentrate at the rail barriers set in sockets across the railway and main road in the centre of the valley. Here they fall victim to flanking fire from anti-tank guns hidden behind false rockface shutters and armour mantlets, concealed at either side of the valley.

Stung by their losses, the panzers send in assault engineers to blow gaps in the rail barriers, but they are pinned down by sustained machine gun fire from more hiddden flanking embrasures, and innocent-looking wooden chalets which turn out to conceal concrete bunkers.

The Swiss have planned their defences for years, and have the ranges marked to the centimetre on panoramic target boards set above each gun mounting. The German advance is bogged down.

Then, the long Swiss 10.5s and the 7.5s open up from defensive positions further up the valley. Once more, their ranges have been zeroed in, and their fire is directed from control centres deep under rock which would not be out of place in a battleship's transmitting station. The trapped Wehrmacht units are unable to effectively reply to the hidden Swiss artillery, and begin to take significant losses.

Allied airstrikes increase the pressure and the XIXth Army, contrary to Hitler's repeated vetoes, is forced to surrender.

Long-range Swiss 10.5cm fortress gun similar to those which stopped Blaskowitz's
XIXth Armee. The rubber tubes hanging from the ceiling
attach to face masks worn by the gun crew, allowing them to breathe
fresh air when firing instead of inhaling the propellant gases

A Swiss 7.5cm fortress QF gun in a concrete emplacement

Hitler flies into one of his uncontrollable rages, especially furious that Blaskowitz, commanding officer of the German force, has failed to commit suicide rather than surrender his person to the Allies.

For a second time, Blaskowitz has disobeyed his Fuehrer's direct order *(11)*. His defiance is noted by other Wehrmacht general staff officers.

British, Polish and American paratroops are dropped on the little town of Arnhem, to try to size the bridge across the Rhine, but the men land among a German armoured division. Desperate fighting continues for days while Allied ground forces battle to reach them. However, the survivors are forced to pull back or surrender.

At this juncture, Hitler decides to bring into play his fourth 'Vengeance Weapon'.

The SS under Himmler and Heidrich, in their self-proclaimed role as arbiters of military and cultural matters in the Thousand Year Reich, have been working non-stop on the programme they hope will ensure the enslavery of their last major opponents, the democracies of Britain and the United States.

They are aided by those German scientists who, unlike the author of the famous Oslo Telegram, have now decided to throw their weight behind the Nazi regime, in the belief that Germany is likely to win the war.

To deal with the British, Hitler orders production of the Luftwaffe-sponsored pilotless flying bomb, the first practical cruise missile. The SS have misgivings about this V1, which is still capable of being detected and intercepted by both fighters and ground defences. As insurance in case the Luftwaffe's new toy fails to destroy London, the SS push forward construction of their giant multi-barrelled London Gun, buried in a hillside near Boulogne. This cannon complex, the V3 weapon, is based on multi-chamber principles and nicknamed the "Tausendfüsssler" or "Millipede".

The SS also encourage the development of a far more potent weapon system, based on the A4 liquid fuel rocket, which is to become the V2 ballistic missile. Its huge warhead, delivered at supersonic speed, cannot be detected or intercepted.

---

11   Blaskowitz had once asked Rommel why he, Blaskowitz, was not a field marshall. The answer was that he had refused to condone the activities of the SS in Poland.

The enemy's only chance would be to track down the launch bases, but since the V2 missiles can be launched from any convenient street corner or woodland clearing, they are very difficult, if not impossible, to combat by traditional means.

The rocket designers, eager to please their paymasters, propose a giant, two-stage version of the A4, which is promised to have intercontinental capability.

Immediately, Hitler seizes on this as a means of avenging himself on the Americans, who provided such critical logistic support to the transatlantic convoys a couple of years earlier – and without even declaring war on Germany.

He will declare war on the United States on his own terms, by way of the first ballistic missile to impact in the heart of New York.

But opinions are divided as to the warhead of such a missile. Conventional explosives would be only a pinprick, and New York could shrug off dozens of such missiles and still survive. It would take a very lucky strike to bring down one of the giant skyscrapers.

The scientists turn to nuclear devices. Their chief physicist, Heisenberg, is confident that, given time, he can construct a fission device, but his calculations will be proved by later experience to be well clear of the mark. However, there is the option of the "dirty bomb", less immediately effective than a nuclear explosion but almost as deadly in the long run.

Unlike the British and American participants in the top-secret Manhatten Project, the Germans have never managed to make one of their prototype nuclear piles achieve criticality *(12)*. What they do have, however, is a significant quantity of highly radioactive uranium taken from the cores of these reactors.

The SS conceive the plan to strike at both the American East and West coasts. Japan is therefore provided with a continuous supply

---

12   One nuclear research bunker was built for an official of the German Post Office in the garden of his home in Berlin, for him to carry out private experiments.... Only the "Atomkeller" hidden beneath a church had any prospect of working as intended, and without any practical bioshielding for the operators, who were expected to clamber on top of the pile and moderate the reaction by manually raising or lowering a graphite block by chain hoist....

of uranium 235, both by means of cargo-carrying U-Boats, but also by long-range German and Japanese transport aircraft flying out of Southern Russia. While the Germans target the cities of the US East Coast, the Japanese will attack the West Coast, contaminating the major naval bases with radioactive dust *(13)*.

In order to continue to prove their loyalty to the cause, the Luftwaffe who are operating the V1 cruise missiles come up with a secret nuclear project of their own.

One evening in late July 1943, SOE in London are receiving an update from an agent in Prague, when the transmission comes to an abrupt end. The Gestapo have correlated their radio detection sets and the heroic operator has paid with his blood for the message. But it is worth untold lives..... he has managed to transmit news of a new prototype – number V38 - of the giant Heinkel He177 Grief bomber which has been specially modified at the Avia works before being despatched to a new Luftwaffe unit, *Sonderkommando 500*, based on an airfield near Chernobyl in the Ukraine.

The V38 is a lightly armed long-range version of the He177, but of immense interest is the enormous amount of shielding which has been built in around the plane's electronic systems. To the Allied scientists who examine the report, it is clear the plane may be destined for a nuclear attack mission.

The SS are the first to strike, however, when on 24th December 1943 they launch Germany's first "dirty" nuclear weapon on board a two-stage A4 missile. The target is to be an unsuspecting New York, over 2,000 miles away. The choice of date is deliberate.

The missile suffers a catastrophic second stage failure, and the warhead falls, without detonating, on Irish soil some twenty miles inland from Cork.

---

13   The question of the Nazis using "dirty" bombs was raised by Philip Henshall in "Vengeance - Hitler's Nuclear Weapon – Fact or Fiction?" (Allan Sutton Publishing, 1995). The book contains a reconstructed drawing of a V2 rocket with a quick-release central compartment which may have been intended for a radioactive cargo.

When local cattle and then inhabitants begin to fall sick and ultimately die, De Valera's Irish Government panics and calls in US scientific help. In the shock of this tragedy and the discovery that Hitler has planned the destruction of New York and the cold-blooded murder of thousands of civilians, the Manhatten Project is hurried to completion, and the Allied riposte is made ready.

Chapter Twelve
ENDGAME

The Wehrmacht and the Luftwaffe have failed the Fuehrer in holding back the forces of the Western Democracies. Now is the moment for Heinrich Himmler to prove his value as Hitler's most trusted lieutenant and thereby ensure his ultimate succession.

He agrees to commit massive SS Panzer reinforcements to the West. At dawn on a misty February day, fifty SS Divisions break out from the Seigfried Line .... English- and French-speaking commandos under Otto Skorzeny (who has rescued Il Duce from his mountain prison) create confusion behind Allied lines and the latter fall back in disarray. The British and American armies are being pushed back against the shorelines, and face total annihilation. The French, fighting for their homeland, and using their M6 heavy tanks, are barely holding their ground.

Kurt Mayer was at the forefront of the Waffen SS counterstroke:

We had been busy training our "client" countries' new armed forces, with the aim that they should take over the day-to-day task of guarding our newly won Eastern possessions. I had been detached to look after an Ukrainian armoured regiment, based near Kiev.

In truth, they had been given very few actual tanks, apart from some old Panzer Mark IIIs with the long 5cm gun, and several captured French tanks, which had been of dubious value even when new. But their principal requirement was for armoured cars to patrol their stretch of the frontier between our SS firebases. The Waffen SS had reinstated in production the old Steyr AZDG 8-Rad armoured car made in Austria before it joined the Reich, and they shared many mechanical and electrical components with our Steyr 4x4 trucks and staff cars – an excellent arrangement.

More problematical were the several dozen old French Panhard armoured cars we had captured in the West a couple of years earlier. These were often on their last legs. But I was amazed to see how the former Soviet tankers in the new Ukranian National Army managed to cannibalise and extemporize and keep these old Panhards running. They had had years of practice in working within – and outside – the completely inefficient and decadent Soviet industrial/military complex.

One day I was amazed to see a mechanic stripped to the waist, hard at work at a blacksmith's anvil, forge welding and straightening a broken suspension arm for his Panhard!

Then came the news of the disaster which had befallen the Wehrmacht in the West, and their shameful withdrawal to the WestWall – giving up all the territory for which we had shed our blood in May and June of 1940. While we in the East had been creating a new Empire, they had grown soft on French wine and French women, in the dubious attractions of Paris.

Mayer on his meeting with the M6 Liberty heavy tank:

We had been briefed on the new heavy tank supplied to the renegade *(sic)* French army by the Americans, in order to get someone else to fight their battles for them. A captured example had been transported East for us to study, before we went up against them in combat. This particular example had been put out of action by a 7,5cm PaK shot which had hit the "shell trap" on the lower part of the turret mantlet, being deflected downwards into the thinner armour at the top of the hull front. Our own Tigers were immune to this problem, with their vertical mantlet armour, but hurried changes were being made to its successor, the imposing Königstiger or King Tiger, in order to alleviate the very same weakness.

Otherwise, by Western standards the M6 was quite well protected. But nothing that our long 8,8cm and 7,5cm KwK and PaK guns could not handle, given our experience against the heavy Russian KVs. I had to admit to being impressed at the quality of their manufacture, much superior to the relatively crude Soviet production – it was rumoured that T-34 drivers were supplied with a sledgehammer to help them change gears – and I particularly liked the power turret traverse, much faster than the hand traverse of our Tigers. This seeming disadvantage seldom troubled us in actual combat, as we inevitably fought from positions of concealment, and left our thick armoured hides to shrug off shots from enemy tanks trying to outflank us on the move.

Our major problems were twofold – the sheer numbers of the Allied tanks and the ease with which they seemed to replace them. As fast as we knocked them out, another squadron would spring up out of nowhere to be knocked out in turn. And then there were the swarms of Jabos, or Allied fighter bombers. Every time we emerged from our ambush positions to pursue our fleeing enemy, we were literally set upon by ranks of circling Jabos, which would swoop down and attack us with bombs, rockets and then cannon fire. We became quite adept at co-ordinating our extensive FlaK protection with the forward movement of our armoured columns, just as we had in the heady days of May and June of 1940. The new *Mobelwagens* with their fearsome Flakvierling managed to keep the Jabos from inflicting crippling damage. Nevertheless, our losses were serious. They did not, however, stop us in our relentless push to crush the Allies utterly and drive them into the sea from whence they had emerged.

Then we would look to exact revenge on those who had helped them, especially the cowardly Swiss who had turned on their German paymasters in such a despicable manner. During a lull in the fighting I was detailed off to attend a planning meeting in Berlin, at which the Waffen SS were to update the plans for *Operation Tannenbaum*, the twice-postponed invasion of Switzerland.............

It is at this stage that Roosevelt gives authorisation for Operation Endgame.

Ever since he has read the report on the abortive New York nuclear missile attack, Roosevelt has pondered on how best to respond. To simply unleash the fission device on a populated city in Germany would seem to lower him to the level of the enemy he despises.

He has received two other disquietening reports. One details the discovery during a local counter-attack, of the bodies of over forty Allied soldiers. They are unarmed, and most have been shot in the back, some several times. Four have bullet wounds in the back of the head, and would seem to have been executed. Two survivors who feigned death report that the men were prisoners of war murdered by the Waffen SS......

And the latest secret report to hit his desk tells of a horrific discovery by a joint French and American reconnaissance group in a forest near Longwy, in North-East France. In the heady days just prior to the SS counterattacks, the unit surprised a group of SS men who appeared to be burning "something" in a furnace in the woods. After the Germans had been shot, the Allied troops had moved in to investigate, and to their horror discovered that the SS men had been trying to dispose of a large number of bodies. Some are half-burned, others lie on the floor of the clearing awaiting disposal in the furnace.

Enquiries with local inhabitants reveal that the Nazis had kept a large number of prisoners in hutted accommodation behind barbed wire at a place called Thil. No-one could tell what they were doing, as the SS and Luftwaffe guards who surrounded the compound invariably chased off locals who strayed too close, sometimes even firing shots to drive them away.

The compound is discovered to be bare. The Nazis have obviously evacuated their own men, but most if not all the inmates have been shot before they could talk to their would-be liberators. The SS men killed in the firefight were in the process of destroying the last of the evidence.

One chilling fact is that the photos taken of the grisly scene, on analysis, reveal the presence of two bodies dressed in Luftwaffe uniforms. It may be that these courageous individuals refused the order to massacre the prisoners in their care, and doomed themselves to share their fate.

Other reports coming in from the front lines reveal the ferocity and merciless nature of Hitler's shock troops, the Waffen SS. They fight like tigers, fight to the death, and take few prisoners.

Roosevelt decides he has seen and heard enough to justify taking what, as he would later admit, will be the hardest decision of his life, namely to unleash the new Atom Bomb.

There are other, more immediate reasons to justify his weighty decision:
- It will save hundreds of thousands of Allied, and especially American, troops facing imminent death or surrender;
- It will dramatically shorten the war, saving untold millions of lives, and especially those victims of Nazi bestiality and oppression.
- The choice of target will hit at two of the pillars of the Nazi machine, the Luftwaffe and the SS.

*Consolidated B-32 Terminator long-range bomber,
developed from the B-24 Liberator.*

A special Bomb Group is established, the 501st based in Mildenhall in Suffolk, flying the first production Consolidated B-32 Terminator bombers. To save weight and gain range and height these new aircraft have been stripped of their dorsal and ventral gun positions, and rely for defence on their high altitude performance and a tail turret armed with a pair of .50 cal machine guns. Internally they have been stripped of armour plate from the crew positions, and the bomb bay has been configured to contain one very large bomb. The RAF who share the base help to respray the Terminators in RAF PRU Blue, a mid blue shade used for deep penetration photographic reconnaissance missions over Nazi Europe.

A pair of the specially converted B-32 "nuclear bombers", with full cabin pressurization and armament reduced to just a pair of .50cal guns in the tail turret. The aircraft will be repainted in RAF "PRU Blue" just prior to the operation which would culminate in the Chernobyl attack.

The B-32 Terminator carrying the first US Atom Bomb deep into the Ukraine, together with its companion photographic aircraft, are ignored at first as a photo-reconnaissance mission, out of reach of all current German defences.

For a week before the actual raid, pairs of unescorted B-32s have been overflying German rear areas at more than 30,000 feet altitude, to feign the appearance of regular reconnaissance flights and cover the true nature of their presence. The Luftwaffe is confident that, when the perfected *Enzian* and *Rhinetochter* missiles come into service in several months time, such impudent incursions will be ended.... The Americans are keen to avoid any heavily-populated areas of Europe for this stroke, and instead the Bomb is dropped on a centre of Nazi power, a huge Luftwaffe resupply base which adjoins a rest and recuperation area for the SS Panzer Divisions, situated just to the north of Kiev in a small town known as Chernobyl – the destination for the He177 V38. The town itself has been taken over for officer and NCO accommodation....

The damage is devastating to the Luftwaffe and SS concentrations. No final casualty figure has been released, but it is probable that over six thousand personnel were killed outright, one hundred and fifty five aircraft were vaporized, and over three hundred tanks destroyed. Radiation burns affect tens of thousands of personnel, and the surviving medical services are simply overwhelmed. The message is clear.

By the greatest of good fortune – or ill-luck – depending on one's viewpoint, the attack has claimed one notorious victim. By mischance Reichsprotektor Reinhard Heidrich is passing through the base to review the latest batch of SS recruits. His body is never found, and he thus enters the realms of mythology....

Roosevelt leaves one day for the Nazi leadership to garner what information they can on the attack, and then on the third day he goes public with the first announcement of the existence, and the use, of the United Nations' most devastating weapon, against which no defence will be possible. Without specifically naming German cities, he plays on the catastrophic effect one of these devices can have on a large urban population.

With their bluff being thus called, and powerless to prevent what they now see as the inevitable destruction of their entire armed forces, the leaders of Nazi Germany begin to see the game is literally up.

Joseph Goebbels has flown to the devastated target area to see the damage and the irradiated survivors for himself. On his return to the capital he falls into a deep depression, fearful that the Allies will make Berlin the next target.

Calling together his family, Goebbels poisons his wife and children, then kills himself. Coming on top of the devastating reports from the Ukraine, and the disappearance of Heydrich, the news of Goebbels' death throws the entire Nazi hierarchy into a panic.

Party members begin to clog the roads leading from the large cities, streaming out into the countryside to seek escape from the nemesis they fear is about to fall upon their heads from the sky.

With the disappearance of the Party apparatchiks, the whole rotten edifice which is the Nazi régime begins to tumble like a pack of cards. Founded on terror and the domineering presence of its chief exponents, when these begin to falter, the lack of underlying substance is cruelly revealed.

Many high-placed Nazi officials slip away to Switzerland, where they have stashed away stolen art treasures and specie. A large increase in Swissair flights to Spain heralds a mass exodus.

Most continue on to South American hideouts, where they will live out their dotage in increasingly straitened circumstances as their loot runs out, and the price of anonymity increases year-on-year.

The underground resistance to Hitler's Nazi régime has been simmering below the surface since before the Munich Agreement of 1938 *(14)*. A group of high-ranking Army officers and influential civilians decide that now is the moment they must replace Hitler, and seek Armistice terms from the Allies.

Chief among them are Field Marshalls Kluge and von Witzleben, Generals Beck, Stülpnagel, von Tresckow, Stieff and Hoepner, Admiral Canaris (Head of the Abwehr), Count von Helldorf (President of the Berlin Police), Dr Hans Goerdeler (former Mayor of Leipzig), Dr Otto John, Pastor Bonhoeffer, von Schlabrendorff and Count Helmut von Moltke. In the turmoil following the American nuclear attack, the resistance come out openly on the streets, the military members mobilizing their forces in and around Berlin and Paris and Vienna. Forming a Provisional Government under Hans Goerdeler, they issue a call via the neutral Swiss for an Armistice with all the opposing Allies.

---

14   Many anti-Nazis bitterly criticised Neville Chamberlain for making the fatal concessions at Munich which led to the dismemberment of Czechoslovakia, emboldened Hitler into continuing his mad schemes of conquest, and provided him with a thousand new battle tanks.

Hitler rallies a group of SS supporters around him, barricades himself in the Reichstag Building and calls for Waffen SS units to come to his aid. Unfortunately the cream of the Waffen SS are tied down in the desperate fighting in France, and only raw recruits are available to bolster his own personal bodyguard, the fanatical *Leibstandarte Adolf Hitler*. There is fierce fighting between the two German factions, which devastates much of central Berlin, but slowly the Wehrmacht units gain the upper hand, and the SS youngsters are wiped out, while their leaders slip away into obscurity.

Leutnant Kunze of the 361st Panzer Grenadier Regiment was a participant in these dramatic events:

After our narrow escape from the jaws of the converging Allied armies coming from Provence and Normandy, we were sent with other Wehrmacht units to the Berlin area for rest and refitting (15). There we outfitted ourselves with the very latest models of PaK guns, including some of the awesome Model 43 long 8.8s. I myself was retrained on the Sturmgewehr 43, our latest assault rifle firing a shorter version of the standard rifle bullet. It was a very fine weapon in use, although in terms of appearance it left much to be desired, being made from many stampings and pressings instead of the traditional machined steel forgings of our older weapons. Such is progress, I suppose. And beauty is in the eye of the user.

We were dazed by the news of the devastating Allied bomb. If they had unleashed these weapons on Germany our cities and loved ones would be obliterated in a split second. This time, when the Allied bomber crews dropped leaflets by night and day, we took the time to read them....
Our Wehrmacht High Command also passed down messages to the troops, to the effect that the SS had betrayed our cherished Germanic principals, by systematically murdering the millions of Jews we had been told were gathered together in work camps for the good of all Germans. The most stunning *volte face* was when our officers told us we would be released from our personal oath of allegiance to the Fuhrer as the leader of all the German Volk.

---

15   *This redeployment allowed the Army High Command to draw on considerable numbers of regular troops when the decision to go head-to-head with the SS and the other organs of the Nazi machine was taken.*

Berlin Radio kept up a stream of news on the chaotic conditions inside the Capital, and it was little surprise when we received our orders to entrain for Berlin to sort out the mess the politicians had got us into.

We passed road block after road block manned by Wehrmacht soldiers loyal to the new Provisional Government. As we penetrated deeper into the heart of the city we came across scenes of desperate combats, groups of burned out panzers, SS and Army mixed up together, and large numbers of bodies from both sides. The civilian Red Cross were trying as best they could to render assistance to the wounded, but such was the savagery of the fighting that the dead far outnumbered the wounded.

Finally we were given orders to attack one of the flak towers, the Gun Tower of the pair near the Zoo, where a bunch of SS desperadoes were holed up. They had commandeered the tower from its normal Luftwaffe unit, and had busied themselves fortifying it against ground attack. The SS, with their boundless enthusiasm and fanatical courage, had failed to grasp the fatal flaw in shutting yourself up in a fortress, surrounded by opponents on all sides: If no hope of relief is in prospect, you merely become a target for all the artillery in the neighbourhood, and lose all tactical advantages of manoeuvre. Your only option is to resist for as long as possible. In the case of the flak tower, this resistance was to be of short duration, although we were not to know that at first....

My commanding officer decided to establish his command post on the roof of the abandoned L-Tower situated just 400 metres away from the Gun Tower. Although this spot promised to give us unparalleled views over our chosen battlefield, it very quickly got too hot for our liking.... The SS, on sighting us, immediately opened up with their FlaK Vierlings mounted on the lower tier nicknamed the "swallows' nests". We had to take rapid cover from the hail of 20mm HE shells which ricocheted off every vertical surface. We called in our divisional artillery, and their fire caused the SS to retreat from the light FlaK batteries. In the meantime, however, they had been busy removing the safety stops from the 12.8cm mountings which were designed to prevent the twin FlaK guns from accidentally firing at their own Command Tower. A half dozen of the much bigger 12.8cm HE shells at point blank range, and we hurriedly evacuated the roof of the L-Tower, and set up our new command post in an abandoned house a hundred metres nearer the Gun Tower.

Around the base of the flak tower were stationed several SS Königstigers and a Jagdpanther, and these were our initial targets. With little in the way of cover these mammoth panzers received countless hits from our 7.5cm and 8.8cm PaK guns, until they were all knocked out. The Jagdpanther was stalked by an individual infantryman armed with a Panzerfaust. The lack of turret traverse meant the crew could not keep him under observation or fire as he approached the tank destroyer from the rear..... With the armour screen out of action, we then turned our attention to the flak tower itself. Ringed by our heavy artillery, the SS garrison tried to fight it out by depressing the twin 12.8cm FlaK guns on the roof mountings, but the guns did not lower below the horizontal, so they had no means of controlling the ground in the vicinity of the tower base, other than with smallarms fired between the armoured shutters of the rows of windows which lined the tower sides.

The Zoo FlaK Tower in Berlin with destroyed SS panzers.

I set up a ring of snipers to drive the defenders back from these windows, and after that we were able to work virtually undisturbed.

We deployed a Goliath remote control demolition tank, and managed to blow off one of the armoured entrance doors. To our dismay we saw that the SS had shored up the inside of the opening with sandbag protection, and obviously intended to fight to the bitter end. A second Goliath soon put paid to this extempore barricade, however, and I was in the squad detailed to follow up and clean out this monstrous tower looming high above our heads.

The basic way to flush an enemy out of a high building is to drive immediately to take over the upper levels, and then push your enemy down and eventually out into the street level, and this is what we planned to do. The alternative of fighting our way upwards would have had the double disadvantage of being fired down upon from above, with restricted opportunities to return the fire effectively, and cornering our enemy on the roof, giving them no escape route......

Craning my neck upwards at the top of this giant, five stories above my head – I began to have serious doubts about the enormity of the task we had set ourselves. And the irony of my situation came home to me, when I reflected on what my old Uncle would have said of my exploits? He made his name in the Great War capturing the main French fort at Verdun single-handed, and here was I about to assault a German fortress! *(16)*.

I need not have worried. Hardly had the dust from the last Goliath subsided than we were astonished to see civilians, men, women and children, of all ages, stumbling out of the still-smoking entrance. Armoured doors at the other sides of the monolith also swung open, to disgorge their own streams of refugees. The civilians had been accustomed to using the flak towers as air raid shelters, so where better to shelter from the desperate street fighting?

Mingling with the thousands of hurrying figures we could see many of the SS garrison. Our commander deemed it prudent to allow these despairing men the opportunity to escape unmolested.

On climbing up the hundreds of steps to the upper stories, we came across dejected groups of the SS defenders, standing sullen and forelorn in corners. Several appeared to have taken their own lives. This sudden collapse and dramatic turn of events puzzled us at first, but from several prisoners we learned that their cowardly Obersturmbannführer – downcast at the destruction of his screen of panzers, and his inability to depress the main gun armament to keep us at bay - had thrown himself to his death from one of the 20mm Vierling FlaK balconies. His unexpected removal from the scene had had a dramatic effect on his "men", who on closer inspection turned out to be mere boys, untrained young recruits of the *Hitler Jugend* 12ᵗʰ SS Panzer Division, hurriedly cobbled together into a garrison for the flak tower.

---

16 Pioneer-Sergeant Kunze of the 24ᵗʰ Brandenburg Regiment had entered Fort Douaumont , the strongest of the ring forts surrounding Verdun, on 25ᵗʰ February 1916, and captured the garrison virtually single handed.

No-one sees the end of the leader of the Third Reich, although two badly burned bodies found inside the Führer Bunker are declared to be those of Hitler and his mistress Eva Braun. Over the next twenty years there are many supposed sightings of the 'Phantom Führer' as his ghost comes to be known. In this way he joins the mythical ranks of fallen Celtic heroes King Arthur and Owain Glyndower, who always wait in the hills and caverns for the day when they will be called on to return in triumph.

Wehrmacht soldiers hoisting the old German flag on the Reichstag building after the swastika has been torn down.

At the very moment of victory in the West, there is high drama. As Admiral Darlan steps out of his car at the Armistice signing ceremony in Paris, a young French Army officer by the name of Bourgignon steps up to him, pulls out a Ruby automatic pistol and shoots him twice in the chest. Darlan is rushed to a nearby military hospital but is declared dead on arrival. Thus it was, just as with President Lincoln eighty years before, that one of the chief architects of the victory is removed from the scene before he can reap the rewards of so many years of sacrifice. At his trial, the assassin claims he has 'executed' the Admiral as a traitor, carrying out the legal sentence passed on him by the French Government four years earlier. Investigations reveal that the killer's entire family was murdered by the Nazis following their invasion of the Unoccupied Zone, and of course Darlan has to bear the responsibility for this move. Nonetheless, and despite pleas for clemency, Lieutenant Bourgignon is condemned to death by firing squad, and executed on July 10th 1944 in the ditch of the Château de Vincennes outside Paris.

In the immediate chaos which follows Darlan's death, General De Gaulle takes the opportunity to step forward and seize the reins of power in France, capitalising on the supporters he has set up in positions of authority prior to the invasion of Provence. Churchill is prepared to go along with this action, despite Roosevelt's opposition, but the latter has to acknowledge the strength of support inside France for De Gaulle, who is perceived as a national hero untainted by earlier co-operation with the enemy.

JAPAN

The Japanese, having lost virtually all their fleet and with their oil supplies from the Dutch East Indies virtually cut off, have been blockaded in their home islands by Allied submarine, surface and air forces for the last fourteen months. One by one their island bases have been subdued, until American B-29s from Tinian and Iwo Jima bomb the Japanese home islands on a nightly basis. Early radar-guided bombing from high altitude gives poor results, so the Americans switch to lower level nighttime raids, carrying mainly incendiaries. The flimsy Japanese buildings of their main cities are swept away in ferocious firestorms, and the civilian casualties are horrendous.

Driven to desperation by their war situation, the Japanese Army in China embarks on several major offensives, which are beaten back by Chinese troops armed and supported by the Americans. In retaliation for these defeats, the Japanese armed forces turn to rape and massacre on a scale unseen in China since the fall of Nanking seven years earlier. Hundreds of thousands of men, women and children perish in the holocaust.

In the Pacific, the Japanese have resorted to a startling new technique, the deliberate suicide attack.

Marine Sergeant Joe Collins was involved in the American push to retake the Philippines:

At first our tank unit, equipped with M4 Shermans, had little trouble in dealing with the isolated Jap tanks we would bump into. They were all of the small Type 95 or the so-called "medium" Type 97, but even on the larger model, the armour was a puny one inch maximum. Our 75mm shells went through that like it was paper. We had to be careful to face them frontally, for as the Brits had found in Normandy, one unfortunate feature of the Sherman was its ammunition stowage beside the crew on either side of the front compartment. A lucky hit by a Japanese 47mm anti-tank round at close range could easily set the tank ablaze. We soon found out why the Sherman had acquired the nickname of "Ronson". Guaranteed to light up every time..... On the other hand, one hit from our main armament would blow the Jap tank into a pile of tangled scrapiron, and at any range.

I remember one vivid encounter. We had fought off a crazed rush by a line of Type 95s, which were shot to pieces by our anti-tank guns before they could close with us. But their sacrificial rush was just that, to take our attention from a second row of much more formidable machines. Their unfamiliar outlines looming through the smoke gushing from their predecessors were low and squat, and they packed a hefty 75mm gun, every bit the equal of our own. We were later to learn that they were Jap copies of the German "StuG" or assault gun.

The action got mighty hot. Our line of 37mm anti-tank guns could make no impression on these assault guns, and the line of gunners was overrun and crushed. We rushed into action to take the pressure off of the survivors, and a crazy melée broke out, with our Shermans mixing it in with the Jap assault guns. It was then that we discovered their achilles heel, that their gun was in a mounting in the front superstructure which allowed only a very small degree of lateral training to the weapon. Fine for taking on a bunker which is a stationary target, but a fatal drawback when facing well-trained Sherman crews using every bit of our high speed, mobility, and the rapid laying of our turrets traversed by powerful electric motors. The traditional Japanese tactic of reckless attack only compounded their problems. Staying hull-down and pivoting the StuG to swing the main gun, they could have caused us much higher losses.

When the dust had settled, and the StuGs had been reduced to shattered, blazing wrecks, a lull decended on the battlefield.

This was deceptive, however, for after around half an hour, we became aware of small groups of infantrymen, scuttling toward us using their own burning tanks as cover. One small group took on our company commander's tank. Of the four men in the group, three were cut down by the hull mounted 30 Cal. The fourth we saw throw himself against the side of the Sherman, arms outstretched, and then there was the blinding flash of an explosion. When the smoke cleared, we could see the stationary Sherman on fire, the turret blown clean off, but of the attacker there was no sign.

A second party made a rush at my tank, but we cut them all down with our MGs. As we passed the group of bodies, sprawled in grotesque attitudes to our right, I risked a quick look out of my turret hatch, and saw that they had several large packs strapped around their torsos. Suddenly it dawned on me what was happening. I yelled over the radio to all our tanks that we were under attack by suicide bombers with explosives strapped to their bodies. Hoping to run up against our tanks, they would detonate the bombs in contact with the hull, immolating their bodies in the service of the Emperor.

During later operations we came across a macabre twist to this tactic, when desperate Japanese infantrymen hid themselves in shallow pits under a flimsy covering of logs, hoping to have a Sherman pass directly overhead, when they would set off their pack of explosives. Unfortunately for them, or rather fortunately for us, it was far more difficult than these desperate men had imagined to set off the bomb at exactly the right moment, especially when they were swallowed up in the womb of the earth, with hastily emplaced logs shutting off most light and air and sound.....and then, of course, if the tank track ran over the covering of logs, they would most likely be crushed outright before they could light the fuze. A desperate tactic and one which killed many of their own men but barely a handful of ours.

These suicide attacks are mirrored offshore, where the massive American fleet comes under attack by desperate Japanese airmen, hoping to offset the qualitative and numerical inferiority of their air groups, by using their planes and themselves as flying bombs. The whole suicide campaign, born of desperation and fuelled by the shame and loss of face felt by the Japanese military following the Indian Ocean debacle and the reverses in China, comes under the umbrella name of "Kamikaze" or "Divine Wind", recalling the hurricane which dispersed a Chinese invasion of Japan centuries before. In this way the Japanese hope to postpone the inevitable day of reckoning, and perhaps even thwart the planned invasion of Japan proper.

Allied reconnaissance planes confirm that the Japanese are stockpiling countless suicide weapons, exploding motor boats, midget submarines and manned torpedoes. What can not be picked out from aerial photos are the hundreds of suicide rocket-propelled bombs, the manned "Okha" or "Cherry Blossom" projectiles, driven at high speed by rocket motors copied from gifted German technology.

The naval suicide craft are being moved to emplacements around the likely landing sites for an invasion of Japan proper. With the major part of her Navy at the bottom of the Indian Ocean, Japan is gambling on the massed suicide craft to sink or repel any invasion fleet which approaches the shores of the Japanese Home Islands.

Japanese Kairyu midget submarines in Dry Dock, Kure. Although not specifically intended for suicide attacks, their fragility and low endurance meant that each and every mission was a one-way journey for the dedicated crews.

Inland from the coastal areas, labourers and even schoolchildren are supplied with crudely made "emergency" rifles, or sometimes just sharpened bamboo poles. With these they are indoctrinated to throw themselves in a mass human wave on any invasion force daring to set foot on the sacred soil of Nippon. Rumours of these suicidal preparations seep out through neutral diplomatic channels.

In the meantime Roosevelt has learned from the Germans of the deadly cargoes of Uranium 235 sent earlier to Japan. Goaded by the genocide taking place in China, and determined at all costs to avoid the bloodbath which must result from a direct assault on the Japanese Home Islands, the Allies take the decision to deploy the second nuclear weapon against a major Japanese city.

1. TATEGAMI SHIPYARD
2. MITSUBISHI DOCKYARD
3. AKUNOURA ENGINE WORKS
4. MITSUBISHI ELECTRIC MFG. CO.
5. NAGASAKI & DÉJIMA WHARVES &
                                    R. R. YARDS
6. MITSUBISHI STEEL & ARMS WORKS
7. MITSUBISHI~URAKAMI ORDNANCE PLANT

STATUTE MILE

Pre-attack reconnaissance photo composite of Nagasaki.

A second special unit, the 509th Composite Group is formed, this time using the Boeing B-29 Superfortress. Their aircraft are modified in a similar way to the European B-32s, but their undersides are painted black, for this critical mission will need to be flown by night. The presence of Japanese jet fighter aircraft makes a daylight flight too hazardous.

The target chosen is Nagasaki, which is the site of the largest Christian community in Japan. Ironically, the uranium for the second bomb comes from a captured German consignment, which is finally delivered to Japan, but not in the way intended.

The attack takes place on the 1st June. The first indication the Japanese leaders have that something unimaginable has happened is when all telephone and radio links with Nagasaki go dead.

Nagasaki after the attack. A photo taken by one of a party of visiting RN sailors.

The results on an urban area are devastating, and at least 40,000 people are killed instantaneously. The flimsy Japanese houses simply vanish, as do their occupants.

Of course the Japanese had studied the reports of the Chernobyl attack, but with oriental fatalism they had chosen to continue the fight to the bitter end.

However, seeing the results of the Nagasaki attack at first hand they for the first time realize the dreadful fate which hangs over them.

They open peace overtures via the Swiss Government, but with conditions.

Roosevelt wants to hold out for nothing less than unconditional surrender, but on the advice of General Douglas McArthur, he softens his stance. Roosevelt concedes that, although their military leaders must be put on trial for war crimes, Emperor Hirohito can remain on the throne. Thus reassured, the Japanese are persuaded to seek an honourable peace.

The Second World War, which began nearly five years earlier, ends on 4th June 1944.

Chapter Thirteen
AFTERMATH

In Germany the victorious Allies are determined to avoid the mistakes of 1918-19, which stored up so much bitterness and provided Hitler with a ready-made *casus belli*.

However, at the same time they are determined once and for all to crush the power of the German Officer Class. Dozens of high-ranking officers tainted with supporting the Nazi party are arraigned on War Crimes charges at Nuremberg alongside those Nazi political leaders who have not managed to escape the net. Whereas the top Nazis are invariably sentenced to the death penalty, with the exception of Rudolf Hess, all the military accused are committed to varying periods of incarceration, and most are quietly released long before serving their full sentence. The process has served its purpose in publically humiliating them and crushing their power base, and reconciliation and reconstruction will be the passwords for the future.

At the same time the country is reorganised politically, a new civilian government being elected for the first time in 1945 with much more emphasis being placed on the individual component German states such as Wurtemburg, Bavaria, Baden and Hanover. Germany emerges as a Federal State similar in many ways to the Swiss Confederation, with numerous built-in checks and balances.

One key element enshrined in the new Constitution is the principle that no German soldier, sailor or airman shall in future serve outside the territory of Germany proper. In future years this would prove a handicap when Germany will be asked to provide support to United Nations peacekeeping expeditions, but overall it is a worthwhile tradeoff.

In keeping with the spirit of conciliation, the tacit co-operation of Sweden and Switzerland with the Nazi régime is quietly forgotten, especially when reports from Switzerland tell of much hardship during that little nation's encirclement by the Axis powers. For the duration of the War the Swiss played no football, having dug up all their pitches to grow potatoes. The rigorous defence of the Swiss border against the escaping German XIXth Army also stands them in good stead.

Nikita Kruschev emerges from the Siberian wilderness and sets about rebuilding old Russia from the ruins. More than 30 million Russians have perished in the War, and the country has been virtually devastated by the unremitting Wehrmacht attacks. He is a stolid pragmatist, and as a quid pro quo for US aid, agrees to quietly drop the worst excesses of the Soviet regime. Over the next 25 years Russia makes halting but encouraging steps to rejoining the ranks of democratic republics, helped by sales of vast natural resources, including gas and oil.

The Post War World will be a very different place. The promised destabilising threat of the Comintern never rears its head, and nascent nationalist uprisings in various parts of the world are firmly suppressed by the colonial powers, unhindered by the spectre of Communist aid and weapons.

France comes out of the Second World War much stronger, politically, economically, and morally, than in 1939. Knowing the sacrifices they have had to make to free their homeland from foreign occupation, the French are much more responsive to the needs and sensibilities of their indigenous populations in Africa and the Far East.

Unlike the dismissive British attitude to their Indian subjects in spite of their losses and the major contribution the Indian Army made during both World Wars, the French are only too aware of the debt they owe to their colonial soldiers, the Goums and other North Africans, the Indo-Chinese, and especially the fearsome Senegalese. All will be rewarded by the establishment of a commonwealth of former colonies. They will share in the Post-War prosperity as Europe rebuilds its shattered infrastructures with American financial aid.

Most critically in the eyes of the Orientals, France may have lost one battle in May-June 1940, but has emerged victorious, and has thereby not lost face.

Over a quarter of a century, the French colonies in North Africa and Indo-China will slowly and peacefully be brought to self-determination and eventual self-rule in a climate of enlightened democracy, supported by American aid and under the aegis of the United Nations.

In particular, the former French colonies in Indo-China are leading the Asia-Pacific Rim countries in industrial production, concentrating on exports of electronic goods and motor vehicles, with solid economic growth all through the 1960s and 70s.

In 1990 the International Space Station celebrates its tenth anniversary, the second phase of Moonbase is nearing completion, and United States attention is firmly fastened on the planned mission to begin the colonisation of Mars, which should be well under way by the time the Third Millennium begins.

And the Memorial Wall of Names near the Lincoln Memorial, in Constitution Gardens, Washington DC, commemorates those intrepid men and women who have given their lives in the exploration of Space, Mankind's greatest challenge and the last great frontier.

Annexe One
TIMELINES

TIMESCALES IN THIS WORK	THE HISTORICAL TIMESCALES
1940	**1940**
18th June: De Gaulle broadcasts from London	18th June: De Gaulle broadcasts from London
22nd June: Franco-German Armistice signed	22nd June: Franco-German Armistice signed
3rd July: Operation Catapult seizes French ships in the UK Somerville meets with Gensoul at Oran Darlan flies to North Africa Luftwaffe attacks Channel shipping - Battle of Britain begins	3rd July: Operation Catapult seizes French ships in the UK Somerville's squadron opens fire on Gensoul's ships, sinking *Bretagne* and crippling *Dunkerque*, *Provence* and contre-torpilleur *Mogador* In Alexandria Admirals Cunningham and Godfroy agree on terms to peacefully demilitarize the French squadron based there Luftwaffe attacks Channel shipping – Battle of Britain begins
	4th July: *Strasbourg* arrives in Toulon HM Submarine *Proteus* sinks French sloop *Rigault de Genouilly*
	5th July: French planes attack Gibraltar
8th July: *Richelieu* leaves Dakar en route to join Gensoul's fleet at Oran	8th July: At Dakar, *Richelieu* is attacked by a British force and damaged by a torpedo

14th July: French fleet attacks Italians off Tripolitania Pétain orders Darlan to return to Vichy Darlan refuses, and instead declares the IVth Republic Germans begin the takeover of Unoccupied France	
16th July: Darlan takes control of Corsica	
20th July: Luftwaffe attacks seaborne reinforcements for Corsica	
25th July: German paratroops seize Corsica	
30th July: Luftwaffe units withdrawn from Southern France to take part in the Battle of Britain	
13th August: Adlertag (Eagle Day)	13th August: Adlertag (Eagle Day)
15th August: Defeat of the Italian Navy off Cape Matapan	
15th September: Luftwaffe's greatest effort against Britain	15th September: Luftwaffe's greatest effort against Britain
17th September: Hitler decides to postpone Operation Sealion indefinitely	17th September: Hitler decides to postpone Operation Sealion indefinitely

	23rd September: Free French fail to take Dakar French destroyer *Audacieux* set on fire and beached *Richelieu* fights off Royal Navy squadron HMS *Resolution* is torpedoed by the submarine *Beveziers*
	20th October: Mussolini invades Greece from Albania
	8th November: Free French attack Libreville Vichy submarine *Poncelet* sunk and sloop *Bourgainville* set on fire by her sistership *Savorgnan de Brazza*
11th November: Fleet Air Arm Raid on Taranto cripples Italian battlefleet	11th November: Fleet Air Arm Raid on Taranto cripples Italian battlefleet
	23rd November: President Franklin D. Roosevelt appoints Admiral William D. Leahy as U.S. Ambassador to Vichy France to try to prevent the French fleet and naval bases from falling into German hands.
30th November: Battle of Britain officially ends	30th November: Battle of Britain officially ends
9th December: British under O'Connor begin counter-attack on Italian army threatening Egypt French North African forces from the Mareth Line attack the Italian rear	9th December: British under O'Connor begin counter-attack on Italian army threatening Egypt

23rd December: Marshall Bergenzoli captured by French forces in Western Libya Marshall Graziani with 200,000 men surrenders to the Franco-British forces Duke of Aosta surrenders Italian Somaliland	
29th December: Italy sues for an armistice Mussolini falls from power and is imprisoned on Monte Grasso	
1941	**1941**
17th January: French naval force defeat the Thais in Battle of Kham Ran Bay	17th January: French naval force defeat the Thais in Battle of Kham Ran Bay
	7th February: General Bergenzoli surrenders to O'Connor's forces in Libya
	20th February: Free French forces attack the Italians in Ethiopia
	22nd February: Africa Korps lands in North Africa
1st March: Operation Barbarossa is launched	
	27th March: Defeat of the Italian Navy off Cape Matapan

	31st March: Rommel attacks in the Desert
	6th April: German invasion of Jugoslavia and Greece
	28th April: Last British forces evacuate Greece
	18th May: Duke of Aosta surrenders Italian Somaliland
	20th May: German paratroops attack Crete in Operation Merkur
24th May: Allied squadron sinks *Bismarck* and *Scharnhorst*	24th May: *Bismarck* sinks *Hood*.
	27th May: *Bismarck* is sunk
31st May: Hitler orders the disarming of the remaining Kreigsmarine heavy ships and the transfer of their guns to railway mountings. The U-Boat fleet loses all production priority. Doenitz is ordered to withdraw the survivors of his undersea fleet from the battle of the Atlantic and husband his manpower resources to await the new secret submarine designs promised by Dr Walther.	31st May: Last British evacuations from Crete
3rd June: Death of Josef Stalin Nikita Sergeyevich Khrushchev seizes supreme power in Russia	

	8th June Free French join the British attack on Syria
	15th June: British launch Operation Battleaxe against Rommel
	17th June: Operation Battleaxe fails
	22nd June: Barbarossa starts
30th June: Stalingrad, cut off miles behind the front lines, is finally captured after weeks of bitter street fighting	
3rd July: Hitler makes triumphal visit to the ruined city of Stalingrad, to which he restores its original name of Tsaritsyn	
	12th July: Vichy General Dentz surrenders Syria
2nd September: Powerful French & British naval squadrons begin their transfer to the Far East	
	23rd September: Fall of Kiev Germans take 600,000 prisoners
23rd October: Leningrad is captured by Germano-Finnish troops, and renamed Petrograd. 50,000 Russians inside the city have died in the bitter fighting	
25th October: Moscow declared an open city	

30th October 1941: Yamato runs trials	30th October 1941: *Yamato* runs trials
31st October; Hitler visits Moscow, views a victory parade in Red Square from the vantage point of Lenin's Tomb	
	18th November: British launch Operation Crusader against Rommel
30th November: Wehrmacht units seize dominating positions on the heights of the Ural Mountains, just before the Russian Winter finally puts a halt to all military operations for several months	
	2nd December: Leading Wehrmacht units are in sight of Moscow
	4th December: Zhukov's Far East divisions spearhead the Russian attack which saves Moscow
	8th December: Japan attacks Pearl Harbour, the Philippines and Malaya
	10th December: Force Z overwhelmed by Japanese air attack. *Repulse* and *Prince of Wales* sunk.
12th December: Japanese-inspired revolt against Dutch rule begins in Jakarta	
16th December: *Yamato* commissioned	16th December: *Yamato* commissioned
19th December: Dutch troops arrest Suharto and other leading rebels	

	23rd December: Japanese land in Sarawak
	24th December: Wake Island captured by the Japanese Submarine *Surcouf* brings St Pierre & Miquelon over to the Free French
	25th December: Hong Kong captured by the Japanese
31st December: Japanese 'peace-keeping' forces begin landing in the Dutch East Indies, ostensibly to support the Dutch	
1942	**1942**
1st January to 5th January: Dutch East Indies fleet overwhelmed by superior Japanese naval and air forces. Cruisers *De Reuter* and *Java*, destroyers *Banckert, Evertsen, Kortenaer, Piet Hein, Van Ghent, Van Ness* and *Witte de With*, submarines *K7, K17, O16, O17* and *O20* are sunk.. Only the light cruiser *Tromp* and 11 submarines survive to escape to Australia and temporary internment.	
6th January: Dutch troops surrender their weapons and are confined to barracks Japan declares Dutch East Indies will form a Japanese 'protectorate'	6th January: Japanese forces land in Brunei

	10th January: Japanese land in Borneo
	21st January: Rommel drives the 8th Army out of Western Cyrenaica
	24th January: Japanese land on Celebes
30th January: Allies begin large-scale supply of Chinese armies via India and Burma *Yamato* visits Thailand *Musashi* runs trials	
	8th February: Japanese forces invade Singapore Island
	13th February: Japanese land on Sumatra
	14th February: Koenig's Free French Brigade take over the defence of Bir Hacheim
	15th February: British forces in Singapore surrender to a smaller Japanese army
	18th February: Loss of the giant submarine cruiser *Surcouf*
	19th February: Japanese land on Bali Japanese aircraft raid Darwin in Australia
	20th February: Japanese land on Timor

	27th February: Allied fleet defeated in the Battle of the Java Sea
	8th March: Dutch forces in Java surrender
10th March: *Musashi* commissioned	
	26th May: Rommel attacks the Gazala Line
	5th May: Operation Ironclad, British forces attack and capture Madagascar. Vichy naval forces lose sloop *D'Entrecasteaux* and submarines *Beveziers*, *Le Héros* and *Monge*
27th May: Attack on Heydrich's car in Prague	27th May: Heidrich assassinated in Prague
	10th June: Free French evacuate Bir Hacheim after heroic defence
	20th June: Tobruk captured by Rommel
5th August: *Shinano* runs trials with only main 18.1in armament in place	5th August: *Musashi* commissioned
	19th August: Von Paulus' 6th Army begins the assault on Stalingrad
	24th October: Montgomery launches the Second Battle of El Alamein

	8th November: Operation Torch, Allies land in French North Africa French fleet opposes the landings and suffers heavy losses
	11th November/ Germans invade Unoccupied France
	27th November: The French Fleet, bottled up in Toulon, is scuttled to avoid capture by the Germans
	22nd December: Admiral Darlan assassinated in Algiers by Fernand Bonnier de la Chapelle
1943	**1943**
	1st February: End of resistance of the 6th Army in Stalingrad
	13th March: Bombs placed on Hitler's aircraft by Tresckow and Schlabrendorff fail to explode
19th March: Battle in the Indian Ocean USA declares war on Japan	
1st April: Japanese forces attack Philippines Japanese forces attack Hong Kong	
4th April: Hong Kong garrison surrenders	
16th April: Siege of Bataan	

30th April: Allied relief fleet arrives off Manila	
7th May: Seige of Bataan lifted Japanese forces retreat into central Luzon and outlying islands	
	13th May: Surrender of all Axis forces in North Africa
	12th July: Red Army raises the seige of Leningrad. 200,000 Russians have died in the fighting and bombardments, and 633,000 have starved to death Failure of Operation *Zitadelle* in the Kursk Salient, the largest tank battle in history
20th July: Operation Aphrodite, the invasion of Provence	
21st July: Wehrmacht units move south to counter the French advance	
29th July: USA declares war on Germany Operation Overlord, the invasion of Normandy	
13th August: Von Blaskwitz's Army Corps surrenders after attempting to fight their way through Switzerland	

15th August: Wehrmacht units begin their withdraw from France to avoid the Allied pincer movement, and recoil to the old Westwall/ Seigfried Line positions	
15th September: Allied units are halted by the Westwall defences. They consolidate their positions to build up supplies for the final push into Germany proper	
24th December: SS launch two-stage A4 against New York Missile fails in flight and warhead impacts in Southern Eire	
1944	**1944**
2nd February: Operation Wacht am Rhein: Waffen SS counterattack in the West	
21st February: First Atom Bomb dropped on Chernobyl Death of Reinhard Heidrich	
23rd February: Goebbels flies to the site of the attack and visits survivors	
24th February: Goebbels flies back to Berlin That evening, Goebbels kills his wife and children and commits suicide	
25th February: Panic in Germany Nazi officials flee major cities Secret meeting of the German resistance in Berlin	

29th February: Provisional Government formed in Berlin German soldiers are officially relieved of their personal oath of allegiance to the Führer Provisional Government requests Armistice with the Allies Civil War in Germany between the Wehrmacht and the Waffen SS; Street fighting in Berlin	
2nd March: Adolf Hitler commits suicide in his bunker behind the Reichstag Former German flag raised over the ruins of the Reichstag	
4th March: Armistice signed in Paris ends the war in Europe Admiral Darlan assassinated in Paris	
1st June: Second Atom Bomb dropped on Nagasaki	
4th June: World War Two ends with the Japanese signature of the surrender document in Tokyo Bay	
	6th June: Operation Overlord – "D" Day
	22nd June: Massive Russian assault on Army Group Centre

	20th July: Bomb attempt on Hitler's life
	1st August: Warsaw uprising starts
	15th August: Allies launch Operation Dragoon, the invasion of Provence
	14th October: Death of Rommel
	16th December: Germans launch counterattack in the West - Operation Wacht am Rhein, the Battle of the Bulge
1945	**1945**
	12th April: Death of President Franklin D Roosevelt
	28th April: Adolf Hitler commits suicide
	8th May: VE Day – Victory in Europe
	6th August: First Atom Bomb dropped on Hiroshima
	9th August: Second Atom Bomb dropped on Nagasaki
	15th August: VJ Day - Japan surrenders

ANNEXE 2: NAVAL COMPARISONS OF 1940					
	Modern Battleships & rebuilt units (1)	Obsolescent Dreadnoughts (2)	Battlecruisers	Carriers (3)	Heavy Cruisers
Royal Navy (5)	Warspite Valiant Nelson Rodney + *Queen Elizabeth* *King George V* *Prince of Wales* *Dule of York* *Howe* *Anson* *Lion* *Temeraire*	Malaya Barham Revenge Ramillies Royal Sovereign	Repulse Renown Hood	Furious Hermes Argus Eagle Ark Royal Illustrious + *Formidable* *Victorious* *Indomitable*	Hawkins Frobisher Australia Canberra Berwick Cornwall Cumberland Kent Suffolk Devonshire Shropshire Sussex Dorsetshire Norfolk York Exeter + *London*
US Navy	Colorado Maryland West Virginia + *North Carolina* *Washington* *South Dakota* *Indiana* *Massachusetts* *Alabama*	Arkansas New York Texas Nevada Oklahoma Pennsylvania Arizona New Mexico Mississippi Idaho Tennessee California		Lexington Saratoga Ranger Yorktown Enterprise Wasp + *Hornet*	Pensacola Salt Lake City Northampton Chester Louisville Chicago Houston Augusta Portland Indianapolis New Orleans Astoria Minneapolis Tuscaloosa San Francisco Quincy Vincennes Wichita

Light Cruisers		Destroyers	Submarines	Major Auxiliaries (4)
Modern	/ Old			
Leander	Adelaide	176	64	Albatross
Neptune	Caledon			Adventure
Orion	Caradoc	+76 building	+ c 15 building	Erebus
Achilles	Cardiff			Terror
Ajax	Ceres			Forth
Sydney	Coventry			Maidstone
Perth	Curacoa			
Hobart	Cairo			
Arethusa	Calcutta			
Galatea	Capetown			+ 4 Abdeil class
Penelope	Carlisle			building
Aurora	Colombo			
Southampton	Danae			
Newcastle	Dauntless			
Birmingham	Dragon			
Glasgow	Delhi			
Sheffield	Dunedin			
Liverpool	Durban			
Manchester	Diomede			
Gloucester	Despatch			
Edinburgh	Emerald			
Belfast	Enterprise			
Bonaventure				
Fiji				
+25 building				
Brooklyn	Omaha	73 new DD in	99	Utah
Philadelphia	Milwaukee	service		Wyoming
Savannah	Cincinatti		+ 14 building	Langley
Nashville	Raleigh	(plus 231		
Phoenix	Detroit	4-stackers)		
Boise	Richmond			
Honolulu	Concord	+ 16 building		
St Louis	Trenton			
Helena	Marblehead			
	Memphis			
+ 5 building				

	Modern Battleships & rebuilt units (1)	Obsolescent Dreadnoughts (2)	Battlecruisers	Carriers (3)	Heavy Cruisers(6)
Imperial Japanese Navy	Fuso Yamashiro Ise Hyuga Nagato Mutsu + *Yamato* *Musashi*		Kongo Hiei Haruna Kirishima	Akagi Kaga Ryujo Soryu Hiryu + *Shokaku* *Zuikaku* *Hiyo* *Junyo*	Furutaka Kako Aoba Kinugasa Myôkô Nachi Haguro Ashigara Takao Atago Maya Chôkai Mogami Mikuma Suzuya Kumano Tone Chikuma
French Navy	Richelieu + *Jean Bart* *Clemenceau* *Gascoigne*	Provence Bretagne Lorraine	Dunkerque Strasbourg	Béarn + *Joffre* *Painlevé*	Duquesne Tourville Suffren Colbert Foch Dupleix Algérie
Italian Navy	Conte di Cavour Giulio Cesare Vittorio Veneto Littorio + *Caio Duilio* *Andrea Doria* *Roma* *Impero*				Luigi Cadorna Armando Diaz Muzio Attendolo R. Montecuccoli Trento Trieste Fiume Gorizia Pola Zara Bolzano

Light Cruisers		Destroyers	Submarines	Major Auxiliaries (4)
Modern /	Old			
	Tenryu	108	55	Chitose
	Tatsuta	(Including	+ 38 building	Chiyuda
	Kuma	Torpedo Boats)		Mizuho
	Tama	+ 12 building		Tsurugisaki
	Kitakami			Takasaki
	Oi			Nisshin
	Kiso			Ryuho
	Nagara			
	Isuzu			
	Yura			
	Natori			
	Kinu			
	Abukuma			
	Naka			
	Sendai			
	Jintsu			
	Kako			
	Yubari			
Duguay-Trouin		67 including	73	Paris
Lamotte-		Torpedo Boats	+ 34 building	Courbet
Picquet		+ 11		Ocean
Primaguet		building		Cdt Teste
Jeanne d'Arc				
Emile Bertin				
La				
Galissonnière				
Georges				
Leygues				
Gloire				
Jean de Vienne				
Marseillaise				
Montcalm				
+ 1 building				
Bari		116	c 105	
Taranto		including	+ c 10 building	
Alberto Di		Torpedo Boats		
Giussano				
Alberico Da				
Barbiano				
Bartolomeo				
Colleoni				
Giovanni Delle				
Banda Nere				
Duca D'Aosta				
Eugenio Di				
Savoia				
+ 11 building				

	Modern Battleships & rebuilt units (1)	Obsolescent Dreadnoughts (2)	Battlecruisers	Carriers (3)	Heavy Cruisers
Kreigs-marine	*Bismarck* *Tirpitz* *'H'*		Scharnhorst Gneisenau	*Graf Zeppelin*	Deutschland Admiral Scheer Hipper *+ 2 building* (7)

NOTES:

[Units in italics are under construction]

(1)   New designs having entered service or working up. Rebuilt units or conversions in the mid to late 1930s

(2)   Unconverted units or rebuilds prior to the mid 1930s

(3)   Seaplane Carriers and Aircraft tenders are included in the column for Major Auxiliaries

(4)   Monitors, Minelayers, Large Depot Ships, Seaplane Carriers, Aircraft Tenders & Training Ships

(5)   Including Dominion Navies (Canada, Australia, New Zealand)

(6)   Plus older Armoured Cruisers retained as coast defence ships or local flagships

(7)   Including the 'Panzerschiffe'

Light Cruisers		Destroyers	Submarines	Major Auxiliaries (4)
Modern /	Old			
Köln Leipzeig Nürnberg + 3 building	Emden	28 including Torpedo Boats + 22 building	c 60 + c 40 building	Schleswig-Holstein Schleisen Brummer Bremse

Annexe Three
REALITY VERSUS FICTION

In the foregoing narrative, I have resisted the temptation to introduce any new 'inventions' or a *deus ex machina*. I have merely altered the timeframe, and thereby the emphasis given to the various technical developments.

Admiral Somerville's biography was actually written by Donald MacIntyre, and appeared in 1961 under the title *Fighting Admiral*. Somerville always regretted the action he was bullied into taking at Mers el-Kébir. That great British hero, Admiral Nelson, is still today considered by the Danes to be an unspeakable villain for his attack on their Fleet at the Battle of Copenhagen.

Admiral Gensoul had indeed worked closely with Royal Navy experts on equipping the French Navy with the most modern anti-submarine gear.

The French battlecruiser pair were specifically designed to deal with the smaller *panzerschiffe*, and in turn led Germany to try to counter them with the two *Scharnhorsts*.

The Royal Navy helped the French with the design of the *Richelieu* Class, as it was felt they might be the first modern Allied ships capable of facing up to the powerful *Bismarck* Class battleships, then under construction by the Kreigsmarine. In any one-on-one situation, the undergunned and slower *King George V* Class ships could hardly expect to firstly catch, and secondly destroy a *Bismarck* single-handed, as was so painfully demonstrated in the *Bismarck*'s action with the brand-new *Prince of Wales*. To that end *Richelieu* was armoured on a much more massive scale, especially with regard to her horizontal protection and the turret and barbette armour. Many of *Richelieu*'s features were copied from the RN *Nelson* Class, including the forward positioning of the main armament, the tower bridge structure, and the placing of all vital control and power lines beneath the main armour deck.

The *Richelieu* was actually slightly smaller than the *Bismarck*, but saved weight and space by adopting two less main armament turrets. Being some three knots faster, *Richelieu* could bring *Bismarck* to battle and then pursue her to a conclusion.

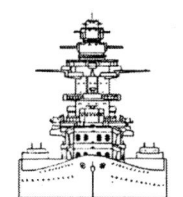

The small target presented by Richelieu head-on, compared with the length of Bismarck broadside-on.

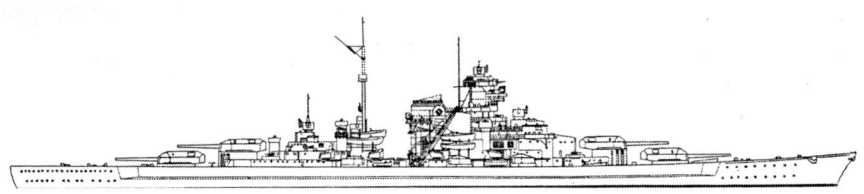

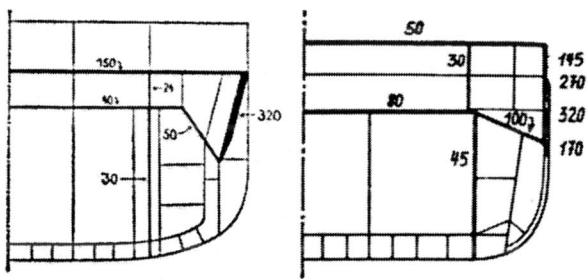

Richelieu's side and deck armour compared with that of Bismarck.

Hitler's orders to his Admirals always stressed the need to preserve their few capital ships by turning away when faced by a superior or even an "equivalent" enemy force – whatever that was supposed to mean. Lutjens in the Battle of the Denmark Strait was forced to fight *Hood* and *Prince of Wales* because Admiral Holland had the Germans cornered. Faced with *Richelieu* the *Bismarck* would always retreat, thus opposing two twin stern turrets to the full eight-gun forward armament on the French ships, which had been designed with this very chase scenario in mind.

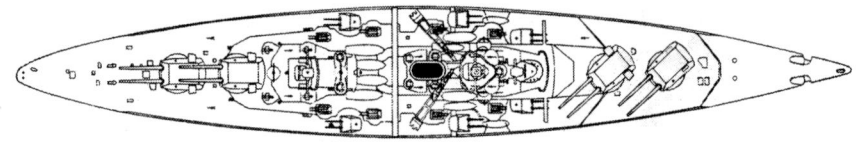

Bismarck's limited A-arcs of turrets Anton and Bruno trained astern

If *Bismarck* were to turn to bring her full armament into play, she would expose most of her side profile to shellfire. And *Bismarck*, being basically a larger, faster version of the Great War *Baden*, exposed all too many of her vital control systems above the main armour deck, the Germans not having had the opportunity to test Great War designs to destruction, as had the Royal Navy.

The close pairing of the guns in the French quadruple turrets had caused problems in the battlecruisers *Dunkerque* and *Strasbourg*. Firing all guns together in a broadside resulted in mutual interference of the shells in flight, leading to serious dispersion patterns. The US Navy had suffered from similar problems with their triple turrets. The Royal Navy, with extensive experience of triple and quadruple main gun turrets, was well aware of these problems and was able to suggest solutions. The eventual answer was to build in a split-second delay in the firing of alternate guns in the quadruple turret. Again, the shape of the shells used in the earlier French battlecruisers was far from ballistically perfect. The Royal Navy experience following intensive investigations into the performance of RN heavy shells in the battle of Jutland would have helped the French overcome these teething troubles.

French destroyers and escorts were primarily designed to overcome their Italian counterparts in the Mediterranean - where seakeeping and endurance were secondary considerations - leaving the Royal Navy to face down the much smaller German Kreigsmarine. Whereas Italian light cruisers achieved record speeds on trials before their main armament was fitted, the corresponding French ships beat them on speed with full armament on board, in service.

The fighting abilities of the French Navy were never in doubt. On 11th March 1943, escorting Convoy HX228, the Free French corvette *Aconit* rammed and sank two U-boats. The fictional destroyer USS *Keeling* is the ship featured in C.S. Forester's novel "*The Good Shepherd*". The planned film of the book was to star Humphrey Bogart in the rôle of her C.O., Commander George Krause, but the project was cancelled when Bogart died.

The P-40s ordered by France *were* transferred to Britain and held in reserve against the expected German invasion, complete with their metric instrumentation and French throttle layout. René Mouchotte joined the RAF and flew Spitfires, rising to become a Squadron Leader in the Free French Air Force. Flying from Biggin Hill, he went missing during an attack on the V2 bunker at Eperlecques.

Kurt Mayer was an expert panzer commander. After the Second World War he was accused of war crimes committed by men under his command during the Canadian attack on Buron in 1944, but always protested his innocence.

The story of the lone KV-1 holding the panzers at bay is described by Kenneth Macksey in his book *Tank Versus Tank*.

The latest revelations about the death of Stalin leave open the possibility that he may have succumbed to poison. It was too tempting to name that reckless adventurer Kruschev, who during the actual historical Second World War was the man sent into Stalingrad to animate the defence, as the perpetrator.

Germany sent many technical missions to Japan, with the aim of helping her in the Axis war, but also to try to persuade the Japanese to attack Russia. Ernst Heinkel was officially barred from producing fighter aircraft for the Luftwaffe – thereby depriving Germany of the excellent twin-jet He 280 fighter of 1942, and later forcing night fighter squadrons to secretly assemble unregistered Heinkel *Uhu* aircraft from cases of spare parts. However, Heinkel *was* allowed to build fighters solely for export, and sold several He 113 fighters to Japan, as well as the earlier He 112. Because Japanese pilots favoured manoeuvrability over pure speed, these state-of-the-art fighters ended up used as instructional airframes for mechanics, but they must have been a source of inspiration to budding Japanese aircraft designers.

Gaius Julius Classicianus was the Roman Procurator Fiscal sent by the Emperor to oversee the taxation of his new British subjects. When the military governor proposed to punish the rebellious Britons with fire and the sword, and devastate the island of Britannia, it was Classicianus who used his influence to veto this approach, thus saving the islanders. After his death, in gratitude they erected a memorial to Classicianus, which is on display in the British Museum. In practical terms Classicianus was probably motivated more by financial reasons – such as the loss of taxes to the exchequer - than by humanistic considerations. All the same, the end result was undoubtedly beneficial.

After their disastrous defeat at Midway, the Japanese were forced to convert *Shinano*, the third vessel of the *Yamato* Class, into a giant aircraft carrier. With no Battle of Midway, they could have pursued their original plan.

Right up until after the Second World War, the Allies remained unaware of the fact that the *Yamato* Class carried a main armament of 18.1-inch guns. It was only after a proof barrel and several shells were discovered and measured at Nakajima in 1945, that the Americans could appreciate how lucky their battleships had been at the conclusion of the battle of Leyte Gulf. There the fast battleships had been sent on ahead of the carriers to trap the retreating Japanese heavy ships. They would have come face to face with *Yamato* and her 18.1-inch guns and risked suffering heavy – if not fatal - damage.

Arming the first three *King George V* Class ships with smaller caliber main armament than any likely opponent was a short-sighted political decision, made in the pious hope that other maritime powers with 16inch gunned ships would follow suit in the interests of "world peace" or some such similar notion.

When the Japanese, the Americans, the French and the Italians all ignored the gesture, it was too late to cancel the orders for heavier ordnance and start again. The successors to the *KGV*s, the *Temeraire* Class, would revert to the standard RN 16inch gun as developed for *Nelson* and *Rodney*. In reality, the *Temeraires* would never be completed.

The notion that the Americans could, and would, supply modern large caliber naval guns to other countries was rooted in historical fact. When the Greek battlecruiser *Salamis*, building in Germany, was put on hold during the Great War, the 14inch guns being constructed for her in the USA were delivered to Britain and used to arm several coast bombardment monitors, including the ill-fated *Raglan*, sunk by the *Goeben* off Imbros. Therefore, there would be no technical objection to the USN supplying the RN with modern 16inch guns.

That a modern capital ship could be sunk by just one bomb was dramatically demonstrated when a Dornier Do217 sank the Italian batttleship *Roma* with a radio-controlled glide bomb while she was en route to surrender at Malta. Barnes Wallis' *Tallboy* bombs were of course used by the Lancasters of 617 Squadron to sink the Tirpitz.

The complex flight attack formation used by Stukas was described in a talk to the Etchingham Military & Aviation Preservation Society by Mr Frank Gardner, a survivor from HMS *Kashmir*, who had been on the receiving end of just such an attack by I/St.G.2 off Crete in May 1941.

The early years of the Second World War provided several examples of the fact that French soldiers, when properly equipped and led, were more than capable of besting their Axis opponents.

In Norway, General Béthouart's Chasseurs Alpins had pushed their Wehrmacht counterparts up against the Swedish frontier, and the Germans were saved from the ignominy of surrender or internment only by the unleashing of the Blitzkreig proper, in the Low Countries and Northern France.

The young professionals of the Maginot garrisons repelled attack after attack by Wehrmacht commanders, eager to gain the Iron Cross for capturing an artillery *ouvrage*, and the Italians were comprehensively repulsed in their attacks on the *ouvrages* of the Alpine Front.

In 1942, the British Eighth Army was saved from destruction in the retreat to El Alamein only through the dogged resistance of the French defenders of Bir Hakeim, commanded by Koenig, who repulsed repeated attacks by crack units of the Afrika Korps, even after Erwin Rommel arrived to direct the operation in person.

General De Gaulle was a leading exponent of using the tank in Blitzkreig-style tactics. He was the author of several tracts on the subject prior to the Second World War. These were eagerly read by German generals but not the French. As with Basil Liddel Hart in the UK, a prophet in his own land.....

The Americans did build a couple of dozen M6 Heavy Tank prototypes, but eventually set up their massive production lines to produce the M4 Sherman instead, for the reasons given in the text. By the time the tank crews facing German panzers cried out for bigger and better tanks, it would have caused fatal delays to switch the factories over to newer designs. So the Western Allies, in the main, were forced to use the Sherman of 1942 through to the War's end. The Americans attempted to make up for the Sherman's shortcomings vis-à-vis the Panzers by introducing specific Tank Destroyers.

The author's Cousin was in charge of the SAS Six-Pounder gun which split the top of the church steeple in the town of Le Muy which was holding up the advance of the American paratroopers. *Officially* the SAS were not present at the invasion of Provence, and it does not feature in their Battle Honours.

Blaskowitz's IXth Army did not actually attempt to escape through Switzerland. They surrendered to the pursuing French troops of De Lattre de Tassigny on the Swiss frontier. The Germans had been made only too aware of the strength of the Swiss preparations for invasion. However, the opportunity to give the formidable Swiss defences, on which they had expended vast effort over four years

– constructing over seventy underground fortresses and dozens of bunkers disguised as innocent wooden chalets - a chance to show their mettle was irresistible.

The story of the last U-boat to sail from Germany in World War Two, the long-range minelayer U-264, has been revealed by her radio operator Hirschfeld. She carried in her cargo hold a dismantled Me262 jet fighter, examples of the latest German radar sets, and prototype aircraft cannons. Her minelaying tubes were filled with lead cases containing highly radioactive uranium 235, destined for use by the attack bombers of Japan's submersible aircraft carriers. *Ostensibly* designed to attack the Panama Canal, by the War's end it was probable that these *Seiran* attack planes would be carrying "dirty" bombs to spread radioactivity over America's West Coast cities and dockyards.

The hypothesis that both Nazi Germany and the United States of America were able to accelerate their respective scientific warfare programmes is feasible if the former had enjoyed a walkover on the Eastern Front, and the latter were not actually engaged in the fighting – other than in the Atlantic - prior to the Summer of 1943.

Similarly, the Allied control of the Mediterranean saved massive diversions of effort in that region, as did the late commencement of hostilities in the Far East.

Hitler's scientists came up with many schemes to attack the USA, including the long-range bomber which it is claimed actually flew to within a few miles of New York on a training mission, the futuristic "stratosphere bomber" powered by rocket engines, various schemes for "Mistel" combination aircraft whereby the transatlantic "carrier" plane launched a much smaller attack bomber, U-boats towing containers for launching V2 missiles from close off the American coast, and of course the two-stage V2 rocket.

De Valera's Irish government was the only Western democracy to send a message of condolence to the Germans in May 1945 in sympathy for the death of the Fuehrer. How ironic that in my narrative they should have to suffer by being the first victims of a nuclear attack, even if by accident. Many prototype V2s failed in tests, and the first concrete Allied knowledge of the weapon – foretold by the famous Oslo Telegram – came from the wreckage of an early V2 which fell by accident on an island in the Baltic.

The discovery of the SS burning the bodies from the concentration camp near Thil in North-Eastern France is described in detail by Eugène Gaspard in his book *Les Travaux du IIIe Reich Entre Alzette et Fensch* (published by G Klopp, Thionville).

Consolidated were asked to come up with a development of their B-24 Liberator bomber, as a fall-back insurance in case the highly advanced Boeing B-29 Superfortress proved a failure.

Powered by the same engines as the Superfortress, the B-32 Terminator used the same Davis high wing as on the earlier Liberator. Early prototypes had full pressurization, but on the simplified production models this feature was dropped. The gun positions reverted back from the remote control positions as in the B-29, to manually powered turrets. The two dorsal turrets were fitted with tear drop streamlined extensions to reduce drag.

In August 1944, the B-32 was renamed the Dominator. However, a year later, because of objections made at a United Nations conference, even this name was dropped as being "politically incorrect" for the postwar environment. After that, the aircraft was officially referred to as simply the B-32.

B-32s flew the last combat missions of the Second World War, photo-reconnaissance sorties over Japan after hostilities had officially ended, and they also engaged in the last aerial combat during one of those missions, on 17th August 1945, fighting off attacks by Japanese fighter pilots who could not accept the political decision to surrender. In the course of these attacks their crews sadly reported the final airforce combat fatality, a photographer on board aircraft 42-108578 "Hobo Queen". More deaths resulted from a final mission 11 days later, when one B-32 crashed on takeoff and the crew of a second baled out due to technical problems on the way back to base.

The original photo used to depict a pair of stripped "nuclear bombers" depicts the unarmed version of the B-32 built for training aircrews.

ILLUSTRATIONS OF THE ATTACK ON THE FRENCH FLEET AT MERS EL-KÉBIR 3rd JULY 1940

High drama in the port:

In the centre, behind the oiler, the battleship Bretagne's aft magazinzes explode, killing almost 1,000 of her crew

To her left the battlecruiser Strasbourg begins to move, avoiding a salvo of shells falling in her berth

On the left of the photo, the battleship Provence has just fired her opening salvo, firing between the masts of her flagship alongside (out of the picture)

In the left foreground the destroyer Tigre or Lynx heads for the gate in the anti torpedo nets

To the right the large seaplane carrier Cdt Teste will help rescue survivors from Bretagne. Cdt Teste will be undamaged.

A painting of the same scene: Flagship Dunkerque struggles to free her
moorings but is about to be hit and crippled by a salvo of three 15in shells.

Hit on destroyer Mogador by 15in shell

The battle seen from high ground: Bretagne burns furiously before capsizing. Mogador's depth charges explode. She survived, badly damaged aft.

Mers el-Kébir today

Annexe Four
COUNTERPOISE

There is a much more unsettling alternative scenario arising from the tragedy of Mers el-Kébir.

Churchill often acted on a gut reaction, and as a man of conviction he always followed through with an idea. This was his great strength, but it could also be his glaring weakness. Often he wielded British forces as if they were the lead soldiers he must have manoeuvred on the table top as a child. With no regard for the value of the human lives he was sacrificing. That is the responsibility, and the curse, of the war leader. To Hitler, Churchill was the derisible "amateur strategist". Darlan dismissed him as a drunkard.

Fortunately for posterity, Hitler was first and foremost a soldier, and a vengeful one at that, and a politician only second, however successful he sometimes was in the latter role. If he had been a more astute politician the Mers el-Kébir affair could have been turned dramatically to Germany's advantage.

We have to imagine the immediate aftermath of the unprovoked attack. The Vichy authorities send their bomber force to raid Gibraltar and other British targets. The Author's Mother was convinced that she and other civilians had seen French aircraft, with their roundels clearly visible, strafing the streets of Swansea in South Wales during a bombing raid on the port facilities.

Hitler announces his masterstroke. Following up on the Armistice, a full, formal peace treaty is drawn up and presented to the French for their signature. One bitter blow – thousands of young French troops, including the crème de la crème of the French Army, the Maginot garrisons, are to be kept as prisoners of war in Germany for the foreseeable future. They can be seen as hostages to the good behaviour of the French, but in reality they are put to work on German farms to replace the farmers and labourers drafted into the ranks of the Wehrmacht.

There are, however, several surprises for the downtrodden French.

There will, it appears, be no occupation of French territory. German forces will pull back to the pre-May 1940 frontier. The undamaged Maginot works can be reoccupied by the French and kept in working order, but their stocks of ammunition must be removed, under German supervision, to rear storage areas. Most significantly, the French Government can return to Paris.

French armament factories are encouraged to continue producing the vast quantities of ultra-modern weapons, vehicles and aircraft they had been building up until the defeat. The Wehrmacht buys up all the trucks French industry can produce, light tanks are converted to artillery and ammunition tractors, medium tanks are built in the latest versions such as the Somua S-40 with two-man turret and the up-armoured Char B1ter which had only just seen the light of day as prototypes just prior to May and June 1940. Turret top hatches in the German style are incorporated, and all tanks are provided with radios. In particular, the Wehrmacht orders large numbers of the successful Panhard 178 armoured car, and the later 8-wheel EBR. French transport aircraft are purchased to help swell the Luftwaffe's cargo fleet, and several French firms begin licence manufacture of specific German aircraft types, such as the Junkers 52/3m and the Fiesler Storch. Payment is in hard currency, and the economy receives a tremendous boost.

The Marshall is able to begin his social reconstruction programmes in earnest. As a quid pro quo, he is encouraged to maintain an anti-British stance, by which the French Navy and coast defence guns stand ready to ward off any incursion by the British fleet.

Much to the surprise of the defeated nations, the German armed forces withdraw from not only France, but also Holland and Denmark. German occupation forces remain in Belgium and Norway, ostensibly because of the threat posed by the British, although in reality the latter are incapable of offensive action.

Hitler offers the British a peace treaty of their own, but his offer is rejected. Cunningly, he orders all German forces to cease offensive actions against Britain. There is no Battle of Britain, and no Blitz on London or other cities, hence no excuse for RAF retaliation against Germany. The German fleet is ordered back to port, and the U-Boat campaign is curtailed. Although the offer of a peace agreement had been refused, in reality the British are exhausted and in no state to continue the fight. So an uneasy truce descends on the West, much like the old Phoney War period.......

In the Mediterranean theatre, Mussolini is cajoled into withdrawing from French territory and handing back the surrendered Maginot works. Before leaving, however, the Italians manage to dismantle and make off with several of the latest French armaments from inside the *ouvrages*, much to the disgust of their returning owners.

In return for his cooperation, Mussolini receives the promise of a licence to build the Mercedes Benz range of high-powered aircraft engines, plus other German hardware.

The uneasy truce extends over the whole Mediterranean theatre, with the British and Italians facing each other threateningly in the Western Desert.

In Metropolitan France, Petain's French State moves against the Communist opposition. To help crush his political opponents, the Marshall forms the para-military force known as the Milice, to be used for internal security.

The French are encouraged by the Germans to form a "Legion against Bolshevism". At the height of its popularity, almost 100,000 trained troops will have volunteered, who will be equipped with modern French armaments and vehicles. They have trained extensively with Luftwaffe ground attack formations, in preparation for their role in the forthcoming attack on Russia, Operation Barbarossa.

In the order of battle for Barbarossa, *Army Corps Charlemagne* is allocated the southern sector of the front, tasked with securing the Crimean Peninsular before striking eastwards towards the oilfields of the Caucasus. The French military are particularly pleased to be revisiting the battlefields of the Crimea where their forefathers covered themselves with glory, in actions such as the Malakoff and other names perpetuated in the streets of Paris.

Naturally the USA is offered no excuse to support England in its last-ditch struggle, which is not actually taking place. As a final blow to divide his democratic opponents, in a public speech Adolf Hitler specifically praises the British Empire and guarantees its continuation – a move designed to alienate Roosevelt, and which succeeds.

And, once again, everything changes……………..

Bibliography

Michel **BERTRAND**	*Les Forces Navales Françaises Libres* (Gazette des Armes)
Siegfried **BREYER**	*Battleships and Battlecruisers 1905-1970*
	Soviet Warship Development Volume 1
R A **BURT**	*French Battleships 1876-1945*
Alan **CLARK**	*Barbarossa*
Jean Labayle **COUHAT**	*French Warships of World War II*
Hervé **COUTAU-BÉGARIE** & Claude **HUAN**	*Mers El-Kébir (1940) La rupture franco-britannique*
Theodore **DETMERS**	*The Raider Kormoran*
Michael **FOEDROWITZ**	*The Flak Towers in Berlin, Hamburg and Vienna 1940-1950*
David **FRASER**	*Knight's Cross, A Life of Field Marshall Erwin Rommel*
Terry **GANDER** & Peter **CHAMBERLAIN**	*American Tanks of World War 2*
Louis **GARROS**	*Le Coup de Dakar, septembre 1940* (HISTORAMA No. 168)
Eugène **GASPARD**	*Les Travaux du IIIe Reich Entre Alzette et Fensch*
Tony **GIBBONS**	*The Complete Encyclopedia of Battleships and Battlecruisers*
Martin **GILBERT**	*The Routledge Atlas of Russian History*

Philip **HENSHALL**	*Vengeance, Hitler's Nuclear Weapon: Fact or Fiction?*
Richard **HOLMES**	*Bir Hacheim, Desert Citadel*
Richard **HOUGH**	*The Fleet Without a Friend*
Jean-Gabriel **JEUDY**	*Chars de France*
Philippe **JUBELIN**	*Flying Sailor*
Philippe **LASTERLE**	*Marcel Gensoul (1880-1973), un amiral dans la tourmente* (Revue Historique des Armées No. 2 – 2000)
Kenneth **MACKSEY**	*Tank versus Tank*
Roger **MANVELL**	*The Conspirators, 20ᵗʰ July 1944*
Lt. James **MATTHEWS**, MM, Chevalier de la Légion d'Honneur & Roger **BRANFILL-COOK**	*Tiger Killer*
René **MOUCHOTTE**	*Carnets*
Alan **RAVEN**	Ensign 1 – *King George the Fifth Class Battleships*
David **THOMAS**	*Battle of the Java Sea*
J P **THÉVOZ**	*Le général de Lattre et la Suisse* (HISTORAMA No. 179)
Lt-Col Philippe **TRUTTMANN**	*La Muraille de France*
M J **WHITLEY**	*Cruisers of World War Two* *Destroyers of World War Two*
Magazines & Periodicals	*Purnell's History of the Second World War* *After the Battle*

ISBN 142514179-X